MW01126543

ONLY THE DETAILS

ALAN LEE

SPARKLE PRESS

Only the Details
by Alan Lee

Copyright © 2018 Alan Janney
Second Edition
Printed in USA

Cover by Inspired Cover Designs
Formatting by Polgarus

Paperback ISBN: 9781726116831
Sparkle Press

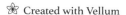 Created with Vellum

"Every man's life ends the same way. It is only the details of how he lived and how he died that distinguishes one man from another."

- Hemingway

A note about italicized words—

Technically I'm supposed to italicize most words spoken in another language. Those are the rules as set down by knowledgeable grammar persons. Take Manny, for instance —a lot of his dialogue is in Spanish. But I don't *want* to italicize all those words. I'd rather save italics for emphasis. I remember reading Hemingway's *For Whom The Bell Tolls* and being exhausted by all the emphasized foreign words. So in my novels, I only use italics *properly* when the reader might get confused by the foreign language mixed in with English. Some foreign words are italicized, and some aren't, and it's my book and I can do that. =)

As Stephen King said, the rules of grammar are meant to be broken. At least I think that's what he said—I might be botching it.

A note about medicine—
Some creative liberty was taken.
Some artistic license was invoked.

PART I

PART I

"Jiminy Christmas," I said. Again.

I'd said it a lot that day but the phrase felt right. Don't tinker with a good thing.

I sat in my reclining swivel chair, feet planted firmly on the floor. I wanted to cross them on the desk like any respectable and debonair detective would do but my sneakers had been unresponsive for several hours, the cowards, stunned into insubordination.

My laptop was open and impatient, beckoning for attention. Outside, cars passed with their headlights on, windshield wipers sloshing the drizzle. The cheery glow emanating from Orvis across the street was brighter than the afternoon sunlight.

In my hands I held an official marriage certificate pinched gingerly on the edges between my fingertips, like it was hot.

It was *my* marriage certificate.

Whose marriage certificate?

Mine.

That's impossible, you say.

You're right it is. I'd never married anyone.

And yet...legally I had a wife.

I had a *wife*.

She was a humdinger, too. A dame worth killing for. An attorney with a predilection for mixing cocktails. She read books to children at the Rescue Mission and drove too fast through school zones. She adored my son and hinted about seducing my roommate. She'd never told me she loved me but she'd admitted it to a poker table full of professional malfeasants. Hard to decide if she looked more like royalty wearing an evening gown or black activewear.

A girl I deemed deserving of my dedication and devotion.

Did I want to marry her? I assumed so, yes. One day.

Though probably not yet.

However...here I sat. Contemplating the evidence of our union.

"Jiminy Christmas," I said.

My net worth had probably skyrocketed. So that was nice. And she'd mentioned marital consummation and honeymoon bliss as she dropped off the document earlier that day.

Did I desire honeymoon bliss?

Yes. Yes I did.

But did I deserve it?

Yes. Yes I did.

Mackenzie August. Husband of Veronica Summers.

The real question was...was a question I'd been avoiding. I had a maxim in life and it was unspoken but I followed it closely anyway—be an independent and complete human being. Or phrased differently, I stayed true to what I believed and I did not compromise.

My life was well-organized and clean. Because that was necessary. Because I'd learned through pain it must be. Because I'd compromised myself before and ended up a wreck.

What did I believe? Live simply. Do justice. Walk humbly. Commune with my creator. Love deeply. Honor my father. Train up my son in the way he should go. Pay my taxes. Don't drink cheap beer. Iron the collars of my shirt so they didn't curl. Important things like this.

So the real question was...

...was I being true to myself if I didn't get the marriage annulled?

...was I compromising if I let a woman marry me without my approval?

And I didn't love the answer. I took umbrage with the truth, because I was besotted with the woman I unwittingly married. Did that matter?

I fretted that it did.

It went against my quest for independence. Not the marriage itself, but the vehicle in which it arrived. My signature had been forged. The ceremony was faked for inheritance reasons. Should that matter if the other name on the certificate was Ronnie Summers? Even if the motive was altruism?

It did matter. I'm glad no one was there to ask me why.

Mackenzie August, a navel-gazing mess.

Someone knocked on my door.

If I was the kind of incompetent man who got startled, I would have been.

A cute girl stood there. Not a girl, but younger than me. Maybe twenty-five. She had one of those haircuts that looked feminine but didn't reach her ears. Blonde.

Untucked slim-fit checkered flannel shirt, sleeves rolled up. Jeans. Bright white teeth. All American.

"Sorry to interrupt," she said.

"No you're not."

"A little, I am. I should say, I hope you don't mind if I disrupt your daydreaming."

"Better," I said. "More honest."

"You look like a man in a good mood. You were grinning at the ceiling."

"I do not grin. And if I did, it would be a volitional expression of good humor. Not the reflex of a milksop," I said.

"Jeez, okay. Why are you purposefully displaying your good humor?"

"I got married today."

"Oh wow. Congratulations!"

"Not necessary. It's easy to do, turns out. How can I help?"

"You're Mackenzie?"

"I am."

She pointed down the stairs. "I bought Metro. Or, the space next-door where Metro used to be. I was going to ask if you had five minutes to lend a hand, but seeing as it's your wedding day…"

I stood. Laid the marriage certificate carefully on my desk. Like it might eat me.

"I miss Metro. Their lunch menu was solid."

"Mine will be better," she said. "Guaranteed."

"What do you need help with?"

"The water main. I'd like to switch it on. So stupid but I can't find it. I'll give you a free lunch when we open next spring."

"Deal."

"Great. Thanks."

I came around the desk. She backed up, letting me descend the stairs first.

I grabbed the handrail.

"What class of fare will you be serving?" I asked.

She didn't answer.

There was a prick at my side. Just above the belt.

She was gripping and lifting my jacket with her left hand. With her right, she had plunged a needle near my hipbone.

"Take it easy," she said. She popped the needle free from my skin and replaced the shirt. "It's a harmless injection. You're fine—I'm a physician."

Alarms sounded in my head. Obviously.

But my body was too sleepy to care.

"You'll be completely out in less than thirty seconds. Might want to sit down."

"You're a physician," I said. "Not a restaurant entrepreneur."

My hands wouldn't work.

She said, "A fabricated story to get me in. I gave you a cocktail of Propofol, Vecuronium, and ketamine, plus an accelerant. I doubt you'll need rescue breathing—you're a bigger man than I was told."

The door at the base of the stairwell opened and a man took the stairs two at a time.

My brain was shutting down.

My limbs refused to lift.

The man caught me. Pinned me to the wall and held me steady, so I wouldn't tumble.

"Kidnapped," I said. The word slurred. Head slumping.

"Yes," she said. Her blue eyes were close to mine. "Sorry."

I wanted to fight.
But I felt so serene and lethargic.
Mackenzie August. In big trouble.
Falling asleep.
On the stairs. On my wedding day.

2

There was no awareness of time or movement. No dreaming or struggling. Simply lights out.

I came to slowly as if from a dead sleep. Vision returned before comprehension.

My hands were in my lap. Great hands, really. I watched them. They twitched when requested. An enormous accomplishment and I grunted with pride.

Someone had fitted me with bracelets. Silver, thankfully. Gold aged me.

I was sitting in a chair. Or rather, after a second inspection, a restraining harness held me upright, pinned to a chair. My head lolled lazily on my chest, so I watched my hands some more.

Hey, I recognized some of the bracelets around my wrists—handcuffs. How about that.

The girl. In the stairwell. I remembered.

She was *not* a restaurant proprietor. She had *lied*.

I tilted my head up, degree by degree.

Oooouch.

I was in an airplane. A private jet, medium-sized, five

windows to a side. The front hatch was swung open, letting in cold air and the unmistakable noise of engine whine. The plane sat on a tarmac at an unfamiliar terminal.

Across from me was a man. Tall, erect posture. Bearded, and pale enough that I could see some veins. He wore black boots, blue 5.11 tactical pants, and a black Rothco undercover vest over a henley shirt. Ballistic plates sewn into the vest, probably. I knew the outfit—commonly worn by guys in his line of work. He held a pistol in his right hand.

He leaned forward. "You can hear?"

"Sure," I croaked.

"You know who I am?"

"Listen to me. Carefully," I said. More of a whisper. I licked my dry lips. "I have to pee."

"I don't care."

"You're going to." I paused to take a deep breath and stretch my jaw. "In less than sixty seconds, my guess."

"You know who I am?" he said.

"The bathroom attendant."

"I am a bounty hunter."

"Hunt me a bathroom," I wheezed.

"You do not follow the orders? I shoot you," he said with a strong German accent. *Follow zee orders.* "I get paid either way."

"I'm going to pee either way," I said with a strong American accent. Plus a hint of Cajun and anesthesia.

"Hold it."

"No."

The cute girl with short blonde hair appeared. "I'm taking him to the bathroom."

"Could be a trick."

"My patient, my rules. It's inhumane otherwise. Everyone pees. Besides, urine stinks of ammonia and I don't want to travel with it," she said. "He'll still be cuffed and have very little muscular control."

She released my harness and I slumped forward onto the floor, unable to halt my fall. Face first on the carpet, I said, "I don't feel dangerous."

It took me a minute to climb to my feet. Another handful to get my bladder operational. Then still several more to fully void it.

Old age and I were going to have issues.

"Nice plane," I said, shuffling back to my chair. My ankles were cuffed too, and the German bounty hunter kept his gun on me. I'd have shuffled even without the shackles, so feeble were my faculties. "But the other passengers ruin the ambiance."

There were no passengers other than Ernst and the dastardly physician. I hoped he got my meaning—Germans have terrible senses of humor.

The physician strapped my harness back on, sort of a locking seatbelt around my torso and elbows. She brought me a cup of water and some pretzels.

"No," said the German. "No pretzels."

"Why not?"

"Because I say. No pretzels."

"No pretzel for infidel," I said, with a hint of German.

He hit me. An insouciant smack to the face.

"Hah. Can't feel it. Anesthesia and all," I said.

It was a lie. That smack hurt.

"Ernst, do not strike my guest," said a new voice. Firm but soft. "I need him in peak condition. Plus, what are we, animals?"

It was Duane, one of the minor Kings. I'd met him at a poker game. Looked like Euro muscle but rich. Raspy voice, thick neck. His eyes and cheeks were puffy, like he used to

fight. Or had a food allergy. His shirt was tailored intentionally tight and it shimmered green. He was followed by a guy
in a navy jacket, tattoos on his neck. And Tattoo Neck was
followed by a woman.

The jet had sixteen seats—a group of eight up front and
a group of eight in the back, four on each side. Each group
of four seats faced each other. I was strapped into the rear
group, port side.

I was facing forward. The bounty hunter sat across,
facing me, gun in his lap. Duane sat across the aisle, facing
me. The woman sat beside him and Tattoo Neck sat in the
forward group of eight, not part of our group. Poor guy.

Duane nodded. "Mackenzie August."

"Duane Moneybags," I replied.

"Chambers. My last name," he said.

"Moneybags suits you better."

He shrugged, partially raising one eyebrow. "Maybe. You
know why you're here?"

"I have many guesses."

"Let's hear'em," he said.

"First guess, you're mad I beat you at poker."

"Beat me at poker. No."

"Second guess," I said. "I called you a few months ago
about a thing in Virginia Beach, and it was late and I ruined
your REM cycle."

"No, it's not because you called too late."

"Because I killed Toby Moreno."

He shook his head. A tiny movement.

Heavy hitters like Duane wasted no energy on exaggerated motion. In fact I wasn't sure he even shook his head.
More of an indication that he might, if he was a lesser man.

I said, "Because I killed Calvin Summers?"

"No."

"You're mad I busted up some of your prostitution racketeering."

He shook his head again. "That's not why you're here. But that thing displeased me."

"You're mad because I killed Angelo the coyote."

He took a deep breath, held it, slowly released it through his nose.

The woman beside him was a knockout. Her imperial eyebrow arched higher with each of my guesses.

I said, "You're mad because while in Virginia Beach I talked to Sergio and—"

"Okay, Jesus Christ, shut the hell up. Only now remembering this. What a pain in my ass you are," he said.

"That was all the past eighteen months too."

The blonde physician stood beside me and placed a hand on my shoulder. "The medicine is still in his system, Mr. Chambers. He's loopy."

"You didn't kill those people," Duane told me.

"Calvin and Toby and Angelo? I helped. I was in the area. Maybe credit me with an assist."

"This man." Ernst the bounty hunter indicated me with the barrel of his pistol. "Talks too much."

"Mackenzie August thinks he's funny," said Duane with a flat smile. "I'll tell you why you're here. You're here because I respect you."

"Well," I said, tugging against the seat restraint. "That's apparent."

"That's apparent," repeated Duane. "A contract was put on your head. A hundred grand."

"A hundred thousand? That's *it*?"

"Hits are usually twenty-five. Maybe forty. You should be pleased."

"A hundred is, like, two Mercedes SUVs. I'm worth more

than that. Besides, everyone knows," I told Ernst, "German cars suck."

The beautiful woman beside Duane smiled. Realized she probably shouldn't. So she covered it with her fingers.

Duane shrugged and exhaled through his nose again. "Anyway. I intercepted the contract. Tacked on twenty-five more if you were brought back alive. So here you are."

"Thanks, Duane. A real pal. Best buds."

"Real pal," he said. "You're being farcical. But that's why you're alive, August. Because of some respect."

"Where are we?"

"Ronald Reagan airport. Washington," he said.

"Where we going? If it's not Disney, I'm out."

"We are flying to Naples."

That was sobering.

Naples. How about that. On my wedding day.

I said, "Can I bring someone?"

The woman smiled again. Her eyes sparkled, matching her diamond princess necklace.

Duane looked at the blonde physician standing behind me. "Meg, get this man some water. Something to eat."

"Ernst insists he doesn't eat."

"Ernst." Duane said his name but didn't look at the German bounty hunter. "Have I paid you for this man?"

"You paid me."

"How much."

"One hundred twenty-five," said Ernst.

"He belongs to me now. We understand?"

"He is yours, Mr. Chambers," said Ernst. "But still I'm waiting."

"Yes. That's right." Duane snapped his fingers. Tattoo Neck materialized and placed a small metallic box in Duane's outstretched hand.

I wondered what would happen if I snapped my fingers.

Duane used his thumbprint to unlock the box. The lid lifted on silent hinges. He took out a small cloth pouch, bright white. From it he extracted a diamond. Returned the pouch, closed the box, which beeped, and gave the box to Tattoo Neck.

I tried snapping my fingers but couldn't. Oh well.

Duane placed the diamond on the bounty hunter's outstretched palm. The diamond's culet had been dyed a bright red. Only a pinprick of color but noticeable.

"You did good, Ernst."

Ernst nodded his thanks. Dropped the diamond into a black leather pouch and zipped it in a vest pocket.

"Well," I said. "He did well."

No one cared about the lapse in grammar, the savages.

Duane said, "You stick around, Ernst. For the agreed handling fees. But I make the decisions. We understand?"

Ernst snapped a nod. "We do."

Vee do.

"Meg." Duane sighed, world-weary crime boss. "Now that's done, food and water."

Meg the physician acquiesced to playing the role of stewardess.

Someone else stepped onto the plane, blocking some of the engine's noise.

My least favorite person—Darren Robbins. Big handsome guy, great hair. Once a quarterback, always a quarterback. He wore a black wool overcoat, a dark suit underneath, Ray-Bans, and leather Armani shoes.

He looked me over.

I looked him over. Deprecatorily.

Duane stood and shook his hand.

"I wanted this man dead," said Darren Robbins. He hadn't taken off his leather gloves.

"Yeah, well. I wanted him not dead."

"You have the right to intercept the contract, Duane, I know the code. But this is a sensitive issue. The whole enterprise benefits if this rookie thug is gone."

"He will be." Duane shrugged, something he did with frequency. "It'll happen. But first, maybe he buys us some credibility. Makes me some money. Who knows."

"It's important he doesn't escape, Duane. You know this?"

"You scared of August?"

"I'm wary of any uncaged rabid dog."

"He's wearing the bracelet. Stop the fucking whining. What's he gonna do? We're good here. Go back to your desk and stamp stuff, huh? Tom, he's in some shit, right? He needs his lawyer. Go help Tom."

Darren removed his Ray-Bans and used them to point at me. "Does Marcus Morgan know? About this?"

"No, Marcus doesn't know," said Duane. "He'll find out and it'll be too late, and he'll complain and it'll be done. Okay?"

Darren walked farther into the plane. Sat on the seat across from mine. I leaned forward as far as I could. He inclined his head towards me. Raised his glasses and tapped me on the nose with them.

"I warned you, August," he said softly. "Did I not? I told you there's a world you couldn't imagine. A reality beyond yours, and that you shouldn't stick your nose into it. But you made an amateurish mistake. Punched out of your weight class. Tangled with what belongs to me, and now there are consequences. You cannot possibly imagine what's about to happen to you."

"You're forcing me to attend a Justin Bieber concert?"

"I wish I could go to Naples. To watch realization dawn on your pug-like face. To witness your regret. But I can't. I have a life, you see. Whereas yours? About to end."

"Pug-like? Perhaps you confused canines."

"What's today, Monday? I'll have Veronica Summers in my employ by Thursday. On her back, forcing a smile."

"Hey. Enough," said Duane. "I'm going to Naples and August is too. Get your ass off my plane, Robbins. Unless you wanna fly to Italy."

"Yes. He does," I said. "Untie me. We'll sit together."

Despite himself, Duane grinned.

"Look'it the bastard. Even tied up, he's running his mouth. I like our chances."

Darren Robbins stood. His eyes, an ugly brown mud color, locked onto Meg. "And you are?"

"In the employ of Mr. Chambers," she said.

He slightly curled his lips inward and pinched them between his teeth. A subtle mannerism many humans do in deep thought. But Darren Robbins, doing it while inspecting Meg the cute blonde physician, made it look cheap and seedy.

She cleared her throat and looked away.

Still looking at her, he addressed Duane. "You paid the hitman?"

Duane nodded. "Ernst, yeah, I paid him."

Robbins reached into his jacket pocket. Took out a leather folding envelope, like a wallet. Withdrew something sparkly. Another diamond, red dot at the base. He tossed it to Ernst, who caught it and put with the other.

"Ernst," said Darren. "Make sure August doesn't escape."

Ernst nodded. "Yah. If the prisoner tries, I will kill him."

If zee prisoner tries, I vill kill him.

"Move, kid," said Duane. He nodded towards the door. "I wanna take off. You hear me?"

Darren continued, talking over Duane's shoulder. "I mean it, Ernst. August tries to escape, don't attempt to recapture. Duane here, he's a softy. You kill August. Bang, one to the temple."

"Enough," said Duane. "Go. Off my Gulfstream."

Darren turned and left, quickly replaced by a beaming stewardess. She didn't look surprised at my predicament. She closed the hatch, sealing off the noise, and started mixing cocktails.

The jet eased forward, moving to the runways.

"Layers upon layers," I said to no one. "Of villainy."

The beautiful brunette woman in the seat nearby crossed her legs and stared steadily at me.

3

The jet surged down the runway, tilted upwards, and banked east into the purpling dusk.

My head remained foggy but I felt confident my day didn't seem to be going as planned. I wondered if I still had forthcoming matrimonial bliss.

Twenty minutes passed in silence as we shot farther over the Atlantic. Duane had mentioned a bracelet. Sure enough, I wore a thick black clunky band on my left wrist. It had a dark digital display and flashing green light.

Meg the physician was sitting across the aisle, running her finger on the screen of an iPad. Everyone else was forward.

I said, "Tell me about the bracelet."

Without glancing up, she replied, "Don't try to take it off."

"That's not an explanation. That's a warning and an imperative."

She smiled, still not looking at me. "It contains two transdermal patches. Essentially tiny needles capable of delivering medicine rapidly—a cocktail similar to B52. The patches can be activated by this iPad." She raised the tablet and waved it. "And by a device on my keychain. Mr. Chambers has similar devices. A patch will trigger if you attempt to take the band off, or if you get too far away from the device on our keychains, or if the battery dies."

"The patches will pump a sedative into my wrist," I guessed.

"Bingo. It's an ingenious device. Cost a fortune."

"You're not a physician."

"I have the framed diploma to prove it," she said. "Georgetown."

"You skipped the day concerning the Hippocratic Oath, doctor."

"Have I harmed you?"

"Profoundly," I said.

"How?"

"It's my wedding day."

She winced. "Fair point. Don't think about it that way, though. Instead, see that working for Ernst and Mr. Chambers has already paid off half my student loans."

"That's nice. Debt from education can be crushing."

She nodded, frowning at her screen. "It totally is. Almost criminal. It'll be gone soon, though. In the mean time, I'll enjoy the private jet lifestyle. Can you believe how decadent this is? I think the Kings own several."

"Play your cards right, get hired on full time?"

She grinned. "Dare to dream."

Ernst came back. He said, "You are hungry?"

"If you insist."

He pulled his pistol from the holster. A black SIG P210. He pressed the barrel into the soft fleshy part under my jaw. "You do not move."

You do not moof.

Even I, brave stalwart and fearless warrior, begin sweating with a gun shoved under my chin.

The stewardess bounced our way, beaming politely.

"Who's hungry?" she cooed. "I have salmon!"

The pistol remained until she swiveled my tray into place, deposited the steaming plate of food, and retreated. Only then did Ernst remove the barrel.

"Unless the customer service improves," I said, "our republic is doomed."

"Eat."

"Ja," I said. "It's German for yes."

Know what's difficult? Eating with cuffed wrists, elbows pinned back, fastened upright to a chair. I bet I looked like a Tyrannosaurus Rex with a fork. My fourth bite fell off the utensil and smeared a little butter on my shirt.

I sighed. "I'm not an alpha predator, I don't think."

Meg the aspirant mafia physician said, "Pardon?"

"Do you think dinosaurs ever drank smoothies? With a long straw? You know, because of the short arms."

She examined me like an anesthesiologist would if she was concerned about over-medication.

Duane himself came back to the rear seating area about the time I gave up on eating. He sat down opposite me and twitched at his tight clothing until satisfied and comfortable.

"You have questions," he said in a rasp. "Ask."

"What'd you think about the finale of *The Sopranos*? Surely you've got an opinion."

He responded with a stony glare.

I tried again. "When's the last time you used the phrase 'Going to the mattresses'?"

"I won't offer again. I'll go up front and you'll know nothing."

"What's with the diamonds?" I said.

"Think of them as a credit. Not to be given lightly."

"Decentralized currency. Used only within the underworld?"

"Decentralized currency," he said. "Yes."

"There's only so many diamonds thusly marked in existence."

"Correct. The more you have, the more powerful you are. Essentially."

"Does Marcus Morgan have any?" I asked.

"A few. Though he wasted some on you, no offense."

"Offense taken. Why are we going to Naples?"

He took a deep breath and let it out through his nose. Watched me with the heavy eyes. "You heard of the Camorra?"

"Part of the mafia."

"No. Not part of the mafia. Well, maybe. The term mafia, it's too general. It used to mean the Sicilians."

"What I meant, Duane," I said, witheringly. "Was that the Camorra is an organized crime syndicate. It operates in Italy. Even the hoi polloi such as myself know that. I used the lowercase mafia to indicate the general underworld, not the uppercase Mafia to refer to the Sicilians."

"Whatever. The Camorra is a system of interlinked clans in the southern part of Italy. Not as hierarchical as the Sicilian Mafia, so there's often unrest. You get the idea, they're corrupt. Anyway. The Camorra lords host an annual event. Called the Gabbia Cremisi."

"Sounds spooky," I said.

"Spooky. Yeah, it's spooky. The Gabbia Cremisi is a tournament. They invite eight of the biggest players to participate."

"When you say players, do you mean lowercase mafias?"

"Yes. Got'damn it. You called them, ahh, organized crime

syndicates. The Triads, and Cosa Nostra, and the Yakuza... who else, the Camorra of course, and the Brothers Circle from Russia...who am I forgetting? Doesn't matter. And the Kings, we're invited. Eight total. To the Gabbia Cremisi. Means red death, or something."

Without looking up from her iPad, Meg said, "Crimson Cage."

"Right. Crimson Cage. It's a week-long tournament. Each of the mafias submits a single entrant into the tournament. They fight it out. The winner brings glory to his tribe. So to speak."

"To summarize," I said. "Eight of the most wicked criminal organizations on earth gather once a year to see whose champion is the toughest. That it?"

"Sure. Yeah. Though sometimes the mafias bring political prisoners; have fun watching them die, you know. Been going on fifty years or more."

"And you want me to be your plus one, to watch?"

"The Kings, we get invited every year. And we decline. I've gone and watched, but never had an entrant before. Now? Now we got a fighter," he said.

"Me."

"You."

"You want me to fight and kill people and bring you glory," I said.

"Yeah. That'd be good, don't you think? Or at least some entertainment."

"That's lunacy, Duane Moneybags."

"You should be dead now. But I purchased you from the bounty hunter. And from Darren Robbins. Now you can go out with some honor."

"I won't fight."

He did a kind of disinterested shrug. "Maybe."

"What happens to the winners of these events?"

"You won't win. These guys, they're assassins. You'd have to kill...what, three of them? There's eight total. A single elimination thing. I'm hoping you get one victory. Bring the Kings some credibility."

"Some of the fighters are champions and assassins, and some are prisoners?" I said.

"Most volunteer. It's a great honor."

I indicated the cuffs and chair restraint. "I don't feel so honored."

"Because you're a walking dead man. I release your chains, you cooperate?"

"Hell no. I'll pitch a fit."

"See."

"Duane. Is this a joke? This feels pranky."

"A joke," he said. "I shoulda let the bounty hunter ace you. You'd rather be dead? I didn't have to intercept the contract. But I wanted a fighter. Paid twenty-five grand for you."

"You think a humble private detective is your best bet for a Kings champion."

"Big guy. Big muscles. I hear the stories. Everyone around you dies. Why not you?"

"For starters, it's football season. I'd like to watch the Cowboys. Secondly, I miss my wife. Third...wait, I have a son. He should be first. I'll start over."

"Your wife," he said.

"She's a humdinger, too. Turn the jet around. I'll try to forget this happened."

"You're already dead, August. Your only hope? Fight your way out the other side."

"I win and I'm free."

"We'll see. The contract makes it tricky. I hope you win.

They don't take us as seriously as they should. Part of the reason? We're newer. We don't have the great name. The other guys, they got names with clout. Camorra. Cosa Nostra. Yakuza. Us? Not many Americans know it. Call us the mob or some stupid shit. Kings don't strike fear into the international heart."

"Duane. I'm getting out of these chains. You understand? With or without your help. You need to decide, is this worth dying over?"

He gathered his feet and stood with a soft grunt. Adjusted his belt. "Because you'll kill me."

"Because I'll kill you. If I have to."

He nodded. Patted me on my right cheek with the cup of his left hand. Turned and went forward.

Meg the physician finally looked up from her iPad. She watched Duane leave and then inspected me.

"It's surprising to me that you're threatening him while wearing restraints."

"Not a threat. A promise."

"You're kinda scary, huh."

"Not yet."

4

The Gulfstream refueled in Portugal. Duane and his merry men and his wife deplaned to stretch their legs and consume cool fresh air. I was uninvited.

We had lifted from Washington at 6pm and flown for eight hours. Landed 9am local time in Lisbon. Forty minutes later, we were airborne and aimed at Naples.

I dozed, which was tricky upright. I didn't do it well.

About the time I decided it wasn't worth the effort, I opened my eyes to find Duane's wife sitting across from me.

Duane was maybe fifty and he looked it.

His wife was maybe forty-five but she'd fooled Father Time. On a scale of Old Maid to Veronica Summers, she was an eight and a half. Which was hard to do. Especially since I never judged women on their appearance.

One had to peer closely enough to see that her face, a charming heart shape, was firm and youthful because of a lift. Something about the tight skin around the eyes. There were faint wrinkle indications in spots surgery couldn't fix. She had the hands of forty-five, but the rest of her looked a peak thirty. Her brown hair was piled in an updo and her green eyes were enhanced with colored contacts. She wore black slacks and a strapless emerald satin top.

"I've heard the stories about you," she said. "The mighty Mackenzie August." Her accent wasn't American. The R sound was more of an HRH roll and she sustained the E. Probably French.

"The stories of my might are greatly under reported."

"I heard you pulled poor Dexter's throat out of his chest."

"I had to," I said. Her eyebrow arched. "He kept setting his drink on the poker felt. Leaves moisture rings, you know?"

"Can you be witty at a time like this?"

"When better?"

"You do not lack for confidence, Inspector August."

"Never had cause, Mrs. Moneybags."

"The fabled Mackenzie August, in chains. I have been to the Gabbia Cremisi. Twice, once with Duane. My husband, he can make extra money by selling your services to the women," she said. The level of eye contact she maintained was unrivaled. I didn't know where to look while listening to her sensual way of framing words.

"Is that so."

"Your sexual services, you understand. Some women, they are excited by caged monsters. A man in chains, who otherwise might kill her, but instead she gets to enjoy. What could be better?"

"Almost anything," I said. "I'll enumerate them. Let's start at the top. First, beer at a baseball game. Second... Wait, I have a son. I'll start over."

"Have you read the Bible, Inspector August?"

"I have."

She said, "One of the curses at Eden, Eve will desire

control over her husband. Did you know that? But the Bible says man will rule over her because she's smaller. Less of a curse and more of a prediction, no? A man like you is big and strong, and women want to control that power. It gives the woman pleasure—manipulating the man against his will. Did you know this?"

I did my best not to gulp. Dirk Pitt never gulps.

"You're neither politically correct nor woke, Mrs. Moneybags," I said.

"Being politically correct has its purposes. But so does the truth. Here is some honesty, Inspector August—my husband will kill us both if he finds me with you."

"I'll try to restrain myself," I said. "Get it? I'm in restraints."

She stood, smiled down at me, and walked forward to return to her seat. I was like an animal at the zoo, visited occasionally by the aristocracy closer to the cocktail bar.

Meg the physician was reclining in her chair, eyes closed, cocooned in a blanket. She murmured, "I didn't know you had a son when I agreed to medicate you."

"His name's Kix."

"I'd be careful if I were you," she said. Almost a whisper. "With Emile Chambers. Duane's wife. I've only been with them a few months but I can spot trouble."

"Thanks." My cuffs made a clinking sound. "I'd hate to get into trouble."

"This blanket is a Givenchy throw. *So* soft. These people live like kings and queens. Can you believe it?"

"I'm trying."

5

The Gulfstream landed north of Naples at a private strip in Giugliano in Campania. Judging by what I saw out the window, the small airport pushed up against a commercial section of the city.

The jet taxied to a waiting motorcade of black luxury sedans and stopped. The hatch swung open, sucking in thick warm air. Tattoo Neck went out first, followed by Duane.

Ernst the bounty hunter pushed a button on his phone and the black band on my wrist beeped. I felt a prickly pressure on my wrist and heaviness settled over me.

"Oh," I said slowly. "Damn it. I'd prefer you not."

He'd sedated me, the rascal.

Meg said, "I adjusted the dose. A mild sedative only, not the paralytic."

"The medicine, it prevents the funny business," he said. *Zee funny business.* He released the chair restraint and hauled me up. My thighs and back protested, but did Ernst care? No, no he did not. He patted his holster. "Try to escape

and I kill you. Or the bracelet, it zaps you. More medicine.
Understand, funny man?"

"No. Say it again," I said. "But lose the accent this time.
My head's swimming."

He hauled me forward and down the jet's short staircase.
Sun and humidity hit me. The same sun had hung above
America but the interaction felt different. I enjoyed it from
the distance created medicinally.

An entourage greeted Duane and Emile at the doors to
the terminal. Men who looked like Italian diplomats and
women with trays of iced drinks. Emile turned to watch me
while Duane postured and shook hands.

Some of the men pointed at me, questioning Duane.
They seemed pacified by his response. All esteemed parties
raised glasses to one another and drank.

Duane and Emile and Tattoo Neck ducked into a Rolls-
Royce Phantom.

Ernst and Meg and I settled for a black Audi A5, Meg up
front. The driver wore sunglasses and did not remark on my
shackles.

Nor did he welcome me to Italy.

The manners of these Neapolitans.

The lead black sedan rolled out, followed by Duane's
Rolls, and then us, a caravan of three.

"Guys," I said. "Who's tired and loopy? Just me?"

Meg yawned. "I'm jet-lagged. It's the morning in Washington, I think, but I've barely slept."

"You should try it on heavy sedatives."

The driver's head tilted up to his rearview.

"Keep talking," said Ernst, "and I will give you more.
Knock you out."

"These are *not* FDA approved, I bet," I said, lifting the
black band. "You quacks."

The medicine he'd given me was a good idea. Because I was very close to using my handcuffs to choke the driver. First an elbow to Ernst's face, then the driver got the cuffs. It might work.

And yet...no way. I was barely sentient. Too enervated for heroic violence.

We drove south into the city of Naples on Via Miano. The city was flat and wide and multicolored, like a carpet. No skyscrapers in view. I felt disappointed because the steering wheel was on the left of the car, and traffic flowed on the right of the street. Same as America. I expressed my disillusionment and got no response.

Traffic teemed as we neared Naples's more touristy areas.

Meg commented, "Look at the architecture. It's as if Naples knew what Americans think Italy should look like, and they built the city that way. It all feels...ancient. Somehow smaller but more permanent than Washington."

Ernst grunted. "The streets are too narrow."

"So many churches and palaces. I see both Renaissance and Baroque styles here. And the piazzas, look! I hope we have time to sample restaurants. Do you think?"

"I travel the world, to Naples many times. What you need to know about Naples is this—the Camorra runs it. The underworld does not even hide here. Police do nothing."

"It cannot be all bad, Ernst," she said.

I smiled sleepily.

He replied, "You know how the Camorra is called? The System. Crime is the way of life."

The driver nodded his head, a reflexive motion.

We paused at a congested intersection, and saw the first indication of violence.

Protestors were on a street corner, shouting and waving signs. I couldn't decipher the wording. Beyond them, a block away, a store was on fire and the mob danced.

We rolled on.

Meg asked, "Is the Camorra the source of the unrest?"

"Ja. Naples, for the past three years, tears itself apart during the tournament. Rioting and chaos."

"Why?"

The driver glanced in his rearview at the German. Ernst steadily watched the bouncing mirror, answering the gaze. He rolled down his window.

"Breathe the air, Fräulein Doctor. What is it? What do you smell?"

She buzzed her window too. I tried but my fingers mutinied.

She said, "Smells like...sewage?"

"It is the garbage. The Camorra, it makes money off the trash. But Camorra is poorly run at this time. Too many warring clans. Chaos and division. So in many places, the trash is not collected. It piles."

Meg glanced at the driver. "Is that true?"

He glanced at her but didn't respond. Stoicism in shades.

"And there is toxic waste in the dumps," said Ernst. "Unlike Germany. Germany is clean, precise. Naples? It is king of the hill."

We approached a raised part of the fragrant city. The land here wasn't level and part of Naples had been built on a low mountain range. I got glimpses of it as we wove through the thick tapestry of streets.

Our sedans stopped at something like a train station. Another entourage of swarthy gentlemen received us, like the Secret Service would. Tattoo Neck stayed near Duane, looking in all directions. Duane hung up his phone and helped Emile out of the car.

In the distance, sounds of chaos banged through alleys.

Duane pointed up the commercial mountain.

"Look at this. We're taking a funicular. I love it."

A man in a suit held the door for us into the station.

I groggily told him, "But really. Ya'll should clean up the trash. It kinda stinks here."

Ernst jerked me through by the arm.

The lobby was large with travertine floors and tinted glass walls. A minstrel played violin in the corner and the music echoed above our heads.

A handsome and well-tanned man stepped from the security detail and greeted Duane warmly. His sports jacket was white and so were his hair and teeth. He wore three gold rings and an earring. They half-embraced and then the ebullient man kissed Emile on both cheeks.

He said, "I am so pleased you came, Signore Chambers."

Duane said, "Nah, pleasure's mine, Mr. Ferrari. Finally the Kings get to contribute this year, huh?"

"Indeed! What fun we'll have. And Signora Emile, my god, you are more ravishing than ever. How I wish your husband will be killed soon."

General laughter among the wealthy idiots.

"You are too kind, Monsieur Ferrari," she said.

"Ferrari," I said. Kind of a snicker. "He's a car. AmIright?"

The man beamed good-naturedly at me. "Here he is. The American champion?"

"Yeah," said Duane. "Sorry about that. He's—"

"No apology necessary. Of course he is sedated."

"Right."

I said, "Ferrari, anyone ever say you look like Johnny Carson? But an Italian one. What is it about you guys that marks you? The gold chains? Casual arrogance and pinkish skin? You talk with your hands a lot."

Mr. Ferrari tapped his chin thoughtfully and told Duane, "He is large. Looks like you're betting on size and brute strength. A courageous gamble. The recent champions have been smaller and quick."

I debated insisting on how quick I was, but I felt too tired. I needed to sit down.

Mental note to Mackenzie—being medicated doesn't mean you should act like a jackass. To thine own self be true.

So exhausted.

"This guy," said Duane. "Mackenzie. He's been like a freight train in the States. Killing a buncha our guys. Good men, too. You know Toby Moreno? Anyway. Darren Robbins, you may not know him, puts out a contract. Hundred grand. I see an opportunity so I buy him first."

"What is your saying in America—two birds with a single rock, Signore Chambers?"

Duane Chambers looked pleased with Ferrari's approval. Must be a powerful mobster. He said, "Exactly. Get rid of the headache and also I get a champion."

"There's another phrase originating here in the Mediterranean, Mr. Ferrari," I said, my eyes closed, concentrating hard on the words. "Like Icarus, on waxen wings you've flown too close to the sun. Duane made a mistake bringing me here. I'm the quietus you brought on yourself. I'll leave the jongleur alive but that's it."

My eyes stayed closed despite the sudden stillness in the lobby. I focused on not falling over.

"Sorry about that, got'damn," said Duane after an uncomfortable silence. "Like I said, the medicine."

"No apology necessary, I assure you. He is as a *combat-*

tente should be. Feisty. We in Italy honor this quality, Signore Chambers. He gives me chills. But, I confess, the word jongleur escapes me."

Duane chuckled. "Yeah, got no idea."

Meg's voice. "An archaic word for musician."

"Elite," I said. "Elite word for musician, you mean."

Mr. Ferrari laughed. Sounded like he clapped his hands. "Your champion will kill us all but preserve the minstrel! How perfect. A devil who enjoys the arts. I am so pleased you came, Signore Chambers—this will be a slaughter to remember! I wish you the best of luck. My servants are ready to receive you." He placed a fist over his heart. "Mala via masta ne."

Duane returned the salute and stumbled through the phrase.

A funicular is a small train car that climbs upwards, along the rise of a mountain. What a fascinating and modern age we live in. Duane and his inner circle boarded one and us another, along with the luggage carted by men in suits and sunglasses.

I laid prone on the cushions and fought off dizziness. Ernst and Meg and our guards/attendants sat on the other side. Our car lurched forward.

"Herr August, I commend you," said Ernst. "It is not so easy to be dangerous while drugged and in chains."

"Thanks," I said. "I try."

"Who was that man?" asked Meg.

"Niccolo Ferrari. The spokesman for a Camorra lord named Rossi, currently the most powerful man in Italy. Rossi cannot come out of hiding, so he sends Ferrari to represent him."

"That means Ferrari is Rossi's fugleman," I helpfully contributed.

No one cared.

"Pearls before swine."

Meg asked, "Where are we going?"

A man wearing black Ray-Bans answered in an Italian lilt, "Vomero. The city on a hill. Many of Naples's wealthier residents live on the top."

"Police are helpless in Naples," said Ernst. "But on Vomero? Nonexistent. Camorra rules all."

Halfway up, the sedative lessened its tentacles. I sat up and looked out with clearer eyes. The German bounty hunter eased his black SIG from the holster, in case I decided to go Jason Bourne on them.

Which I wouldn't, still far closer to a nap than I was to decisive action.

Meg sat on her knees, pressed against the window and gazing at the unfolding city.

"The colors! What a striking place. So many structures shoved into a small area."

She was cute in the way young, short-haired, energetic blondes often were, and one of our guards openly admired her.

Don't be fooled, I wanted to warn him.

She's a fake doctor. Or at least a nasty one.

A wolf in kitten's clothing.

We ascended higher and hazy Mount Vesuvius thrust into view, looming over the city. Soon the Mediterranean glittered and winked on the horizon.

She said, "Even the rooftops are painted. Such an optimistic presentation. It's hard to believe these people live under oppression."

"It is not oppression, Fräulein," said Ernst. "It is a second level of government. The government taxes and so does the Camorra. The government protects and so does the

Camorra. Play by their rules and you do not notice them. One benefit, you can get anything at any time. Girl. Boy. Coke. Money. The gambling. Anywhere."

The spire to which we rose looked like a dense collection of ritzy condominiums. A shocking amount clustered on the brow of the mountain.

Meg asked, "The rich live here? Not much space."

"Maybe fifty thousand persons on the mountain. In Naples, the rich do not have single-unit houses. They live in luxury apartments or...townhouses, ja?" Ernst waved his gun, searching for the right words. "Private space and personal area is not as prized as in your country. Inspector August's house and yard would make him one of the richest in Naples."

He'd been to my home, I thought.

Our funicular came to rest in the corresponding station and a third entourage waited to receive us. This high, much of Naples was a bright tapestry below.

Duane waved off the waiting sedans. Said he wanted to stretch his legs. Men loaded his luggage into a black car, promising it would be ready for us.

We struck out into the city on the hill. Meg and Ernst pinned me in. She held a device in her left hand that would pump enough syrup into my wrist to render me null and void. Ernst let me walk freely, but his right hand remained on his sidearm. One of our escorts had clearly been assigned to me, almost stepping on my heels.

I asked, "How much are you being paid for babysitting services?"

No response.

"Last month I paid mine twenty bucks an hour," I said. "That seems high, but Kix isn't potty trained yet."

Up here there was no stench of sewage. The residential

buildings, newer and the facades less august, crowded overhead. Music played from open windows and hundreds of
spectators spectated our passing. Men and women hawked
wares from stores—fresh cheeses and wine and meats.

Duane accepted a phone handed to him by Tattoo Neck
and spoke softly into it.

Ernst told Meg, "This section of the city is called
Magliari. Means cheating merchants. These stores on
Pavone, for many blocks, they cater to the Camorristi. Police
do not travel here. Look, do you see?"

He pointed at a gun shop. Black pistols and rifles and
shotguns were on display in the window—the proprietors
were polishing and cleaning weapons at marble benches
out front.

We passed a store offering luxury tailoring. Another that
sold wine and alcohol and cocaine and heroin. Then a lewd
brothel, models available for purchase posing in the
windows. Two impressive banks carved from stone—banks
which Ernst claimed operated solely to exchange currencies
for black market use.

I asked, "Could you trade in your diamonds there,
Ernst?"

He chuckled. "You mean the *aurum*. Yes, I could barter
away aurum. But I would be a fool. And I am not."

I said, "The aurum is an underworld currency. The
diamonds are accepted by all major criminals, aren't they."

"Ja. Anyone can make money. But the diamonds? Price-
less. The penalty for counterfeit aurum is death. Penalty for
stealing aurum? Death. Not to be taken lightly."

We passed a stately stone church that Meg admired, but
Ernst said, "The priests inside, they will burn in hell. They
condone and pardon sin. For a price."

We also strolled by rowdy gambling halls, a counterfeit

goods wholesaler, a store that produced fraudulent identification, another which advertised for protection.

"All declared illegal by state of Italy," said Ernst. "But where is the *polizia*? Below, where it is safe."

Meg, carrying a backpack of medicine high on her shoulders, looked a little shell-shocked. Her face was white and she held herself by the elbows. Duane and Emile paused to fill grocery bags with wine and bread and cheese and olive oil and cocaine. Servants carted most of their purchases, but Duane insisted on carrying a bag. Like a real citizen would.

"The war between Camorra clans is big business. It's gotten worse recently, though..." Ernst trailed off, not finishing his thought.

"When I get out of these chains, I'm robbing the gun store," I said. "When I do, if you're smart, you two will get the hell out of Dodge."

It was such a ludicrous statement by a man so thoroughly ensnared that no one bothered to reply. Or else they didn't know how.

Children trailed us, shouting things in Italian and pointing at me. Probably gesticulating to one another that I would look good in a beard.

"There," said Ernst, pointing up the street into a clearing of light. "Teatro di Montagna."

Meg translated, "Theater on the Mountain?"

The hotel stood at the center of a piazza. Had to be the largest piazza in Naples because the hotel was monumentally huge. And graceless; it looked exaggerated, like a Baz Luhrmann movie, like the Coliseum mated with the Sydney Opera house. It was ornately adorned with towering columns on all corners and glinting domes and theatrical windows. Buses could be driven through the front entrances. Limousines ferried patrons to the waiting army of bellhops and a helicopter lifted off from the roof and swung north.

"I think we're neighbors with Nick Carraway," I said.

Ernst looked like a confused German bounty hunter.

Confused and stupid.

Meg explained, "It's from literature. Your captive reads books."

"Is it a hotel or a theater?" I asked.

He said, "Both. Because it is current home of Gabbia Cremisi. The tournament. And your death, Herr August."

"Swell."

A concierge greeted Duane in the shadow of the Montagna. One man caught my eye—short hair, tight suit, businesslike, one of those great lantern jaws. Probably former *Alpini*, Italian special forces. They always stuck out. Men accustomed to chewing rocks and killing others who did the same. Head of security, I bet. He wore a flashing Bluetooth headset in both ears. Seemed excessive.

An elderly and pompously mustached man welcomed and gripped Duane by the shoulders and simpered and said ingratiating things.

I thought about making an escape. I didn't know how many chances I'd have. But the circumstances—wearing the bracelets of death and surrounded by fifteen guys with guns —didn't seem optimal. Plus, the man in flashing headsets was watching me and I had a healthy respect for him. I nodded at him. He looked unhappy about it.

Duane made a motion. Ernst dragged me to the entrance, and the concierge placed room cards in his hand.

"Signore," said the pompous man with a pompous mustache. "Champions on the second floor. You will follow Gennaro, *per favore*."

Gennaro was a boy of no more than ten and he wore a porter outfit, including cap. He led us through a blast of city air and into the lobby decorated with garish paintings and extravagant chandeliers. The ceilings were high and the floors polished flagstone and thick rugs, pillars connecting with arches. Fashionable men and women paused to inspect me.

Wish I'd worn my slim-fitted shirt, the salmon one. I'd cut a more dashing figure.

In the reflection of a mirror I saw Bluetooth Man following close behind. The healthy respect was mutual.

A woman reclined on a leather couch, her feet drawn underneath her. Her neck glittered with millions worth of jewels. In her left hand she held a glittering leash, connected to the collar of the young tiger lying prone on the floor.

"Guys, there's a tiger," I said. My entourage stayed cool. "Are we going to pretend that lady doesn't have a pet tiger? If so, a little warning next time be nice."

The Italian boy led us upstairs to a labyrinth of grand hallways with heavy carpet and warm lighting coming from chandeliers and wall sconces. We stopped at 207. The boy keyed the wall and the reinforced door whooshed upwards and disappeared into the ceiling. One of our armed escorts preceded us in.

The first room was an immaculate sitting area. The walls were bright beige, the oil paintings original, the bar fully stocked with libations, the leather furniture buttery—Meg ran a hand along a chair and gasped. The exterior wall was a floor to ceiling reinforced window. The floor was carpet, a dark wine color.

The corner of the room was a professional kitchen, complete with a chop block counter, tile floors, magnetic knife rack on the wall, and stainless steel appliances. A stoic Italian man stood there, dressed in standard chef's whites and a toque blanche. My own chef? Behind him, a large aquarium bubbled. Inside the aquarium, pink crabs waved their claws and looked delicious.

The second room contained a bed, the piled blankets a dark red color. The exterior wall in here was also a monolithic window, double-paned, looked out at a neighboring residential building and the city below.

A heavy chain sat coiled on the carpet, one end bolted into the subfloor.

Kinda ruined the luxury motif.

Ernst connected my handcuffs to the chain.

Escape, at this moment, became impossible.

The Italian boy smiled at me and departed. With no more words, the guards and Meg and Ernst left the room. I heard sounds of the door being locked.

My chain provided enough freedom to reach the toilet and the bed. I climbed under the red covers, the clinking shackles proving cumbersome but manageable.

Exhausted again, I closed my eyes.

"And that," I yawned. "Was how Mackenzie's absurd adventure began."

Asleep in seconds.

6

H ow to escape.

The most significant obstacle would be the electronic bracelet. That's what I decided. I didn't doubt its effects—I'd felt them. A cunning and sinister gadget making getaway unlikely.

For lesser private inspectors.

The device formed a tight circle. Two seams—the hinge and the clasp. One button and one display. When the button was toggled, the screen indicated battery power and appeared ready to pair via Bluetooth to a handler. By pressing my wrist firmly against the interior of the band I was able to detect pinpricks from the patches. Tiny needles hidden in the band, ready to be activated.

After a thorough examination I lowered my wrists back to the blanket. Stymied yet undaunted.

Two security cameras watched all this from the upper corners of my luxury suite.

I had napped a few hours and was contemplating my shackles and planning my valiant escape when the door popped open. In wafted the scent and sounds of sizzling sausages. Ernst entered, looking like a stupid German bounty hunter who wished his rest had lasted longer.

Duane followed. He clapped his hands and rubbed them together.

"How's our champion," he said in a rasp.

"Disoriented. Handsome. And displeased."

"You're a late entrant, August. The Ndrangheta had their guy bumped. But who cares. With the Cosa Nostra and Camorra, Italy already had two entrants. Three is too many anyway, so the American Kings took the Ndrangheta's spot." Duane grinned, still rubbing his palms back and forth. "Fucking wops."

Ernst scratched irritably at his beard. "Ndrangheta are upset. There will be trouble."

"Meh, there always is. Forget about it. We need to focus on winning. How you feeling, August."

"Disoriented and displeased, yet satisfied with my appearance. We covered this."

"You're big news, kid. The city is buzzing, what I hear. Who's the new guy."

I noticed a gray line on the dark carpet. The line went around the room like the diameter of a circle. At the center of the circle (near the foot of my bed) was a steel plate to which my chain was bolted. The gray line represented a boundary between the safe zone (outside of my reach) and unsafe zone (within my reach). Duane set a chair outside the line and sat in it. What a wimp.

Mackenzie August, given the Hannibal Lecter treatment.

Duane said, "We got a chance to make some noise, August. Could be good for the Kings. I feel good about this."

"Allow me to deflate your balloon, Moneybags. I will not kill people for you."

"Why not."

"Why would I."

"You'll be dead otherwise," said Duane.

"What I hear, you're planning to execute me anyway. Heard it straight from the horse's mouth."

Duane shrugged, his go-to move.

"Maybe. Maybe not."

"You're the horse. Did you understand that?"

"I do not approve, August. Of your lack of gratitude. You should be dead the last twenty-four hours. But you aren't. I spent twenty-five grand on you."

"A *bargain*."

"A bargain. My fighter, he says he won't fight and that's a bargain. A real man, he shows some respect."

"Poor Duane. Your largesse goes unappreciated. What a sad situation for you. It's breaking my heart," I said.

The Italian boy from earlier wheeled in a cart of food.

I *thought* I smelled sausage. The grease still sputtered.

Easy, August. Never let them see you drool.

I hadn't eaten since...what time was it...a while.

The boy pushed the cart to Duane, smiled shyly at me, and fled.

"Thanks Gennaro," I called.

Duane raised a lid. Some form of pasta with hunks of meat. I also saw coffee and wine. "You need nourishment, August. In case you decide not to be a lamb for the slaughter."

I didn't go for the food.

"Mr. Ferrari providing all this?" I asked.

"Ferrari works for Rossi. This is Rossi's tournament. Hosting the Gabbia Cremisi, it's a great honor. He'll make a fortune in betting. Eat the food."

"What's with the unrest in Naples?" I said.

Duane leaned back. Exhaled through his nostrils and

adjusted the corners of his belt. "Been this way for three years. Rossi deposed the most beloved Camorra lord in a century. There'd been peace for a decade or more thanks to...Ernst, what's the man's name?"

"Di Contini."

"Di Contini. That's it. Di Contini took over in 1997 or something like that. He put an end to the protection racket. Demanded the Camorristi obey the commandments. You know the commandments? The code? Anyway. He gentrified the System. The people loved him. Peace and prosperity for years. Safety in the streets. No more wars. But then?"

"Rossi killed Di Contini and seized control," I said.

"You're close. Police been after Di Contini for years and Rossi tipped them off. The federal police, you know, not the locals. Now Di Contini sits in prison and Rossi tries to hold the warring clans together. But the man, he can't do it. Made too many mistakes, like re-instituting the protection racket. Like moving the tournament away from their beloved Secondigliano. So there's war again. What's worse? Last two years, Rossi didn't pick a champion from Di Contini's clan. First time in decades. The people, they're furious."

"Heavens."

"Guy you met, Ferrari, the man you threatened to kill? You called him Johnny Carson. He acts as the master of ceremonies, has for over a decade. Rossi probably won't show his face."

I said, "The tournament is public knowledge?"

"Sure. Even the police place bets. August, eat the fucking food. Got a big night ahead."

"The fight starts tonight?"

"No. Tomorrow. But tonight is big. You'll see. You'll be interviewed. Meet the other fighters. The drawing. Shit like that."

I said, "I'm not dancing to the music, Duane. And I'm not killing people for you."

"Only shot you got is to win."

"Does this not strike you as strangely similar to the movie *Gladiator*, Duane? I mean..."

Duane's face, which had been an ugly frown, broke into a smile. "*Gladiator*. Maximus? One of my favorites. Yeah, Russell Crowe died in that one. Don't get your hopes up, August."

"I'll do my best." I snapped my fingers. "Food. Now."

He stood. Said, "You don't give me orders. Hear me?"

"Food, Duane. Hear me? Do as you're told."

"Weird game you're playing, August." He didn't want to, but he didn't have much of a choice—he rolled the cart into my circle of reach. "Don't be an idiot, August. Eat the food. You need strength. Believe me."

7

Later that day, my door opened again and Meg entered. She wore a blue dress and she was attaching diamond pendent earrings.

"You look cute," I said.

She finished with an earring and smoothed the dress over her hips. "It's Oscar de la Renta. Made here in Italy. I get to borrow it tonight. It costs three thousand. Can you imagine."

"A good length. I like the split V neckline."

She affixed the other earring. "What's your name?"

"My name is gladiator."

She pursed her lips. "Do you know what day it is?"

"One of Duane's last."

"Did you eat? How do you feel? Any out of body experience? Any strong surges of emotion?"

"You're checking me for some kind of shock," I said.

"Psychological shock, yes. You'd have to possess a super human mental constitution not to. Do you feel disoriented?"

"Sure. It's been a disorienting day."

"You're handling this well, Mackenzie. May I check your pulse and blood pressure?"

"Nah. Trust me, both are gorgeous."

"I'm curious. How are you coping so well?"

I said, "An old trick I learned on homicide detail in the rougher parts of Los Angeles."

"What's the trick?"

"Keep your goal in mind and parse everything you see into one of two options—obstacle or tool. This bracelet? An obstacle. Ernst's gun? A potential tool. It simplifies the world. Brings clarity to chaos. Later, during a moment of peace, you can release the restrained emotions."

"You're remarkably level headed."

"Cogency is a tool. Panic is an obstacle. Get it?"

She frowned thoughtfully. Fiddled with her dress.

Two Italian men entered, each carrying a Beretta ARX. Such a heavy assault rifle wasn't necessary for little ol' me so I assumed they formed part of the pageantry. The men dressed in red sports jackets with a fancy crest.

Duane and Emile followed. Duane wore a black tuxedo, a trendy outfit with silk lapel and stripes. Emile wore a high-necked royal blue evening gown that grazed the floor.

The two men with assault rifles paused beyond the circle.

Emile did not. She kept her eyes on me and strode into the circle.

The men tensed. What if I ate her?

"Emile, Jesus, careful," said Duane.

She deliberately laid clothes on my bed and smoothed them out. Her hand brushed my foot under the covers.

"He is a man in chains," said Emile in her slow French accent. "And he is not stupid. I do not fear him."

"Yeah, well, whatever, maybe you should. August, it's time for the Colloquio."

I asked, "Which means?"

"Got no idea."

"The Interview," responded Emile. "Undress please."

Ernst the German bounty hunter walked in. He crossed his arms and leaned against the frame. Unlike the others, he hadn't dressed for a formal occasion. Still in tactical gear.

"Duane, pass a message for me," I said. I got up and stood on the bed, towering above them. Bounced lightly on the balls of my feet. Emile stepped backwards, closer to the safe zone. "A message to Signore Ferrari. Tell him I enjoy my room so I'm skipping the Colloquio."

"Skipping the Colloquio," repeated Duane. "No. You aren't. We can do this the easy way, August. Or the hard way."

"The hard way."

"Why."

"Because I think you need me sensate and sensational for this thing tonight. You don't want me sedated, which reduces the power of the bracelet. So in order for me to cooperate, you'll have to manhandle me. And Duane, I'm in the mood for you to try."

The two men with assault rifles glanced at each other.

Who was this idiot in handcuffs?

And why was he so devilishly attractive?

"Meg," called Duane. Softly. "How quickly do the sedatives wear off?"

"Depends on the dosage, Mr. Chambers. Thirty minutes, at least," she replied.

"Shit."

I bounced on the bed, my chain clinking.

"Enter the circle, Duane."

"Why you doing this, August. You know you can't win," he said.

"Doesn't mean I won't try. Besides, I'm grouchy."

"Good. Save the anger for your opponent."

"Those poor men in the tournament? They are not my enemy."

Duane sighed and rubbed his eyes. "The other bosses, I bet they aren't having this issue. Christ. Ernst, what do you suggest?"

"Electroshock. Wears off quicker than medicine," said the German, still leaning casually at the door.

Electroshock sounded nasty.

No thanks.

I leapt into the air. Straight at them, no warning. The chain caught my wrists and jerked my flight to a halt, but I'd planned on it. My feet whipped forward and caught the closest guard in the chest.

They hadn't anticipated the extra length my outstretched legs provided.

The man made a sound like, "Huuffggg!" and collapsed backwards, dropping his assault rifle.

Meg screamed.

Duane swore. Ernst went for his pistol.

I landed heavily on my butt. Used my heels to pull the discarded Beretta close.

Got it. Hellishly awkward to hold in cuffs. But I'd caught them arrogant and unprepared.

I tried to rise but the second guard struck with the butt of his rifle—a crisp blow to my temple that staggered me.

I rolled away from him, the chain snaking around my left ankle.

Got to my knees, one hand on the assault rifle's grip.

The upright guard froze.

First things first—Ernst and the guard.

Before I could squeeze, my arms sagged. Finger refused to contract. A sudden heaviness.

"Oh Meg," I said. More of a groan. "Not cool."

Meg was hiding around the corner but she held her sinister device out like a shield, her finger on the button. The bracelet on my wrist was flashing.

She'd moved quickly, activating a patch. The transdermal injection got into the bloodstream quick thanks to the accelerant she mentioned.

My limbs were jello. Sinking.

Duane's face was purple. "Motherfuckers! You let him get a gun!"

Emile was pressed flat against the wall, her hand at her throat. Unlike Duane, the blood had drained from her face.

The upright guard approached me again.

"Don't hit him," said Duane. "I need him undamaged."

He hit me anyway.

Ernst's words were a little fuzzy and not just because of the accent. Took me a moment to sort through the fog.

"You are quick, Herr August," he said. "I am impressed."

Our procession walked down a long hallway. My feet moved on autopilot. I wore black silk pants and a red and blue silk kimono.

How had that happened?

Good thing I looked great in silk.

Ernst and a guard each had hold of an arm. Otherwise my legs would've collapsed.

"Aren't you embarrassed," I said. A little thickly. "That it takes all of you? For only one of me."

"Good," said Duane. "The bastard can talk again."

From behind me, I heard Emile's voice. "Your outfit. I chose the colors. Do you approve?"

"Listen quick, August. This Colloquio, it's like the kick off for the Gabbia Cremisi. The opening ceremony. You follow?" said Duane. "It's important. Billionaires thick on the ground. Persian Gulf sheiks, oil sultans, European royalty, Singapore gods so rich I can't imagine. Renting rooms for ten grand a night."

Emile purred, "They are here for you. Indulging a guilty pleasure."

"And *this* is the outfit you picked out? A kimono?" I said.

"A joke. You still think this is a joke," he said.

"I am unimpressed, Duane, by things which impress you."

"Unimpressed. We'll see. You get weighed. Interviewed. Eat dinner with the other contestants. Tattooed. Then there's the drawing. That kind of thing."

I blinked. Intelligently.

Did he say tattooed? Probably not. Just the medicine.

"Do a good job. Don't embarrass the Kings. Then we'll talk about what happens after the tournament. You follow me?"

A little. Maybe. Or maybe I was dreaming.

My handlers walked us to a large door. Duane and Emile and Meg departed to join their wealthy peerage.

It was dark. Strangers stood nearby. I heard noises, a hot hum out of sight. Ernst and the other guy smelled like sweat.

We waited.

I swayed.

"What's going on?" A ball of pain knotted in my head, near the spot struck by the guard.

"You will be introduced," said the German. "Is almost our turn."

"How do I look?"

"Bad. Like you are stupid and a man had to hit you in the temple. Twice."

I said, "You're unkind, Ernst."

The wall in front of us rotated upwards. Like magic. Noise and light rushed in at our feet, then rose to our knees, our waist.

Ernst pushed me forward.

Despite being a stolid and unflappable gentleman, I felt a little shocked. This room was gigantic, like a big top circus venue or an NBA basketball arena. The central area/floor was as big as a skating rink and surrounded by a high wall on all sides, and above that stadium seating rose to the rafters. A live orchestra played violins and cellos and a piano in the corner on a silver stage. Spotlights swiveled. Thousands of people watched and cheered in the stands.

Theater on the Mountain.

A theater in the round.

A preposterously large stained-glass dome capped off the ceiling. Lions eating prisoners.

"We're not in Kansas anymore, Ernst."

"What?"

I heard my name blared over speakers. Nicollo Ferrari stood in the middle, beaming and talking into a microphone. His teeth and jewelry flashed, and his voice echoed. Were people cheering for me?

Noises and lights boomed omnipresently. My medicinal fog was evaporating but that allowed my sensorium to flood.

Ernst helped me navigate to the center. The arena's floor was empty and clean except a hefty baronial table at the center, sitting on a rug of sheepskins. The table was set with a white table cloth, red cloth napkins, candles, goblets of wine, focaccia and olive oil. Other men sat around the table.

Ernst got his mouth close to my ear.

"Sit. Behave."

"Meh."

"There are dozens of guards. And we can still sedate you again. Do not be a fool."

"No promises."

I sat on an ornate high-backed and polished wooden chair. Because I was disoriented, not because I was told.

I listened as other men were introduced.

The world reordered itself slowly.

Eight of us sat at the table. Around and above us, ten thousand watched. Maybe fifteen or twenty thousand—hard to make out details.

All eight entrants wore a kimono in the colors of their country. All eight wore the electronic bracelet. Five men were without shackles. Three, including me, wore handcuffs.

The stadium appeared to be divided by entrant. By comparing the flags and symbols and the appearance of the entrant, I was able to differentiate the attending "mafias."

I represented the Kings. Our section of the stadium was only half occupied. Embarrassing.

The Cosa Nostra's (or Sicilian Mafia's) cheering section overflowed deliriously.

Next to me sat a giant the size of a sumo wrestler. Yakuza, from Japan. I glanced over his shoulder—his section was half full too.

A Mexican cartel was here. Not only did their entrant wear cuffs, he was also chained to his chair like a wild man. I couldn't identify which cartel.

The Colombian had a large following.

The Russian Brothers Circle's section was half full.

The Triads's entrant set solemnly, wearing handcuffs.

The biggest cheering section was for the Camorra, obviously. Their entrant sat across from me, a fit and darkly attractive man.

I counted on my fingers.

Kings, Cosa Nostra, Yakuza, Mexican cartel, Colombians, Russian Brother's Circle, Triads, and Camorra.

That was eight.

"This is deeply abnormal," I told myself.

I was right.

The man across from me, the Camorra's handsome champion, smirked. He lazily dipped focaccia into the oil. Ate it. Wiped his mouth and replaced the napkin on his lap. His posture erect, his motions deliberate.

"You Americans," he said. "Like an animal stuck in the headlights."

"You Italians," I replied. "With your outlandish coliseums and fights to the death."

"You do not wish to be here."

"Given the choice," I said, "I'd rather be golfing."

"In your country there is no system. No...corruption. Here, the rules are different. We take great pride in the Gabbia Cremisi."

"We have corruption," I said, talking loudly to be heard over the booming voice and violins. "For example, major league baseball doesn't have a salary cap."

"You are jesting."

"In America, we do our best to disempower and usurp the corrupt. Not throw pageants for them," I said.

Without turning, the man pointed behind his chair at the cheering section beyond.

"The leader of Naples. What is the word in English?

Mayor? And chief of polizia. And judges. They all watch and bet. As I said, pride."

I took a moment to inspect the congregation.

Hundreds of beautiful women in skimpy sequined outfits moved up and down the stairs, bringing refreshments to the crowd. An elderly couple near the front row raised their hands and were brought a bottle of champagne. Near the top, private luxury boxes were alight and occupied by the wealthiest of the wealthy. Some of the most powerful persons on earth were in there. I bet behind me, in the Kings section, Duane and Emile watched from a luxury box.

The giant sumo wrestler to my left reached over and took my bread, jostling me in the process.

Rude.

The handsome man across from me said, "Do you know the Gabbia Cremisi?"

"I do not."

"It is great fun. The most important part is the betting. Money will be placed based on your answers. So do not get the Colloquio wrong, American," he said.

"Are you betting on yourself?"

"Of course!"

"Of course!" I shouted back. "Roma victa!"

Servants dressed in white brought us platters of food. Slices of salami and prosciutto and pepperoni and culatello, with chunks of mascarpone and parmigiana and gorgonzola, plus bowls of fresh fruit. Also the best looking tiramisu and cannoli I'd ever seen.

The sumo wrestler tucked in. Eating his food while eyeing mine.

I slid my plate of desserts slightly farther away.

"This is grotesque. Right?" I asked the giant. "Does this

not strike your moral compass as absurd? Surreal? Like an elaborate hoax?"

The sumo wrestler issued a soft growl.

The Italian opposite me said, "I know this man. A famous fighter from Japan. He does not like Americans."

"How odd. We're likable and benevolent and many of us have plastic surgery to look better."

"You think this is like, what did you say...an elaborate hoax?"

"I think this is absurd."

"Think about history, American. Violence is part of life," he said. "Down through the ages, humans have hunted human. Killed for sport. Tournaments like this are not uncommon."

"Yeah but now we have Netflix."

He smiled, which was a good look for him, and rolled his eyes. "You are too...what is the word? Peaceful?"

"Gentrified. Docile. Striking."

"You believe any part of society outside your experience is inferior."

"I believe human trafficking and profit from the death of others should not be a part of any reality."

Photographs of the entrants were being displayed on an enormous screen above. All of mine were taken from social media.

Betting lines were displayed on a separate screen and men circulated the audience, accepting money and returning receipts.

"What are my odds?" I said. Out of curiosity. Not stubborn chauvinistic macho pride.

"Not good," answered the Italian gentleman.

"Eight-to-one?"

The man tilted his face upwards to inspect the screen. "More like fifty-to-one."

"Fifty," I repeated. Maybe I'd heard him wrong—my head was pounding.

He nodded. "Fifty."

I said, "I am outraged. You Italians, always backing the wrong horse. What are your odds?"

"Four-to-one."

"I hate everything. You're the favorite?"

"Of course."

The next phase of the ceremony began.

The Colombian, a wiry man with sinewy forearms, was taken by guards to talk with the master of ceremony, Niccolo Ferrari, on stools under a convergence of spotlights. He and Ferrari communicated through an interpreter. The section from Colombia cheered, a small sound in the big space.

During the interview, the Colombian's numbers dropped; the betters didn't like what they heard. Too meek, perhaps.

He was then led to what looked like a massage chair. He removed his kimono and sat. A woman drew a design on his back with marker and prepared her equipment.

I realized, "She's going to tattoo the word Colombia on his back."

The man across smirked darkly.

I hated people who smirked.

He said, "Indeed."

"Ferrari will be mad when I decline, I bet."

He laughed and sipped his wine until it was his turn to be interviewed. He stood and flourished his kimono like a cape. Bowed to the audience, ignoring his guardian escort. The crowd reacted as if he was Lebron James or Chris Pratt or someone else equally amazing.

He sat with Ferrari and chatted. I didn't understand the Italian, but clearly the man was a favorite.

The Russian one seat down called, "American. O Principe, he is not friend."

I said, "O Principe?"

The Russian, a solidly built man with dead brown eyes, jerked his thumb towards the handsome Italian talking with Ferrari. "The Prince. He will cheat. He will slit your throat."

"You know O Principe?"

"O Principe was champion. Three years past. Do not think him friend."

"That Italian guy is nicknamed the Prince and he's already won this tournament before?" I said, shouting to be heard. And also shouting because that was lunacy.

The Russian nodded and said no more.

The sumo wrestler took some greasy salami from my plate.

I didn't care.

The universe had gone mad.

Suddenly the spotlights swiveled my way and the world went ablaze. The guards came. Grabbed my arms and hauled me up.

I passed the Prince en route. He had removed his kimono and bypassed the tattoo chair. I checked—he already had *Italy* scrawled between his shoulder blades. Underneath that was the word *Principe.*

The amount of things that made no sense was accumulating.

The guards shoved me onto a stool.

Ferrari read off a note card and spoke into the wireless, using English.

"Ladies and gentleman of the tournament, I present to

you the American. The King's champion, a Yankee named *Mackenzie*."

My section cheered behind me.

His words repeated over the speaker in Italian. From a corner of the arena came the sound of booing.

He wasn't preening for the crowd, but instead acting like an auctioneer rattling through information. "A late entry into the Gabbia Cremisi. A soldier for the Kings, from the States. A police officer. A former MMA fighter. Now he works independently. Yes?" He looked up from the note card and held out the microphone.

The Italian translation issued from the overhead speakers.

I leaned forward until my lips touched the mic.

My voice erupted everywhere. "Put me where I can feel the pillars that support the temple," I said. "And let me die with the Philistines."

Ferrari looked stumped.

The Italian translation drifted from the speakers and some of the audience chuckled.

The lights were bright and blinded out most of the onlookers, but those I could see wore headphones, probably getting a real-time transliteration in their language.

Ferrari said, "Are you quoting something?"

"Yes. But botching it."

"Very well." Ferrari cleared his throat and availed himself of another note card. "The stories are told, American, that you have been killing off the Kings one by one in the States. What brings you success in the fights? And what method will you use to kill your opponent in the cage?"

Into the mic, I said, "I won't kill any of these men. Except the sumo wrestler if he eats my dessert. The rest seem wholesome. Salt of the earth."

"You refuse to fight?"

"This is not what I do. I'm a detective. I solve mysteries. Find lost children. Report romantic indiscretions. Serve court papers. Pretend to be an English teacher. Work with lawyers to undermine the justice system. You know, real Superman stuff."

"Some of the English phrases I do not understand. I insist you take this seriously, Signore *Mackenzie*, as a fortune will be won or lost during the fights."

"The amount of money spent on this macabre slaughter is breath-taking. Are mafia lords really this well heeled and bored? I can recommend some great non-profits," I said.

"In the audience today are former champions of this great tournament. Returned home as deities. This is a great honor for your master. You continue the tradition dating almost a century," he said. "Surely you want to represent your country with dignity."

"My country is home of the Whopper and *Jersey Shore*. Not so much dignity."

Ferrari did not think me funny. Poor breeding, I bet.

"Are you still medicated, American?"

"Probably."

"You are new to the Gabbia Cremisi so some confusion can be forgiven," he said. "I attended a boxing match in Las Vegas. Floyd Mayweather. You remember? Before the match, the fighters perform...promotions, I think. You have already missed some of the promotion, *Mackenzie*. You'd be wise to catch up quickly. For your survival and for the honor of the Kings. Let us continue. Fighting styles and experience are extremely important to our event. Many fighters train for months. Some of our patrons hire professional fighters to evaluate competition, but little is known about you. What is your preferred fighting style?"

"Rope a dope."

"Tell us about your experience in the MMA."

"I hurt people. They hurt me back. I did well."

He sucked lightly at his lower lip, dissatisfied. "Is there video?"

"Doubtful."

"You wear handcuffs. What crime did you commit?"

I said, "I fell in love with the wrong woman."

There came a gasp from the audience. Great gallons of air being sucked in.

Ferrari nodded understanding. His earring glinted. So did his smile.

"The commandments. You broke one. Never involve yourself with the wife of a fellow Camorrista. Or King, I mean to say."

I said, "Ah but for the right woman a man will break them all."

Another gasp. A feminine sound.

"For her, your beloved, you must fight and win, yes? A *combattente* with something to live for, that is a dangerous man."

"Well, Mr. Sports Car, there's a contract on my head. The jackass who brought me here doesn't know whether I get to live, even if I win. Be easier for him if I don't."

"You misunderstand, American. The winner goes free. And keeps a portion of his winnings. A hero for all time."

I said, "You misunderstand, Ferrari. I've upset many grouchy and ugly Americans. They brought me here to die. Even if I win."

"Not possible. That goes against the commandments."

"Not possible? I was abducted, shipped to Italy, and forced to fight other guys to the death at the Entitlement Olympics. Maybe you aren't the people to act outraged at broken rules," I said. "Also, that photograph on screen? That's my Facebook profile from three years ago. I've put on at least four pounds of muscle since then. Bet accordingly."

More of the audience laughed.

The man who laughed the loudest was the Camorra Prince, the handsome Italian champion.

Ferrari said, "I think the betters will be confused, Signore *Mackenzie*. I cannot remember an interview quite like this. The men who arrive in cuffs, they die quickest. But you? I am not so sure. Thank you, American."

I leaned forward to the mic.

"When I break free, you should run. Also I'm not getting a tattoo," I said.

Ferrari looked thunderstruck, his mouth ajar.

I stood, ducked the guards, and made my way back to the table.

The audience reacted like they loved the drama. Laughter and cheers and boos. The men with assault rifles didn't know whether to wrestle me to the tattoo chair or fetch the next contestant to interview.

I sat down.

The big sumo wrestler had taken my cannoli. He was finishing his, about to start on mine.

I slid my plate back and glared.

More laughter from the audience. They were watching, apparently.

Mackenzie August, compelling theater.

I said, "Take all the meat and cheese you desire, enormous man. I want the dessert."

He glowered. I think. Most of his features were hidden in fat rolls.

The Italian Prince watched and smugly ate bread.

The sumo wrestler reached again for my dessert. I

picked up my fork and slammed the tines into his hand, hard enough to puncture. Blood squirted from the bulging arteries.

"Leggo," I said.

He roared like a bull and threw me from my chair. I slid face first across the sheepskin, which didn't feel great.

The audience erupted. Ferrari shouted into his microphone. "Gentlemen! Gentiluomini! Champions, please!"

Guards swarmed.

I sat up.

The enraged sumo wrestler hauled me up into a bear hug, getting his blood on my silk kimono.

"I realize it's just dessert," I wheezed, my feet kicking helplessly, suspended in the air. "But it's my dessert. And I've had a rotten couple days. The cannoli is symbolic, you know?"

He probably didn't hear my last few words. He was squeezing me to death and I ran out of oxygen. My ribs verged on fracturing. He had four inches and a hundred pounds on me.

I bet Duane wasn't enjoying himself either.

The guards shouted orders and haplessly whacked the giant's shoulders with the butts of their rifles.

Feckless nincompoops.

So much blood pooled in my face I thought it might burst.

If only my wrists weren't still bound by handcuffs I wouldn't be defenseless and the Stay Puft Marshmallow Man wouldn't be suffocating me.

But they were.

However, I still held the fork.

Ah hah!

"Sorry about this," I gasped.

I jammed the fork over my shoulder, driving it like a knife. The tines went straight into his right eyeball, burying deeply into iris tissue.

His howl deafened me. He released and I fell to the floor with a thud.

My wrist band beeped and the light turned green.

"Dammit Meg," I coughed. "I haven't eaten my cannoli yet."

The sumo wrestler's wrist band beeped too.

We'd both been zapped with medication. A powerful dose. It hit me like a tidal wave.

"Hope this improves my betting odds..." I slurred.

Beside me, the giant collapsed into a medicinal coma, both hands clutching the silver fork protruding outwards from his face.

8

"**A** disgrace," said Duane. "A disgrace and a fucking nightmare."

He paced back and forth across the red carpet of my bedroom.

I couldn't see him but I imagined his hands were on his hips. I lay face first on the floor, trying not to move. The knot of pain in my head had increased tenfold.

"Right?" I said. "He tried to take my dessert."

"Shut up, August. Shut the fuck up. I'm *this* close to putting one in the back of your head and being done with this charade. Hear me? This close."

"Are you making a gesture where your thumb and pointer finger are only an inch apart?" I asked.

"An inch apart. Yeah I am. You wish, an inch. Lucky for you the Yakuza brought a second fighter. Otherwise...I don't know. I'd let the Japs take the reparations out your ass, August. Even still, the Kings's first ever contestant and we're already under sanctions. You screw up again and we're out."

"Be a real shame."

"You'd be executed."

"Oh."

His anger and animation had increased the rasp of his voice to a full scrape. "I googled that thing you said. About the pillars of the temple and dying with the Philistines. You're quoting the Old Testament. I read the chapter. Samson, he was brought to the temple in chains and then he killed everyone. The balls on you, August. That's the second time you threatened to kill Niccolo Ferrari, the spokesperson for Rossi."

"Not just Ferrari. Everyone else too."

He kept pacing. "Unbelievable. Just unbelievable."

"Includes you, Duane Moneybags. Unless you release me of your own volition, you're going to die."

"If this costs me, I won't be happy. I put money on you to clear round one. The odds of you winning the whole damn thing are fifty-to-one, but you were four-to-one to survive tomorrow. If the others get you at a better price? If I start getting less payout because of your bullshit, August..."

He didn't finish the thought.

I said, "A fool and his money."

"Shut up. Stop being smart and maybe you get your bed back."

"I hope so," I said, speaking into the carpet. The chain connected to my handcuffs had been reduced to four links, effectively pinning me to the floor. The room looked huge without the queen-sized bed. "That mattress was elite."

"Serves you right, being a pain in my ass. Win tomorrow and I'll return it."

Meg sat crisscross on the floor near my hands, still wearing the blue cocktail dress. Smelled like expensive perfume. She attached a new metal wrist band to my other hand and removed the old band. The new one beeped as it paired to her devices. Then she rubbed antiseptic on my wrist where the patches had pricked.

"I can't believe how fast you drained the sedatives in the bracelet," she said through a yawn. "I bet you have quite the headache."

"Yes I do."

"Hold still, please. I'd like to dab Neosporin on your forehead and stronger anti-bacterial cream on your back."

"Since you insist, I'll remain in genuflection."

"You won't try to escape?"

"Not till tomorrow."

She smeared cream on my face, where the thin-skinned guard had popped me with his rifle. Still loopy from medicine, I barely noticed. She said, "Would you like to see your back? I can take a photo."

"That'd be super."

She rose to her knees and scooted beside me. I heard the sound of an artificial shutter click. Then she held her phone screen in front of my face.

I squinted at the close up of my shoulders.

Tattooed in big letters across my back was the word **KING.**

I sighed. "A humiliating way to get my first tattoo. No one will ever believe the origin narrative."

Duane grunted. "Origin narrative."

Meg said, "Invent a story about being an egomaniac in college and getting drunk on spring break. That's more plausible than being forced into a blood sport."

Emile strode into the room and paused.

"Where is his bed?"

Duane said, "I had it removed. Teach him some manners."

"Duane, do not be an ass. Mackenzie was almost killed by a Japanese monster. He needs a bed."

"Don't be an ass? He jammed a fork into that guy's face. Meg says he's blind for the rest of his life in that eye, no doubt about it."

Emile said, "That man was too fat. No woman wanted to be with him. And besides, my love, the monster would most likely be killed tomorrow anyway."

I didn't want to move my head, so I could only see Emile's dress and heels.

Duane said, "Not the point. We got rules. What'd you find out?"

"Betting is complete for the night. The odds have shifted," she said.

"I knew it. What'd he drop to? Five-to-one? If it's six, I'll kill myself."

Her voice held a tight smile. "The crowd loves him, as they ought. He is three-to-five."

Duane released a wheeze and clapped his hands.

"You're kidding me. How about that, August! The bastards love you. He's the favorite now? Forget about it. Means we got our money in good." He crouched and slapped me on the shoulder. Affectionately, I hoped. "August, you went from underdog to the favorite. All you got to do is kill that little Mexican guy in the chains. Got'damn, I could use a drink. Emile, walk me to the lounge. I want to rub our fortune into those stupid Italian faces."

Duane left, a storm of sudden goodwill.

Emile's dress and heels lingered a moment. Then she too left.

I said, "What'd he mean, the little Mexican guy in chains?"

"You were unconscious," replied Meg. "During the drawing. You drew the entrant brought by the Los Zetas, the Mexican cartel. I forget his name, but he strikes me as criminally insane. A *condenado*, they said, brought for public execution. During his interview he mostly blithered. In America he wouldn't be mentally fit to stand trial."

I didn't respond.

Instead I stayed quiet, absorbing and processing the reality in which I found myself. It was a disorienting and surreal reality and required significant digestion.

Her hand, which had been applying lotion to the angry skin between my shoulders, paused.

"What did you mean, you fell in love with the wrong woman?"

"The guy who put the contract on me, Darren Robbins. His prized possession, a high-end lawyer and sexual toy, left him. He blames me."

"Should he?"

"I was the impetus behind her departure from prostitution, yes. She's the girl who married me."

"Wow. Okay, so," she said. "You're here...because he's jealous?"

"Also because he's fraudulent and vindictive and petty. He abuses women and I think his eyes are the color of sewage."

"Doesn't seem fair."

"Our looks are an accident, Meg."

"Not the eyes, you brat. About him sending you here out of spite."

"I'm learning just how far the scales are tipped in favor of those with money," I said, my voice muffled by the carpet.

"I didn't realize you were here because of love."

"Also, to be fair, I cost Darren a lot of money."

Her words sounded small. "Do you miss your son?"

"He's one and a half. A fun age."

"Do you want me to pass a message to him, in the event that...I mean, you know. If you don't make it home?"

"No," I said.

"No? You're sure?"

"Not necessary. I'm going home."

She started applying the lotion again. I manfully decided against yelping.

"Your confidence baffles me. You were bought as a slave, essentially. Escape is impossible."

"For lesser equipped Yankees," I said.

"You're still doing the obstacle and tool trick?"

"Not a trick. At the moment, many things are out of my control. But I'll use what I have. Things like hope and confidence. I will not pass a message to Kix because that admits the possibility of failure. In my mind, failure is not one of the paths open to me."

"But," she said slowly, like she was speaking to an exceptionally dimwitted child. "You admitted you won't kill your opponents in the ring."

"Makes it problematic."

Her hand had stopped applying the lotion. It felt like she was idly running her fingers up and down my spine.

"You're an enigma, Mackenzie."

"Probably because my stupid tattoo is sending mixed messages."

"You take yourself less seriously than the others. No, that's not it. Maybe it's that you take others less seriously than they take themselves?"

I yawned.

She continued, "I think you offend people because your opinion is important to them and they don't know why. And you deal with facts and sometimes people don't like the facts you notice so they take exception to your observations. To compensate they take themselves even more seriously, which doesn't impress you. How accurate is my diagnosis?"

"Maybe. I'm too tired for navel gazing."

Her hand stopped moving. She rested it on the fleshy right side of my back between my hip bone and rib cage.

She asked, "What is your opinion of me?"

"Corrupt and conflicted."

"I can't help you escape, Mackenzie. I *can't*."

"Mmhm," I said. "Going to sleep now."

"I'm nervous about tomorrow. I want you to survive. Okay?"

"You're pinching me. Quit it."

"Oh. Sorry. Are you nervous? ...Mackenzie? Hello? I don't understand you."

9

A fter lunch the following day, I was led through the plush hallways back to the arena. Being a perspicacious detective meant I could deduce the arena occupied the middle of the Teatro di Montagna, with lounges and salons and restaurants and suites built along the outside. Today, inside the arena, instead of explosions of color and sound, I found echoes and empty seats.

Two guards walked either side of me. Ernst carried a chain attached to my handcuffs; in his other hand, the remote to my wrist band. Meg strolled with Duane and Emile and they chatted about a soirée last night.

A cage had been erected in the middle of the theater, in the space where last night we'd eaten. Like a grotesque shrine to violence. It was larger than the MMA fights I'd participated in, but the netting was a more open weave and the metal thinner.

I said, "Who were the people cheering in the Kings sections yesterday?"

"The Kings do not have many people here," admitted

Duane. "You happened last minute, you understand. Other-wise...who knows. Mostly they were Italians and Chinese who love America. They love American football and action movies starring The Rock and music by Frank Sinatra and Taylor Swift, all that shit. Seating isn't assigned."

"Your cheering section will be larger this evening," said Emile. "Trust me. The women are talking."

Ernst led me into the cage. The others appeared reluc-tant to enter, hovering outside instead, the sissies. The cage didn't form a dome but the walls rose ten feet. Being inside made my chest tighten.

"How it will work," said Ernst. *How it vill vork.* His voice caromed off distant corners. "Three rounds. Five minutes each. First round is the classic fight. Like you have done before."

"Classic fight. And if you're smart," said Duane, "You'll kill him then. Because of your history, right? Your biggest advantage is in the first round. Break his neck. Choke him out. Whatever."

"I'm not killing anyone, Duane Moneybags."

"Second round, the cage becomes electrified," said Ernst. *Zee cage.*

"Electrified," I hooted. "A shocking development."

"Yeah, the current won't kill you, August. But might knock you out. First guy makes contact usually loses, you understand?"

"Third round," said Ernst. "Fighters are given weapons. The weapons always change. No way to predict. Third round is when fighters usually die."

"This Mexican guy. He's a pro with knives, what I hear. He makes it to the third round? You're dead."

Ernst nodded and made a grunt noise. "It's true. I

listened last night. The Mexican is crazy but they say he will fight smart. If he knows you are stronger, he will play the defense until third round and then use weapons."

I said, "Both fighters might still be alive after round three."

"Then another break for water," said Ernst. "After that? No rounds. Just fight until one victor."

Emile removed a phone from her clutch purse and she ran her thumb across the screen. She wore a black bandage dress, a sexier outfit than last night's formal blue. "It's less romantic that way. Attrition is boring."

"Romantic. Gimme a break. You get how this works, August?"

"Affirmative. Twas clearly adumbrated."

"Adumbrated. I dunno what that means. Whatever. Sometimes both fighters, they get zapped at the same time on the fence. Or both get too tired to go on, you know? Can't finish the other off. That's what the Executioner is for."

"Of *course* there's an executioner. I deduced there must be."

Duane circled the cage, arms crossed. "Niccolo Ferrari, he'll poll the audience and the Executioner will finish off the loser."

"Does he carry a large double-bladed headsman's axe?"

Emile nodded. "He does."

"I knew it. Anything less would be uncivilized."

"Won't be so funny, it's your head he's loppin' off."

"I'm not killing any contestant, Duane."

The two Italian guards with sports jackets and assault rifles were standing at the entrance to the cage and they glanced at each other.

"The *hell* does that mean, August. Getting fed up with this. You just gonna lay down and die tonight?"

"I'll play defense," I said. "Until the Hispanic gentleman and I work something out through diplomacy."

"Diplomacy, Christ," said Duane and he continued pacing, but now he also rubbed his forehead. "You're a dead man."

"Whether I win or not."

"What do you want me to do? Huh? Tell me that. The bounty hunter here was paid good money to ace you. Maybe he should've. But I intervened. You been dead for days. I release you, I'm betraying that asshole in Washington. Robbins."

"Then why should he fight, my love?" asked his wife.

"Because of honor, that's why. Some self-respect."

She watched me with eyes too large and luminous.

"We need to release him, should he win. No chains."

"I release him, Emile, and I'm odd man out with the Kings. This is what I do for a living. So how about you let me talk, huh? August, maybe this—maybe you just knock the guy out."

"Render the Hispanic gentleman unconscious?" I asked.

"Yeah, how about it. A compromise."

"Sure."

An energy seemed to light up his face.

"Yeah?"

"Yeah, you give me your word of a release," I said.

He placed two hands on the cage meshing and leaned into it.

"Damn it, August. Robbins got my word. He's a colleague. What's so difficult, you can't understand that?"

"I'm too dull and stubborn, Moneybags. What's the deal with the Prince? Why'd he come back to fight again?"

"O Principe," said Emile. She replaced the phone into her purse. "That man. He is a legend. A god."

"Oooh, you gave me chills," I said. "For real, something about your accent and reverence. Chill bumps. Look."

Duane said, "The Prince worked for a Camorra clan few years ago. He'd get hopped up on coke, pull on a skull mask, and ride the streets on his motorcycle. He sees guys from one of Di Contini's clan, he shoots'em."

"Di Contini was the populist Camorra lord until a few years ago, when Rossi ratted him out to the police," I said.

"That's right. You pay attention. So the Prince gets captured by Di Contini's associates and forced into the Gabbia Cremisi, like you are now. But he wins the damn thing and goes free."

"Much to Di Contini's chagrin, the poor man," I said.

"Right. Anyway. Rossi overthrows Di Contini soon after. The Prince, he's a celebrity now. Like what's-his-name. The fighter in America, you know the guy. MacGyver."

"Conor McGregor."

Duane shrugged. "Yeah, him."

"Prince still rides motorcycle with the mask," said Ernst. "Even now. He will win again this year."

"He entered voluntarily?" I said.

"That's right, August. This tournament, it's a big fucking deal. Money and fame and glory, you know? There's only been one repeat champion, and he was from the sixties. People still talk about him. Man's a myth. Whatever his name was. That's why, tonight, be great if you'd kill the Spic. Bring the Kings respect."

"I need your word," I said. "About my freedom. Otherwise tonight I'll win through diplomacy, escape soon after, and then kill you."

Duane watched me a long time. The skin around his eyes were puffy from fatty foods and too much wine.

"Bah." He turned and snapped for his wife, signaling she follow. He headed for the exit. "You'll change your mind. You get in the ring and that Mexican guy starts kicking your ass? You'll change your mind."

10

I stood at my window and watched rabble assembling below, in the Chiaia district. The mob was directly south of our perch on Vomero, perhaps a half mile distant. I couldn't discern the details but it was obvious a fire had started in the streets.

Trouble afoot.

The designers of the Theater on the Mountain had built this window to be escape proof. And they hadn't failed. Heavy glass, double paned, reinforced sill. Only a wrecking ball would remove it.

Meg walked in, wearing pale blue scrubs, like an emergency room physician. Cheap, easy range of movement, simple disposal when soaked with blood.

She arched an eyebrow. "I like your costume."

I looked down at my outfit. Stretchable fighting shorts in red, white, and blue. That was all. "Shut up. It's cold."

She smeared cream on my back and said, "Where do all these muscles come from? The women are going to love you."

"Years of sports and training and steroids."

"Switch to HGH. I don't recommend ongoing anabolic steroid use."

"I quit in my twenties."

"I'm going to give you some antibiotics. Your skin hasn't healed and infection is possible. It's asinine to tattoo fighters immediately before a match."

"You're right. That's what's asinine about this."

She'd gotten too familiar with me. Too focused on the fight. She'd walked into the danger zone, into my circle on the carpet. I could kill her. Use her as a hostage.

Ernst was in the next room, however. He had controls for the device. Plus I was still chained to the floor, and I didn't think Duane cared much if Meg died. *Ga'head, kill the broad,* he'd say, like a true gangster.

I nodded towards the window, indicating the mob and curl of smoke. "Are the protests about the tournament?"

"Yes. Apparently the riots get worse today because all entrances to Vomero are sealed off with check points."

"The Haves are being separated from the Have Nots, and the Have Nots take umbrage. I can relate."

She held up a small vial.

"Cocaine."

"No thanks," I said.

"Duane and Emile are coke heads. This is from their private supply. It will heighten performance in the ring."

"All good. I prefer clarity of mind."

"So. Here's the thing. Duane told me to insist," she said, lowering her voice. "And if you refuse, there's a device to fit around your head like a gas mask."

"I've seen the kind. You light a crack rock, put it in the filter, and the wearer gets high, like it or not."

"Right."

"Give me the vial," I said.

"You'll snort it?"

"No. Tell them I did."

Meg the physician and drug pusher asked, "Are you nervous?"

"Sure. You?"

"Terrified."

11

From the general hum, and because I was an adroit detective, I detected the swelling crowd. Noise came through as vibration in my feet.

Four armed praetorian escorted me and Duane and his retinue to a holding cell set under the stadium seating, a square room with white walls and dark carpet and linoleum couches.

The guards had swapped assault rifles for electroshock devices.

Duane was in a black tux and bowtie and he watched me warily. The poor guy was on edge about backing a fighter who refused to throw a punch. A disastrous investment.

Emile wore a green evening dress that would've been at home in the Playboy Mansion. Her breasts had a way of drawing the eye and she knew it and enjoyed it.

Tattoo Neck sweated and refused to look at me.

Duane conferenced with someone outside the room and came in. "August, you fight third. That's the best slot, I'm told. First two rounds, the people are on cocktails and dessert. By round three, audience will be drunk. Got it?"

His eyes were a little wild and he fidgeted. His normal rasp had grown to a grunt.

"If you see a cannoli," I said, "Save it."

"A cannoli."

I shrugged. "I have a predilection for them and a sumo wrestler ruined mine yesterday."

"You win, August, and I'll get you a truckload of cannoli. I don't need to tell you how big a victory tonight would be for me."

"I need your word," I said. "I win the tournament, I go free."

"You won't win. So who cares."

"Your word."

Duane huffed. Glanced at our four guards and at Ernst. Crossed his arms, which threatened the shoulder seams, and shook his head—like, the nerve of this guy!

"My love," said Emile. "Be reasonable."

"We're going to our seats," he said. "Just win. Win and we'll talk."

"No deal."

"Got'damn you, August. Rossi might be here. The former champions are watching."

"Gimme that thumbs up, Moneybags."

He stomped to the door, a motion which looked goofy in a tuxedo. He stuck out his fist, thumb pointing at the ground. "Ga'head and die, August. I don't care."

Emile followed him but paused at the door. Placed her hand on the jamb.

"Win, Mackenzie," she cooed in her French accent. "The rewards are worth it. Trust me."

"Herr August," said Ernst after she and Tattoo Neck left.

"You have probably an hour before the fight. Be better for you now without handcuffs."

"Was thinking the same thing, German bounty hunter."

"The doctor's bracelet stays on. But I take the cuffs off. If you behave. You tell me so, I believe you."

"Take off the cuffs, Ernst. I'll give you no trouble for the next hour. Soon enough I'll escape and kill you. But not in the immediate future."

He grinned and removed a small silver key. "You still believe you will escape."

You still belief you vill escape.

"Sure."

"How will you?"

"Extemporaneous chicanery."

He fitted the key into the lock. I heard a click.

"That means?"

Meg stood in the corner. She watched me with no small amount of concern, the bracelet's activator in her hand. Ready to zap. She answered Ernst, "It means he doesn't know yet."

Ernst shot me another glance. Looked as though he momentarily had second thoughts but took off both cuffs.

I did the thing every prisoner has done throughout history—I rubbed my wrists. It was the first time my hands hadn't been cuffed in three days and the freedom felt alien.

Meg, Ernst, and the guards seemed to hold their breath. Was this idiot in the American shorts about to kill them all? Or die trying?

To put them at ease, I lowered onto the couch. I spread my arms along the back cushions and enjoyed the range of motion.

The room relaxed.

Ernst tossed a set of grappling gloves beside me, the kind with fingers cut off.

Before long Niccolo Ferrari's voice began thrumming through the walls. A muffled thunder. He spoke in Italian and an English translation followed. Anyone who didn't speak those languages wore the headphones, I bet.

Fighters were introduced, a process which lasted four minutes. The first round began, unmistakable due to the rise in pitch.

I watched the analog clock on the wall. The fight began at 9:30pm.

"Il Principe combatte," whispered one of the guards to the other. In a dazzling display of unprofessionalism, they bumped fists.

Ernst said, "The Prince is fighting. The crowd is loud, do you hear?"

"Yes I hear, Ernst," replied Meg, breathing heavier.

Two minutes in, the audience issued several short blasts of emotion, followed by thunderous applause. The walls shook and dust drifted from the ceiling.

Good grief.

"Two minutes," gasped Meg. "How do you terminate a human body in two minutes without some sort of tool?"

The guard whispered again. "Il Principe."

Mackenzie August, a little spooked. I wished for a television so I could watch.

Soon new fighters were introduced.

At 9:45, the next fight began.

The second hand slowly fell through the Roman numerals for five minutes, and then there was a lull. Break in the action. Fighters to their corners, probably. Take water. Talk with trainers. Catch their breath. Ferrari's voice blared out and at 9:53 the fight rejoined.

The second round passed without incident.

Three minutes into the third, the volume ratcheted up. Meg put her hands at her ears.

At four minutes, a burst of sound—screaming and groaning and boos, and then Ferrari's voice returned.

"The second fight," said Ernst, "is over. With the weapons, it doesn't take long."

"Holy shit, this is terrifying," said Meg. Her face had lost color but hives swelled on her chest and neck. "I can't believe I agreed to help with this."

I stood up and began hopping. Better to exercise the nerves than let them stress and fester.

The guards and Ernst watched the ceiling, their heads involuntarily tilted to the side as they listened.

The door burst open. A man stood there, panting a little. He wore a radio headset. He shouted something in Italian and we were moving.

We plunged through dark tunnels and up a staircase, into another small room. The sound of dense humanity grew more intimate.

Ernst said, "My advice? Get him to the mat. The Mexican is smaller than you. Don't let him reach the weapons or Fraulein Doctor will have nothing to patch up."

"I don't want to do this," Meg was telling herself. "This is absurd. I don't want to do this."

Soon Ferrari's voice boomed out again. The door rattled.

I thought Meg would pass out.

The Mexican was introduced first. I caught his name as Jorge.

Ferrari's voice ramped up for me. Had I become popular? Maybe stabbing the sumo wrestler in the eyeball had been a great career move.

I heard my name.

Our door flung open. We went through the tunnel and turned into dazzling brilliance. The stadium, which had been less than half full for the Drawing, rose like sheer cliffs of sound and color. Spotlights twirled, radiating a multitude of hues.

Yan-kee!

Yan-kee!

Yan-kee, chanted by twenty thousand.

That was unfortunate.

The orchestra played louder, accompanied by an electric guitar.

Ernst walked beside me, shouting.

"Once the cage closes, it won't open until the fight finishes. I stay in your corner and give you water. The doctor cannot help until the end."

I nodded.

We stopped at the stairs leading into the raised cage. Ferrari chattered but I couldn't listen. My sensorium was struggling to stay afloat.

Next to the stairs stood an enormous man wearing an executioner's black mask and shroud. Tattoos were sleeved up and down his arms. In one hand he held the haft of a double-bladed axe.

Struck me as unnecessarily theatrical.

I thought about telling him traditional executioners didn't wear the shroud or mask, but this seemed an inopportune time to dispel myths.

Ferrari was dressed in a white tuxedo and he circled the arena outside the cage, reading from cards into his wireless. His hair glinted with Macassar.

Meg pressed a boxing mouth guard into my hand with trembling fingers.

"For your teeth," she cried.

I nodded.

She continued, "Don't die, Mackenzie! Finish him quickly!"

"I agree with the doctor." *Zee doct-air.* "Kill the bastard! I hate the Zetas."

I jumped up the stairs and the cage door closed behind me. In the corner I saw a crimson stain on the mat.

Jorge wasn't a big man, but he also wasn't little. Thin with corded muscles that flexed and bunched as he breathed. His hair was a little shaggy. He was being restrained by a strap, pinned to the cage wall by handlers on the outside. He wore loose brown linen pants.

I turned in a circle, fighting against a drowning sensation. The crowd was mostly blinded out and to my eyes it acted like a single entity. The throng breathed and heaved and roared as one. In the front row, the same elderly couple cheered and waved their arms.

At the top of the stadium, the halo of private boxes kept an imperial watch. I glared against the spotlight, searching until I found the American suite. Duane looked tiny from the distance. He'd taken off his jacket and stood with hands on his hips, ignoring the others with him.

I raised my gloved hand. Gave him a thumbs up.

It seemed like one of those moments frozen in time. Thousands of onlookers watched and wondered at it, and I felt I was having an out-of-body experience.

What was the American champion doing?

Duane shook his head.

I shrugged.

Ferrari said things I didn't listen to.

I jumped and paced my side of the cage.

Dear God. Let me live. Keep both of us alive.

Reduce this temple to a junkyard.

An electronic bell rang and the crowd roared.

Yan-kee, Yan-kee.

The strap around the Mexican's chest released and he bolted forward. I dropped into a shallow squat, a forward stance.

He halted just beyond my reach and shouted. Jumped up and down and smacked his forehead with the palms of his hand. His body was crisscrossed with scars and his face bore burn marks.

"Take it easy," I shouted. "I got an idea. And we both get to live."

He frothed at the mouth and drool dribbled down his chin. What had Meg told me? He was probably insane, and had mostly dithered during his interview. And now he was bursting with narcotics, I bet.

He snapped a few kicks at me, easily blocked. Circled and backed away again.

Yan-kee, Yan-kee.

Jorge jumped and punched at nothing.

He was mentally unstable, no doubt about it. He'd been brought to die, not to win—a *condenado*, condemned to die by the cartel. Kinda like me.

"Jorge," I shouted. "Get over here. Trust me." I crept closer to him, staying defensive.

He danced away.

"What's Spanish for—stop acting like a dervish?" I asked.

I got too close and one of his kicks connected. Caught me in the temple and I staggered.

He saw an opportunity and leapt. We collided and toppled, me underneath. He threw punches and elbows faster than I thought possible.

Meg was screaming to get up.

"So listen," I told him, dodging and blocking and getting hit in the ears. Had he been a professional fighter, I'd be dead. "Here's my idea. It's called a non-violent protest."

Jorge screamed and tried biting my neck.

That was a little much. I shoved him hard enough to toss his body to the side. I rolled to my feet.

Yan-kee, Yan-kee.

But now the crowd wondered if I was a wimp. Were they rooting for a foregone loser? Their tone sounded less confident.

My ears hurt. That was the longest sixty seconds of my life.

I glanced at the American suite. Flashed Duane a thumb pointed skyward.

He didn't respond. Only watched, fists clenched in his hair.

By now the crowd knew something was up. They glanced back and forth between Duane and me. I'd announced that Duane planned to have me executed even if I won, which reduced some of his bargaining power.

Some of the audience raised their thumbs.

Hah.

Ernst shouted, "Kill him, American! Now!"

I needed to cause Duane more pain. Keep up the public negotiation. The Mexican presented no true danger, not until round three. But I could act.

I resumed the stance and crept closer to Jorge, who danced and backpedaled cautiously. His eyes looked wild in every direction.

"New plan," I called to Jorge. "Kick me again. That worked great."

The Mexican bicycled beyond my reach. Would he run for the next nine minutes until he got a weapon?

No es bueno.

I lowered to my knees, kneeling in the middle of the ring. Jorge paused. Glared suspiciously. The audience's volume lowered a notch.

"C'mon, Jorge. I need a solid kick." My words came out slurred because of the mouth guard. "I need some blood. Duane'll hate that."

The Mexican's trainers screamed at him, but their fighter refused to approach.

"Fine." I closed my eyes and covered my face with my hands. "Now Jorge, come kick me before—"

He didn't kick me. He landed like a jaguar from a tree. Drove his knees into my back and his strong right arm wrapped around my neck. He bent me backwards, my spinal column arched.

A choke hold. Hadn't expected this. Zero oxygen flowed.

Meg and Ernst shrieked.

From my position, I could see Duane's box. It was inverted, far far below me.

I held out my hand. Thumbs up.

What'll it be, Duane? I can only hold this for twenty seconds or so.

The crowd erupted. Ten thousand people stuck up their thumbs.

Yan-kee! Yan-kee!

Duane jumped up and down and fumed. His wife swatted him with her clutch purse. Marital drama acted out in miniature.

Jorge's grip tightened. My spine cracked and popped painfully.

Starting to panic. No air.

My hands went to the arm around my throat. Like I was in trouble. Which I was.

The crowd watched me. Watched Duane. Watched me. Frantically pumped their thumbs. Watched Duane.

Finally...

Duane raised a fist.

Stuck his thump upwards and waved it desperately.

You win! Now get up, August, you idiot, he shouted.

I assumed.

Jorge's hold, while effective and dramatic, was not executed well. The man had never received training. I twisted and rolled, enough to get my elbow into his face. Hammered him once, twice, and he released. Busted nose.

I got up. Gasping sweet delicious oxygen.

How much time left? Maybe a minute and a half? I didn't want to reach round two.

I closed, strafing right and left to pen him in.

"Don't take this personally." I coughed, a little light-headed. "You're going to lose. But at least this way you'll wake up."

He tried to stay away but couldn't. I boxed him in, got him in a corner. Smaller and untrained and scared, he had no chance. I blocked a kick and punch, and put a major league uppercut into his jaw. Followed with a hard left into his cheek. A combination Mike Tyson would be proud of.

He dropped. Knocked clean out. No movement, other than twitching fingers.

The throng, which had been on its feet, jumped and roared loud enough to rattle my ears.

Yan-kee, Yan-kee!

I went to my side of the cage and lowered into a criss-cross sitting position. Spit out the mouth guard.

Ernst shouted, "You must kill him!"

"I don't have to do anything," I said. Tugged off my gloves. "Fight's over."

I panted and sweated and rubbed at my neck.

It became clear that Jorge wasn't going to move soon.

The electronic bell rang. Round over. Niccolo Ferrari's unctuous voice filled the stadium. In his box, Duane made emphatic gestures.

The Executioner opened the cage door. He lumbered in, followed by Ferrari. The silver-haired master of ceremonies shouted happily into the microphone and I understood: I was declared the winner. And no one had died.

A commotion stirred the stands, somewhere on the border of the Kings's section. A fight was breaking out. A big one, dozens involved. Guards swarmed that direction, including the head of security. He was easy to spot, with the flashing Bluetooth headsets.

"Ignore them," shouted Ernst through the cage. "Happens all the time. Twenty thousand criminals? There will be fights. You did well, American."

Meg came into the cage. Knelt beside me to examine my ears and neck. She said, "Your tattoo is bleeding. So stupid."

Ferrari smiled and indicated me, and his voice kept droning on.

"I was so scared," said Meg, her breath hot on my ear. "That stunt of yours was bullshit."

Ferrari lowered the microphone long enough to clap for me. Everyone else did too.

I raised my fist and pumped it.

That's when I noticed the Executioner standing over Jorge. His double-bladed axe dropped—a sick thunk.

Jorge's head neatly rolled free.

12

"Pop, bam!" Duane threw a faux punch combination at me, ducking and weaving. "Upper cut, right cross. Lights out for the Mexican."

"Left cross."

"Whatever. It was gorgeous. I could kiss you on the mouth," said Duane in a soft rasp.

I sat on my bed. Meg kneeled on the bed behind me, toweling my hair dry, while Duane, Emile, Ernst, and Tattoo Neck watched—a weird celebratory post-fight debriefing.

It was almost midnight. The adrenaline had worn off and was souring my stomach. Sounds of a raging party throbbed through the walls. Or maybe it was a rave. I never knew the difference.

"How is he, doc? How's our cash cow?" asked Duane.

"Without injury and almost entirely unhurt. And this is the freshest he's smelled in days."

"First of all," I politely corrected her. "My natural scent is divine. Secondly, my neck is sore. Third, I don't love the cash cow nickname."

"You're a monster, August. An absolute monster. Can't

believe how quickly you dismantled the Mexican." He
grinned so broad that his eyes disappeared inside puffy
cheeks. He wasn't fat, just swollen. "You played me; I know
you did. Faked the fight to get your release. But it worked. I
caved, August. You won, fair and square. And I'll keep my
promise."

An Italian boy wheeled in a large cart of food, including
a thick white china plate stacked with cannoli. He rolled it
to a stop along the wall.

"Thanks, Gennaro," I said, the lone avuncular adult.

He grinned, shot me a thumbs up, and left.

"How about that, August. All the cannoli you can eat.
The chef out there doesn't make it, so I ordered some. You're
welcome. That's what you get. I'm cashing maybe a million
tonight. How about that? I need to make a call. What time is
it in DC? Got'damn, I'm in a good mood."

"I can tell. You won't shut up."

"I did you another favor. Immediately after the fight, I
put you up for bidding. You're gonna get laid tonight,
August. You're welcome for that, too," he said.

"I decline."

"You decline. Hah. That's good. Girls bidding good
money for you. If she's ugly? Well, close your eyes. Or
maybe it's a guy? I dunno. Emile, you know?"

Emile was watching me. A predatory gleam in her eye. I
tried not to shiver. She said, "A silent auction was held for
each of the four victors. Bidding closed twenty minutes ago,
and the results were delivered to our door. Mackenzie
fetched...a surprisingly high amount."

"Surprising?" I frowned.

"Oh yeah? A big number? Good for you, August. You
survive this thing and I gotta share some of the winnings
with you. Maybe I should kill you myself, then." Duane kept

smiling, drunk on his good fortune. And his powerful narcotics. "You know who won the auction?"

Emile nodded slowly. "I do. She will be here soon."

"Here soon. Good. August, you get laid and I get paid. Hah. What a life this is. To the victor go the spoils, am I right?"

"Duane," I said. "I suggest you snort less cocaine. Also, send the girl away."

He didn't pay attention.

"Good thing I put the bed back in. C'mon, let's go. There's a party on every level of the Teatro di Montagna tonight. I hear the Colombians are furious. Gonna be half a dozen fights. Girls so thick you could walk on them." He stopped at the door. "Meg, take the night off. Ernst, stick around. Mackenzie tries to escape? He hurts the girl or uses her as a hostage? Zap him. Got it?"

Ernst glowered at me, like his job was my fault.

Meg said, "I'm going to bed. This was brutal."

Emile remained the longest, watching me with an expression I couldn't decipher. At last she said, "I entered the auction too. For you. And lost, obviously. Despite bidding a record amount."

"I'm flattered."

"You should be."

"A fool and her money."

"If I'd won, and Duane found out..."

She left the sentence unfinished.

MY DATE for the evening arrived at 12:15am. She was preceded into my bedroom by Ernst and also a Camorra praetorian, hand on his sidearm.

All three looked at me, curiously. I was lying on the floor, stretching the chain and my legs as far as they could go, trying to get my toes under the food cart.

"The hell are you doing?" asked Ernst.

Zee hell.

"You selfish nitwits didn't push my food close enough," I said. "So I'm getting it myself. Obviously. I'm so close."

"So that's what you were shouting about."

My date wore a clingy strapless red dress that reached the middle of her calves. Her heels glinted a metallic gold, and her gloves were gold too. Her brown hair fell in curls around a pretty face. If I judged women on their looks, which I would *never* do, I'd say her face was a little too thin, as though she dieted to the extreme. Maybe forty years old? Forty-five?

"Here," she said, a little breathless. "Allow me."

She laid her hands on the cart and wheeled it into my circle of freedom, and quickly retreated.

"See how easy that was, Ernst?" I said.

The guard said something in Italian. "Lo vuoi immobilizzato?"

She cleared her throat and spoke in a soft quaver. "No, I don't think...that won't be necessary. Mackenzie said he's here because of a woman. He won't hurt me."

Ernst said, "You have one hour. We'll be in the next room. The door stays open."

They left and the girl's face paled.

Ahh, alone at last.

And not the least bit incredibly awkward.

I got to my feet, chain clinking, and said, "Do you mind? I haven't eaten yet."

"Oh! No, um, please."

"What did he ask you?" I said.

"He asked if I wanted you, ah...immobilized."

She stayed near the wall, leaning against it, unsure what to do with her hands.

I removed the lid from a plate—sausage and cheese.

"What is it with the Italians and their different types of sausages?"

Her anxious face relaxed into a smile. "That's Ciauscolo and Cotechino. I could...feed it to you, no?"

"Your accent is Italian," I said and I fed myself. Like all good heroes do.

"I was born in Rome. This is my second time at the Gabbia Cremisi. My husband, he...he works with the Sicilians, importing...I don't know how you say it in English. Fake brands?"

Her English wasn't bad. She pronounced *The* as *De*, and the vowels sounded similar.

"Counterfeit goods. Does your husband know you're here?"

"Yes." She exhaled a shaky, embarrassed breath. "You're his gift to me. And his apology."

"Good for him. A stiff apology is a second insult." I finished another sausage and tried the artichoke.

"I thought you might die in the fight," she said.

"Me too, briefly. My ruse nearly backfired."

"Because your owner, the man from the Kings, wouldn't let you live, no? It's all we talked about at the *feste*."

"Duane is not my owner. In fact, I'm going to kill him soon. But otherwise, you're correct."

She pushed from the wall and dared to scoot an inch closer. About her was an air of delicacy. Way too breakable to be tossed into a room with guys like me. These people were lunatics. "You're here for punishment. Not for glory?"

I indicated my food tray. "Cannoli? I can't eat that much.

Or. Let me rephrase. I shouldn't eat that much. My son said I put on a few pounds."

"If...if you like, I will."

"Doesn't matter to me. I'm being friendly. You're hungry or you're not," I said.

She toed the circle on the carpet.

"You will...you will not hurt me, no?"

"What's your name?"

"Aurora."

"Aurora, I will absolutely not hurt you. I didn't even want to hurt Jorge, the guy in the ring."

She scooted a little closer. Tentatively took a cannoli. Held it gingerly in her hands.

She'd paid a lot of money for *this*?

She said, "And your name is Mackenzie. Mackenzie the American King."

"Well...that's a bit much. But yes. Mackenzie the American King, you can call me that."

Might teach that nickname to Manny, my roommate.

She said, "Tonight you fought so well. So big and strong and fast. Everyone says so. You are here because of a woman, no? Tell me about her."

I said, "Ronnie. She walks in beauty, like the night of cloudless climes and starry skies."

"I do not understand, Mackenzie."

"She's cute."

"You miss her," she said.

"Very much."

"Tonight," she said and she replaced the cannoli. "You can have me instead, Mackenzie. To forget."

"Aurora," I said.

"The wives tell two stories. One, that you are gentle and compassionate. The other, a wild and dangerous animal."

"In bed?"

"Sì."

"Don't trust your sources," I said. "I never dated a mobster's wife."

"Maybe the woman, Ronnie, she tells stories."

"We haven't."

Her brown eyes widened. "You and she...have not?"

"No, but don't spread that around. It'll hurt my reputation. I prefer wild and dangerous to abstinent."

She was trying to be seductive but the hand-wringing ruined it. "I think you will be both, Mackenzie. Can I come to...your bed?"

I was on the verge of telling her 'No thanks, this is the weirdest' when Gennaro walked in again, pushing yet another cart.

Not having a closed door was less than ideal for Aurora's purposes.

Gennaro rolled the cart to the line and gave me another thumbs up. "Un regalo dal Teatro."

"Oh!" cried Aurora. "Champagne!"

"What'd he say?"

"He says it's a gift from the hotel. A drink is exactly what we need, Mackenzie."

Gennaro nodded towards the bottle and winked and left.

A wink? Curious.

"And it's Salon Blanc de Blancs Le Mesnil-sur-Oger. The best for us, Mackenzie, no?" She took the large bottle from the silver bucket of ice and used a little towel to wipe it down. "You rest. I will pour us drinks. We will be happier."

She pronounced it *hap-peer*.

I rubbed my forehead. This felt so goofy. Would I owe her a refund?

She peeled off the foil and untwisted the wire cap.

Pop!

She laughed, high and throaty, and let the foam spill over her hand.

"Aurora," I said.

"Yes Mackenzie?"

She tipped the bottle up to fill a crystal flute. Underneath the bottom of the bottle, something silver flashed.

Zounds. A clue.

"Um," I said.

She filled the second flute, tipping the bottle slightly further and giving me a better view. Stuck to the underside of the champagne bottle was a universal handcuff key.

I'll be darned. Someone was sending me a gift.

Gennaro? Someone working with the boy?

She handed me a flute and we clinked.

"Saluti, Mackenzie!" She tipped hers back and drained it. She covered her mouth and grinned. "Scusami!"

I raised my glass and smiled, thinking about the key.

"I need another, no?" she said.

"Bring the bottle. I've never had Italian champagne before."

"Whatever you wish, American King."

She wheeled the cart to the bed and poured herself another.

My brain, well-oiled machine that it was, spun. A handcuff key. What to do, what to do. Remove cuffs and then... subdue Aurora? I needed to incapacitate Ernst and get that damned triggering device. The handcuff key wouldn't work on the black wrist band.

I lifted the bottle awkwardly with the handcuffs. Held it by the base. Pretended to scrutinize the label and surreptitiously scrapped the bottom until the key fell into my palm.

Smoother than Ethan Hunt, in my unbiased opinion.

"Don't you like it?" she asked.

I set the bottle down, picked up my flute, and drank half. Grinned.

Disgusting. Like every other drop of champagne ever fermented.

"Delicious. Must be expensive."

She said, "Yes. Just like you." She finished her second flute and turned, her back to me. Gathered her long brown hair with both hands and said, "Mackenzie, my American King. Please help with my zipper, no?"

Zip-peer, noh?

I glanced at the two security cameras in the corners.

"Sit on my lap," I said.

She scooted backwards.

Using the thumb and forefinger of my right hand, I pinched the key and slipped it into my left handcuff and twisted. The lock popped free.

She lowered onto my lap, still holding her hair up.

I raised my arms to accommodate her, the chain clinking on her dress. As best I could, I acted in a nonchalant manner for the sake of the cameras. I transferred the key to my left hand and released the right cuff.

Free.

I lowered the shackles onto the bed in such a way that it looked as though I still wore them, and wrapped my arms around her waist. She shivered and made a giggling noise.

"Mackenzie! My dress, please?"

I squeezed her, which she enjoyed, and I got my lips next to her ear.

"Aurora."

She returned the whisper. "Yes?"

"I find you coquettish and alluring."

"Is...does that...that is good?"

"Means you're pretty."

She shivered again. "Grazie, Mackenzie."

My voice was low. "Any man would be lucky to have you."

"But I give myself to you, Mackenzie. Not to any man."

I twisted enough to reach past her to the cart. Picked up the champagne. Refilled her flute and mine, emptying the heavy bottle.

"Unfortunately, Aurora, I have to go."

"Go?"

"Yes."

"You...you are leaving?"

"I am," I whispered. "I'm already free. Don't take it personally. I could kill you now. But I won't, because I think you're great. And you shouldn't take this as a rejection."

"I don't understand."

"I'm going into the next room to try and kill the guards. I probably will, because I'm great. If successful, I will remove the band on my wrist."

"And," she said, her voice shaking. "Then sex?"

"Then I'm going to kill everyone else too. Everyone but you."

"But...why?"

"Be rude to kill you, after all the money you bid," I said. "Plus I like your hair."

"No, I meant, why try to escape? You cannot. Teatro di Montagna, it is like a castle. Instead, Mackenzie, lie with me and win the Gabbia Cremisi. It is safer that way. The hallways are guarded."

"I have to try."

"Even though you know it is impossible?"

Em-poss-seeble?

"Even so," I said. "If I don't try, I lose part of myself.

Resisting helps me maintain autonomy, even if it fails. That's odd, I know, but trust me—I'm smarter than I look."

She turned her head far enough so that her lips brushed my skin. "But I want to tell the other wives. I want the glory of sex with a champion. It was a gift to me, Mackenzie. An expensive one."

"A bargain, really."

"Please."

"Tell the wives I think you're beautiful."

"Mackenzie." She pouted.

"And that we had a nice time. And that we fell in love and you helped me escape," I said, blubbering whatever ridiculous thing came to mind.

"Oh?"

"I was so enamored, my strength grew and I broke the chains so we could be together."

"Or instead," she whispered. "We could have sex, no?"

"I wish, Aurora. But I have to go."

"You wish?"

"Tell them the story."

"Oh fine, Mackenzie. This story will make my husband just as jealous."

I nodded solemnly. "That's what matters."

She didn't seem in a hurry to get off my lap so I scooted from underneath. Raised my flute of champagne and drained it.

So gross. Champagne drinkers are idiots.

She clapped her hands and blurted, "Oh, you are free! But how did you take off the...the...?" She made a motion like locking her wrists.

I held my forefinger to my lips. She copied the motion and shot me a thumbs up.

Had to move quick, in case the camera watchers were diligent.

I peeked around the door.

My chef was gone. Aurora's escort was reclining in a leather chair, feet up, ankles crossed, reading a novel, facing the outer door. Ernst laid prone on the couch, napping. Poor guy must be fatigued from watching me nearly perish.

Neither had anything to worry about. Their prisoner wore shackles, right?

Mackenzie August, never to be underestimated.

I leapt into the room and threw the heavy champagne bottle like a tomahawk, the perfect projectile to shatter against the guard's skull and render him insensate.

Except I missed. The bottle connected with his stomach, rendering him merely astonished.

Damn it. Looks so easy in *Last of the Mohicans*.

He made a "Huuuuuhg," sound.

I landed on him, feet first. We toppled the chair over backwards and my bare foot crushed his throat closed.

He gasped and groaned and fumbled for his pistol.

Ernst stirred.

I retrieved the fallen champagne bottle and hit Ernst in the head. A solid connection, which sent painful frissons up my arm. The glass didn't break but Ernst's head nearly did.

The guard successfully yanked his pistol free. Crouching on his chest and throat, I took the pistol barrel in one hand and hit him in the nose with the other until he released.

I removed my foot from his neck. He curled into a ball, hacking and holding his nose. I cocked the gun.

"Oh Mackenzie," squeaked Aurora. "That was magnifico!"

"Thanks. I went for a jog last week, so that helped."

"Kill them, kill them!" She hopped and clapped her hands again. "You said you would."

"Yeah but...look at them." Ernst moved not. The guard coughed and crimson burst from his nose and he whimpered. "They're pathetic."

"So?"

"So I have a heart of gold," I said. "Aurora, did you order the champagne?"

"I did not. A gift from the hotel."

"Was there a note?"

"No, my American King."

Who could the saboteur be?

I went to Ernst and rifled his pockets for a phone. Found it. Used his thumb to unlock the screen. He moaned.

"Oh nuts," I said.

"What? Tell me!" Aurora hurried over on short steps.

"My wrist band is controlled by his phone. But he has a zillion apps." I scrolled through. A lesser man would be thumbing the screen frantically. "Who needs this many apps? Freaking millennials. Check his pockets for a set of keys. Might be a remote on the chain."

"But Mackenzie, maybe we have sex first."

"I'm honored by your aspirations, Aurora, but focus."

I kept thumbing through apps and folders on screen. Most were in German. Argh.

Aurora daintily stuck her hand into a pants pocket.

"This is the most exciting thing in my life."

"Okay," I said. "Okay, this is it. This one says Mackenzie."

The app opened. There were four buttons and an adjustment slider. Probably controlled the dosage? One of the buttons was large and green.

Not that one, I bet.

"Mackenzie," she said.

"I'm going to try one. I've got a one-in-three chance, because I can't make sense of the symbols."

"Mackenzie?" She tapped my shoulder.

"If this doesn't work, it might knock me out. In which case you've been great and I appreciate your help."

"Yes, Mackenzie, but you are in trouble."

"Yes Mackenzie," said a new voice. A sultry feminine and French timbre. "You are in trouble."

Emile. She stood at the open door leading to the hallway. Her eyes were arched and narrow, her mouth a tight angry smile. In her hands she held one of the triggers.

"Oh shit," I said. "Pardon my French."

I pressed a button on Ernst's iPhone. Nothing happened —I guessed wrong.

Emile made a tsk'ing sound.

I leapt at her but I was across the room. Too far.

Aurora released a scream.

My wrist beeped. Pressure from the band.

Emile smirked. I reached her and grabbed her by the throat, my other hand going around her wrist. I forced her backwards into the hallway.

"You will kill me?" she asked calmly.

"No." My fingers squeezed her windpipe, not enough for damage. "But I'll fantasize about it."

"You could do it. You are strong and I am not."

"Don't tempt me."

"Too bad you are my slave, American."

Everything was going heavy.

She tilted her head forward to kiss me on the mouth.

"I own you," she said softly. "You may not leave yet."

My knees buckled. I was sliding to the floor.

"Guards?" she called. "Some help, *s'il vous plaît*."

"Why'd you come back?" My tongue felt thick.

"Sheer jealousy, my love. I came to watch."

"I like Aurora." My words slurred. Kneeling on the floor. "Way more than you."

"Then maybe she needs to die?"

A guard arrived. A man with dark skin, I think, but everything went fuzzy.

He said, "What is...what is happening to him? What'd you do?"

"I have taken back what's mine."

Behind me, Aurora said, "Mackenzie?"

More guards. Suddenly the hallway was swarming with them.

13

The following day, a tailor and I put our heads together and decided on a midnight blue tuxedo with peak lapels and double-buttons. Only slim-fitted couture for me, obviously, because I'm not a savage. In fact, the tailor winked at me and called me a "guappo." A compliment, I assume.

I dressed under strict scrutiny. While putting on my shirt and jacket, my ankles were shackled. While putting on pants and socks, my wrists were shackled.

So untrusting, these German bounty hunters.

Ernst clearly had a concussion. He'd come to, groggy and dazed. Duane threatened to have Ernst drowned if he sought revenge.

"I don't need you fucking up my prize stallion, Ernst, you understand me?" Duane had said in a rasp. "Guys like you, I can buy two of you for ten grand. I need my champion unmolested."

Because I hadn't been successful, and because it generated even more buzz for him, Duane wasn't angry about my escape attempt. He'd affectionately slapped my cheek and said he liked my spirit.

Said it was hard to kill a Gurkha, a reference I didn't understand.

The one negative consequence of my escapade was that the chief of security bolted a second chain into the floor, across the room. One chain for each hand, limiting my range of motion and stretching my arms wide so that even if I got a key my hands couldn't reach one another. He oversaw the installation himself, Bluetooth headsets flashing in each ear, and when Duane wasn't watching he threw me two good kidney punches. While I gasped, he got in my ear and said, "Discipline."

So it was with sore ribs that I finished donning the tuxedo. Duane and Emile and Tattoo Neck and two guards came to escort Ernst, Meg, and me to a party they jokingly referred to as a Bunga Bunga. Duane scrutinized me and tried adjusting his tux to look as svelte and debonair as *moi*. But a man snorting cocaine and cheeseburgers and bourbon arrived to the fashion table at a distinct disadvantage.

"Let's go," I said. "Time for the party. I won't wait for you, Moneybags."

Meg and Emile tried not to smile. Duane hated it when I issued orders he had no choice but to obey. It's the little things in life.

We rode an elevator to the top floor. I wore chains on wrists and ankles, further precautions for Mackenzie August, the Houdini of private investigators. Before the doors dinged, Emile sighed and said, "Another party full of young women to please the old men. *En avoir ras le bol.*"

"You don't like it, go back to the got'damn room," said Duane.

The elevator opened.

We stepped into a party on the roof. One of those without a central point, no spot of gravity, so everyone floated and tried too hard. Speakers blared, women in sequin bikinis served drinks, the younger adults swam fully clothed (or not fully clothed) in a flashing pool, and their elders sipped cocktails and watched. Spotlights created flares in my vision, blocking the celestial beyond.

Party-goers spotted and cheered for us. A cartoonish but significant subset wore vests and cowboy hats and boots, complete with revolvers in tooled leather holsters. Some of the girls wore cheerleader uniforms.

"Let me guess," I said. "Cowboys and cheerleaders are the recognized international avatar for America?"

"Avatar," said Duane. "Sounds right. You claim you're here for a woman, you destroy the Mexican, refused to kill him, win anyway, then almost escape yesterday...you're a legend, August. You got fans."

"This makes me tired," I said. "Let's go home."

Duane wiped some sweat from his forehead. "I heard Rossi himself might be here. He's been absent, 'til tonight. Don't screw this up. You hear?"

We plunged into the jungle.

"The Mexicans went home," called Duane above the throbbing hum and rattle. He shrugged and indicated the party with his thumb. "Otherwise, this place'd be a zoo. I think most Colombians are leaving, also."

Armed guards galore. Mostly Italians but also Yakuza and Russian soldiers, standing with arms crossed. Constant vigilance. Duane told Tattoo Neck that next year they needed to bring more guys.

There won't be a next year, Duane, I get my way.

Whining electric drones with cameras hovered in the air, sending a feed to scattered televisions. Some of the mini helicopters ferried bottles. Others toted cash cannons, raining money.

Above one of the bars a vast digital screen displayed betting lines. I tried to make sense of the Italian and failed.

Two girls dressed in sheer gowns came for Duane, followed by a man clearly operating as an interpreter. He asked Duane to follow him to the higher table.

Emile was not invited.

Duane left without a backwards glance.

We were all still kids hoping for an invitation to the popular lunch table, I thought. What a mess, we humans.

The head of security stood nearby, watching me, his Bluetooth earpieces flashing.

Emile took me by the arm and steered me into the heaving masses. She put her mouth near my ear and said, "This is still very much a man's world, Mackenzie. What is the English phrase?"

"The underworld is a patriarchal society."

"The wives, we are expected to smile and look the other way while the men gamble and grope and screw in private salons. It is an insult."

"I concur, that's insulting. But you haven't earned the right to be offended by the exploitive zeitgeist of the Camorra tournament, Emile," I said.

"I don't know the word, zeitgeist."

"You participate and profit in the underworld. Yet you think pimps should treat marriage as holy? The oppressors should be progressive in their treatment of the oppressed?"

Her grip on my bicep tightened. "I think a woman with an unfaithful husband should feel no reason to remain loyal, Mackenzie. And that the husband shouldn't be surprised at the lack of loyalty."

"Maybe the wife should remain loyal to herself. And to her promises, even if not to the man."

"To herself? What does that mean? Why should she do that?"

I said, "Because she has to live with herself. She has to sleep at night. Because revenge and hedonism will not calm the storm."

"But it might make the storm bearable, Mackenzie."

"Not in my experience, though I claim to be a steward of no one except myself."

We stopped. Her hand released my arm.

"Wait, I have a son," I said. "I need to restate my jurisdiction."

"We are here," she said. "Another chance for you to be judged and shine."

We stood on the edge of the enormous pool. It was lit on all sides by alternating submerged lights and the colors pulsated. Men and women in various states of undress splashed and cackled.

A floating barge drifted our way. The platform was large, roomy enough to hold four chairs. Three of the chairs were occupied.

I recognized the occupants—the three remaining mafia champions.

Ernst clipped a small microphone onto my lapel and slapped me on the shoulder. Hard.

The barge stopped at my feet and guards pushed me onto the platform. I had to either sit in the open chair or fall. The barge returned to drift in the middle of the pool, guided by swimmers. Cones of brilliance followed us, blasted by spotlights on towers.

"And then there were four," I said.

"Ah, the American Yankee," said a darkly handsome man. O Principe, the local favorite. "Good of you to join."

"The hell is going on?"

With leonine indifference, he indicated the microphone on my lapel with his martini glass. "We are the entertainment, of course. We are being recorded and broadcast. Look and see. Many partiers, they sit with headphones, listening. Deciding where to place their money. Even in other parts of the hotel, they listen. The rest will read transcripts in the morning when headaches wear off."

The Prince and I sat opposite each other on the floating barge. To my right, the Russian. To my left, the enormous Yakuza champion. The barge tilted his direction.

The Russian was not a tall man, but solidly built, like an Armata tank. His left ear had been cut off. His left eye was swollen shut. His other eye was lifeless, like a ball bearing. His right arm rested prolapsed in a sling.

I told him, "Here's hoping I get to fight you next."

The Russian did not smile.

He said, "My fight, almost fifteen minutes. Battle with weapons. The Colombian, he died well."

The Prince smiled, showing perfect white teeth. "Died slow and messy, is what I heard. You want a drink, American?"

"I do. Beer."

The man leaned down to an attendant swimming in the water and said, "Birra per l'Americano. Grazie."

A swimmer brought me a Peroni in a glass. I drank some. Perhaps the most delicious thing I'd ever consumed.

"Why do you wear those?" asked the Prince, indicating my chains.

"They aren't worn volitionally."

"Which is why you must, no? A shame, American. You are unable to enjoy the tournament."

"I enjoy my life. Looking forward to returning to it."

He said, "You will win the Gabbia Cremisi?"

"Or leave it."

The Prince laughed, good-natured and rich. He wore a tux, similar to mine, but his shirt was black. His right leg was draped over his left. He raised his martini glass to me. "I admire the courage. But how?"

"I'll pave the streets with the dead, if I have to."

"But you are religious, I hear, no?"

"I'm not good at it."

"The first you must kill..." He nodded at the sumo wrestler. "Riku. The Yakuza champion."

Riku had come out of his fight unscathed, other than a few contusions on his neck. Riku did not deign to look at me.

"Opponents have already been drawn?" I said.

"Yes. And your opponent..." He nodded again at the Japanese man. "In the opening round, he killed the Triad by squeezing him to death."

"What do the rules say about bringing a fork?"

The hardscrabble Russian victor sniffed. Some would call it derisive. "I fight O Principe. I will not last first round. I accept death."

"Shame on you for not ending the Colombian more quickly. Most money is placed on the third minute," said the Prince and he shrugged one shoulder. Almost a feminine movement. "But maybe you live until the fourth?"

The Russian spit at him.

"Minute means nothing. World knows you cheat," he said. "The Russian Brotherhood is not dishonored by you."

"Or maybe the *first* minute." The Prince leaned forward

to me, conspiratorially. "Do you see? Look at their faces. Around the pool with headphones. Millions in betting. Maybe billions. On which minute the Russian will die. How do you not enjoy this?"

"My soul is still in one piece. That's how." I turned to the giant sumo wrestler. "You and me?"

The colossus made a grunting noise.

"I accept your surrender," I said.

He grunted again.

"It was your brother I stabbed in the eye? You guys look the same. Is that racist? Tell him I'm sorry."

"Riku cannot speak, Yankee. Like his twin, the man whose life you saved with a fork, Riku's tongue was removed by the Yakuza."

"That's disturbing," I said. "I am disturbed."

"But look here." Our barge was slowly rotating and the Prince had to point over his shoulder. "You are the favorite at the moment. Two-to-one, over the giant."

I drank some beer. "Even though I didn't kill my previous opponent? Seems aspirational."

"Do you still refuse to fight, American? Be careful how you answer. The world listens."

"I won't kill him, no. Hopefully he's smart enough to realize that we don't need to die. Ferrari and the Executioner would never kill us both if we refuse."

He released another good-natured laugh. "Still looking for a loophole, eh? You Americans can be so—"

"Handsome? Endearing? Muscular?"

"Falsely virtuous. It is cute."

"It's not virtue. It's pragmatism. Also, one day, when I write my first book, I'll entitle it 'Ferrari and the Executioner.' It's a romance."

"Speaking of stories, are the tales about you true,

Yankee? Did you kill the Gurkha with his own knife? Did you pull a man's throat out of his chest in an American card game?"

The Prince was the second man to mention me killing a Gurkha, one of the world's most fearsome fighters, and Duane said I did it last night, in the hallway. Figure that'd be something I'd recall.

I shrugged. "About the Gurkha, I don't remember. Duane Chambers seems to think I did. About the throat, I think that's impossible. But it wasn't fun for either of us."

More and more partiers were losing their clothes and leaping into the pool. The naked and elite milieu gathered around us to listen and scream. In an open-aired lounge above the bar, Duane reclined at a table with other dignitaries. A girl sat beside him, rubbing his shoulders.

I scanned the rest of the audience. Unlike the crowd in the arena, here the throng individuated into persons. The man or woman who slipped me the handcuff key, was he or she here? Watching? Could I expect further help?

It was a mystery.

The Prince grinned and called to the swimmers. They responded with delirious gaiety.

"Why'd you return?" I asked him. "One trip through this madhouse would be enough for me."

"The life I lead is lavish. One week here and I'm wealthy again. Simple as that. Besides, with or without the tournament, I'm not long for this world, as you say in America. Dead meat, no?"

"Don't have to be. I got a spare bedroom. After we get out, come for a visit. We'll grill steaks and not stab one another and talk about life."

He appeared genuinely surprised. "You're inviting me to your home?"

"Sure. I think you and my roommate might be soul mates."

"You have roommates."

"Sometimes I have a lot of them," I said.

"I wonder if your hospitality is genuine. But it wouldn't work. You see, I play the game. The clash of clans, as it were, with the other Camorristi. But, alas, it is a loser's game."

"Meaning?"

"Meaning, I've played too long. There are very few elderly in the mafia. My time is up soon, I think. Finish off Riku here and perhaps you can do the honors," he said, slapping the giant affectionately on the hand.

The sumo wrestler did not return the affection.

"I'm not killing either one of you," I said.

There came a murmur from our audience of listeners.

"Then it is you who are playing the loser's game, my American friend."

14

L ike a pregame ritual, I stood at my window looking over Vomero while Meg slathered my tattoo with ointment. She wore her scrubs, I wore my patriotic fighting shorts.

"Civil unrest has escalated," I noted.

She looked past me, through the glass.

I watched her reflection. Her short blond hair was pinned back with pink clips and she wore no jewelry of any kind, giving her the appearance of a child. Time hadn't begun to etch lines into her face but a frown pushed a furrow between her plucked eyebrows.

The city teemed like an anthill. Up here the denizens walked more often than drove, scuttling to and fro with groceries and children. Their steps were hurried.

"I can't hear it. But I see it. The people are agitated."

"How can you tell?" she asked.

"I'm a trained investigator. I'm deeply shrewd. And three fires are burning today, whereas previously I only saw one. Most of the laundry has been taken off the lines. Look at that woman there, in the hat. She is frantic. Tugging her children, looking over her shoulder."

Meg pointed to the north, almost out of our line of sight. "That fire looks close."

"It started here on the mountain, not below. As I said before, in my sagest voice, civil unrest has accumulated."

"You said escalated."

"Whatever, shut up. Point is, Meg the vile physician, the Camorra clans are warring."

"It's worse this year, I heard. And I am not vile."

I wanted to scratch my nose but I was at the limit of the two chains, my hands stretched to either side. I said, "Something to do with the Prince. He was Rossi's pick for champion, which angered Di Contini's disciples."

"I think it has to do with you, too. You've made a bigger impression than most champions."

"Obviously."

She drew a shaky breath. "This is madness. I can't believe I'm in a hotel dedicated to a blood sport, run by the mafia, on a mountain in Naples, surrounded by protestors starting fires."

"This wasn't covered in your Organic Chemistry class?"

"I can't help you escape, Mackenzie. I *can't*. They'll kill me."

"I haven't asked you to."

Could it have been Meg who slipped me the handcuff key? It was hard to peer under her glassine carapace, but I suspected I'd find treachery beneath. Not sugar and spice and everything nice.

"I know. But..." She finished with the ointment, screwed the lid back on, and stood beside me to watch the city revolt. I didn't worry about the fire or protests reaching us. With enough money you can do anything. And the people inside the Theater on the Mountain had enough.

She asked, "In the cage, will you fight?"

"Artfully phrased."

"I know you're fighting Mr. Chambers and Ferrari outside of it, as best you can, but what about the Yakuza champion?"

"I won't kill him," I said. "Even if he'll never taste pizza again, he shouldn't be thrown into a cage to die."

"What will you do?"

"I have a plan. It's the best plan."

"Tell me."

"Under no circumstances, foul physician. You are party to miscreants."

She groaned and elbowed me. "I'm in your corner, Mackenzie. Literally. You can't win if you won't kill him."

"I can try. And that's almost as important as the outcome."

"In what universe is trying and failing almost as important as living?"

"Don't get me wrong, the outcome concerns me. But I'm equally concerned with how I handle adversity. What would it profit me to win the tournament but lose my soul. Write that down."

She rubbed at the furrows between her eyes and sighed. "Let's deal with facts and imminent realities, Mackenzie. Blood, sweat, bones, and injuries, not philosophy. What will you do when he attacks? He's immense."

"Duck."

"Duck?"

"I'll duck."

"You're an ass," she said. "How can you be so intelligent

and use the sophisticated vocabulary that you do, and say duck? Be serious. This terrifies me."

"Me too."

"Maybe you need cocaine. I might snort a line myself."

"No thanks. Clear eyes, full heart."

"You're quoting that football show."

"*Friday Night Lights?* I'll never tell."

She stomped her foot. "Why are you so maddening? This is *not* the time to be eccentric."

"On the contrary, this is the best time."

"I hope you win," she said. "But maybe the giant could smack you first. A good bell ringing might be what the doctor ordered."

15

Duane's retinue escorted me to the same white room as before. The number of guards had tripled, Duane said, "Because I don't trust those fucking Japs." Above and around us, it sounded like the Rose Bowl was gearing up for kick off.

Duane's nerves had got the best of him again. He paced and sweated and swore. Beneath his nose, flecks of a white powder had embedded into stubble follicles.

"August, the Italian Prince, you know the guy?"

"I do. Handsome fellow. Excellent manners."

"Excellent manners. Whatever. He's going to win tonight. Quick. You hear me? He'll go into the final fight without a scratch," said Duane.

"Which means," said his wife Emile, wearing what looked like a luxury bathrobe made out of silk. She also wore heels. Her eyes drifted over me. Like a predator examining a meal. "You should defeat your opponent quickly. With all body parts intact and functional."

"The other night at the pool, Rossi was there but I didn't talk to him. Bastard hung in the shadows with his new girlfriend. But Ferrari mentioned to me," said Duane, and he wiped his forehead. "Ferrari told me, Rossi has taken note of the American. The head of the Camorra, talking about August. Hear that? I knew this trip was a good idea."

"Release me," I said. "And you may yet still live, Duane."

"Christ almighty. Maybe you should focus on killing the Jap."

"I won't kill him."

He made a shrug. "Yeah. Whatever. Choke him out, let the Executioner do his thing. I don't care, long as you don't die." He shook his finger at me. "I'm letting all the winnings ride tonight. Understand?"

"A fool and his money."

"Stop saying that. It irritates me." He paused, looked like he wanted to say more, but changed his mind. He straightened his tuxedo and shifted uncomfortably.

"You're dismissed, Duane," I said.

"You don't tell me what to do."

"I dismiss you. Leave."

His face did a glower. "I'm going. But not because you say to."

"Take Emile with you. Hold the door for her. Treat her well."

"I do that anyway," he said and she scoffed.

They left, looking strained and uncomfortable.

Ernst pulled a German KM military knife from his belt and pressed the point into my throat. The four guards tensed and their hands went to their electroshock sidearms.

Meg squeaked. "Ernst, what! Knock it off."

"I wish to gut you, Herr August," said Ernst. His nose was almost touching mine. This close, his face and eyes looked swollen and liverish. I bet he'd put on five pounds in the four days we'd been in Naples. "But I am not allowed.

Yet. You try to escape again? I open your windpipe. And enjoy it."

I whispered. "Gross."

"The noise. It makes the concussion worse."

Zee concussion vorse.

"Tylenol, German bounty hunter. Works wonders."

"The Yakuza giant," said Ernst, backing up and sheathing his knife. "He squeezes you. I will laugh as you die."

"What an ugly thing to say. Does this mean we aren't friends anymore? You know, Ernst, if we aren't friends, I don't think I could bear it."

Meg said, "That's another quote isn't it."

"Yes but I'm botching it."

Ferrari's voice filled the world and the tumult above our heads increased. The wall sconce shook and the light vibrated.

At 9:30, judging by sounds, the Prince and the Russian joined in combat.

At 9:32, judging by sounds, the Russian lost.

My guess, the Prince bet on himself through a shell investor for the second minute. Long enough to land a few punches, get position on his severely wounded opponent, choke him out, and make a fortune.

Two guards near the door bumped fists.

The man wearing a radio and mic arrived in a huff and beckoned us follow. We trudged through the dark hallways, chasing the chants, and into the same little holding cell as before. The roof rattled from footsteps above and dust filtered down.

My praetorian guards drew their electroshock weapons. Ernst jammed a key into my ankle and wrist shackles, setting me loose.

"Don't be a hero, American," he said.

"I cannot help what I am, German."

"I mean, don't do anything stupid."

"Of course. I'd hate to get into trouble."

Ferrari's voice shook the floor beneath my feet.

Riku was announced first. A smattering of cheers and a cascade of boos. I kept my head down, eyes closed, listening and tugging on fighting gloves.

"**Signore e signori. Ora ti presento...**" called Ferrari. "**Dall'america, Il tuo combattente preferito...**"

The crowd had already started.

Yan-kee, Yan-kee.

I took deep breaths, steeling myself as if ready to leap into freezing water.

He announced my name and we walked into the living arena. The crowd had grown, I thought. The volume of bodies looked impossible. And dangerous. Screams and cheers rained down, as did roses and batteries. I kept my head lowered. Focused on my feet.

Ferrari maintained the soliloquy.

The orchestra played. It'd sound like *The Godfather* except for the electric guitar.

Ernst and Meg chattered in my ear but I didn't care.

I stopped at the stairs, face to face with the Executioner. His cowl mostly hid his face. From what I could see, he'd applied eye black. I punched him on the shoulder and said, "See you in round two."

I jumped into the ring and the gate crashed closed.

The sumo wrestler had inexplicably grown taller. Didn't seem fair. He had five inches on me and fifty pounds, at least. Maybe closer to a hundred. That was hard to do. In my head I kept referring to him as a sumo wrestler, so seeing him sporting a mawashi loincloth was no surprise.

The coiffed master of ceremonies jabbered. I stayed in my corner, hopping, Riku in his. Fights were already breaking out in the throng. Guards ran past the cage and dove up the stands.

The electronic horn sounded.

He made a ceremonial bow and dropped into a traditional sumo stance.

"Riku," I called. "Don't you think your superior reach and size puts you at an unfair advantage? Be a sport, put one hand behind your back."

He didn't. The black band on his left hand blinked. How much medicine would have to be pumped into that Goliath to subdue him? I'd suggest a two-liter.

I got to the center of the cage first. He came on slowly. A bulldozer picking up inertia.

"Riku. Please tell me you understand English."

The crowd shouted so loud I barely heard myself.

"Wait. That was uncouth. You can't say things. Because they cut your tongue out. Blink once if you understand English, how about that."

For a giant, he moved well. His lunge caught me off guard—a heavy shoulder slamming into my midsection. I went over backwards as before an avalanche.

"Round two," I wheezed manfully. "Let's survive until round two. Deal? I got an idea."

He was on top. Slowly covering up more of my body with his mass. Like being suffocated by a two-ton bean bag.

The audience ramped up the delirium.

Yan-kee, Yan-kee, Yan-kee.

Get up, Meg screamed.

Riku's modus operandi was effective. Lesser men would be subsumed easily. I'd misjudged his weight; he weighed closer to four hundred than three hundred. He laid in a superman pose, me prone beneath. He channeled his weight, focusing on my chest, and rolling—soon he'd be covering my mouth.

Nasty way to go.

If Kix learned his father had died because a fat guy sat on him, he'd never have enough confidence to become a starting pitcher for the Nationals.

I got my hands under his shoulders and essentially did a bench press. I pushed on him until my arms were straight, not easy because he squirmed and pressed at my elbows. But it gave me enough room. I got one leg from underneath his bulk and squirmed free.

I stood, drank in oxygen freely, and decided not to almost suffocate to death in these fights anymore.

Ninety seconds gone.

The flaw in Riku's plan became apparent. It took the man a while to regain his feet, a period of time I didn't allow him. Anytime he got one knee up, I was there to knock him down. I rammed him, kicked him in the head, shoved, got behind and punched. No trick in my arsenal was too juvenile.

"Stay down," I told him. "It's all gonna be great, Riku. We're going to laugh about this one day. Round two, okay?"

I badgered him for the remainder of the five minutes. Our bloodthirsty fans wanted violence and they grew irritated.

At four and a half minutes, sudden bursts of noise got my attention—pistol shots. Two of them.

Someone in the stands firing a weapon.

At *me.*

The cage wall in front of me sparked. The second shot whined angrily past my shoulder, like a bumblebee moving a thousand miles an hour. The bullet tore into the cage's mat. The shot had originated from the cheap seats.

I circled to my right. No easy and immobile target, I.

This never happened to Tom Brady or Maximus.

Ferrari ran across to the stadium, shouting into the microphone. He pointed high towards the Yakuza section. More gunfire. His chief of security charged. The spectators there contracted and expanded like a living thing. I hoped for mob justice.

The electronic horn sounded. Round over. And then Riku decked me from behind. An illegal sucker punch.

I staggered forward, dazed. Two enormously strong arms wrapped around me. Pinned my arms and lifted me off the ground.

Oh crud. The squeeze of death. Like a blubbery vice clamping.

The first thing to break would be my humerus. Both of them. Or maybe ribs? Hard to pinpoint the agony.

Or maybe my head would pop off.

The Executioner watched this with mild interest but he made no move to intervene. Not a stickler for the rules? The round was over. And someone had shot at me.

"Riku," I said. But no sound was created.

I jerked my head backwards. My skull connected with his nose. Cartilage crunched. Again and again. He couldn't evade the battering because his fat shoulders, holding up his arms to suspend me, created a valley in which his head was trapped. He rotated his face side to side but not enough.

No one came to stop the fight.

I kept hammering.

No air. I grew weary of suffocation. Though I supposed it was the simplest way to terminate a life without tools.

I got him again. His nasal bone broke. His sinuses and

turbinates had to be filling with blood. Soon his face and gums would be pulped enough that he'd start losing teeth. The pressure on my arms had stopped accumulating.

Even if my skull cracked, I'd keep punishing him. I had no choice. And I had no more than a few seconds anyway.

The orchestra wailed, and the electric guitar screeched, somehow making it worse. How I hated them.

I hit him again. Felt like his face caved inwards.

He didn't want to release but pain caused his strength to abate just enough. I twisted and dropped free. Crawled to my corner.

Riku's face was ruined. He knelt in the middle, hacking. Beneath him, a spray of red.

"Mackenzie," cried Meg. I heard her as if in a tunnel. She pressed a bottle of water through the small opening in the cage mesh. "Holy shit, Mackenzie, I thought you were dead."

"Give me time. I can still manage it."

I drank some. Squirted some on the back of my head. Tender and bloody.

The Executioner stood in the cage, baring the axe. I hadn't seen his entrance. Took him long enough. He seemed satisfied that Riku and I had come to an understanding that round one had concluded.

Ferrari babbled.

The crowd seethed and Riku splattered.

Ernst was listening to Ferrari. He said, "Careful, American. The fence is turning on."

Meg stepped back.

I felt the charge. It sort of ignited the air with a corporeal hum. Like listening to air molecules melting. The speakers blared fake crackling, a crowd pleasing indication that the electricity had activated.

"It might kill you," Ernst reminded me. "But if it doesn't, Riku will."

The Executioner grabbed the cage door, stepped out, and pulled it after him.

So the cage door wasn't electrified. Interesting.

I panted. "This is no longer fun."

"Was it ever?"

"The amount of things which are illegal yet permissible in Naples is breathtaking."

The horn sounded.

Round two.

Riku hadn't bothered to retreat to his corner. He stood in the middle, a nightmare with no nose.

"Hope this works," I told the cosmos.

The cosmos intimated maybe I shouldn't have blindly followed the cute restaurant entrepreneur down the stairs a week ago. Or before that, not threatened to kill Darren Robbins.

He who lives by the sword.

"Let's end this, Riku," I said.

He came. I kept my feet going sideways, step over step, circumnavigated the humming wall. The hairs on my neck raised. He closed the distance, following me and inching nearer.

I slipped.

Or I pretended to slip.

His eyes sharpened. Sensing opportunity. He charged. Heavy steps, intending to fall on me. But I hadn't lost my balance, merely a ruse. I dove at his feet. He stumbled over me, his momentum out of control. Hard to stop four hundred pounds of blunder.

He roared. Put up his hands. Plowed into the fence.

There was an audible snap. His connection flared a brilliant white. The black wristband exploded off his wrist, corkscrewing over the cage's wall. I felt the discharge in my bones.

The audience gasped. Inhaled disbelief, exhaled approval.

Riku's body slumped away from the metal fence. An electrical burn was already raising on his hands and face.

He moved not. It hadn't been a graze with the fence—it had been a big time connection.

The stadium shook.

Yan-kee, Yan-kee, Yan-kee.

That's right. Say my name. It was growing on me.

I sat crisscross at his feet. Close enough to the wall to tingle. Two steps from the cage's gate.

"American," cried Ernst. "You must—"

"Nope. I won't." I shook my head. Stayed seated. Head bowed. Tugged off my gloves.

Ferrari waited. So did the Executioner. Watching...

Men in the Yakuza corner shook their heads, shoulders slumped.

Riku wouldn't rise soon. And if he did, I'd push him into the fence again.

Three heartbeats later, Ferrari's voice erupted from a hundred speakers. Our spectators responded.

I was declared the winner.

I gulped. This part I'd been dreading.

Meg looked as though she wanted to collapse. Ernst nodded with grim approval. Still I sat. As serene as Gandhi, I hoped.

The Executioner ascended with heavy steps. He threw open the gate. His axe rested on his left shoulder, gripped tightly in his fist.

Dear Lord. Let me live.

He stepped into the cage. The Grim Reaper himself, come to finish the grisly job.

"Not sure you deserve this, Riku," I said.

I slapped my left hand against the exposed flesh of the Executioner's right ankle. With my other, I grabbed the metal mesh of the cage.

Pow.

A brief sensation, like snatching hold of a category five tornado. The Executioner and I both jolted. Immense pain.

My black bracelet burst.

My bones started to shake apart.

The breakers in my mind tripped and the world reset...

16

When I came to, I was crying. Or I felt like I had been.

I sat in a chair. Back in my room. My bed had been removed—more punishment from Duane. My arms were shackled and stretched tight to either side.

Meg was on her knees, applying cream to my blistered right hand.

"Am I crying?" I asked.

"Hello sleepy head," she said. "Crying is common for a victim of electroshock. Energy overwhelmed your nervous system."

"Am I naked?"

"You are." To Meg's credit, she blushed. As one should. "Mr. Chambers is angry with you."

"You're got'damn right I am," Duane said. From somewhere. "You electrocuted the fucking Executioner. The *Executioner*, August. The hell were you thinking."

"Was thinking it might prevent a beheading."

"Your heart went into arrhythmia. I restarted it, to be safe," she said.

That is a hell of a thing for one human being to casually say to another. I shook my head, tried to dislodge cobwebs.

"You can't attack the Executioner, August."

"The heck I can't. He cuts people's heads off, Moneybags. What happened with Riku?"

"Riku? The Yakuza champion? Got no idea. Who cares," he said.

"Me. Obviously. Did they kill him?"

"No," said Emile. She stood at the door, rubbing her thumb across the screen of her phone. "I saw him walking away."

Duane said, "He lost. Should be dead. They won't kill him?"

Emile shrugged. Sighed. "I don't know, my love."

"The back of my head," I observed. "Feels unhealthy."

"I sewed up a small gash," said Meg. "The subcutaneous fat and fibrous tissue are pulverized. It'll hurt for a week, at least."

"Hurts less than the Yakuza's face, though. Or at least it better."

"A nice trick, August." Duane shook his head and rolled up the sleeves of his shirt. "You knew. Knew the Camorra wouldn't punish us now, even if you zapped the Executioner. They'd have no final fight, if they did."

"I leveraged my popularity, yes."

"Speaking of popularity," said Emile in a purr. "Mackenzie set a tournament record."

Tattoo Neck stepped into the room. Handed Duane a phone. He read a message and handed it back. Said in an aside, "I don't wanna talk. Not now. I'll call tomorrow." Then, to his wife, "Record? What record?"

"A woman bid a large amount of money for Mackenzie."

"Oh yeah. Good. A record? Jesus, that smoothes things

over. Hear that, August? You're getting laid again. Aren't I generous."

"Send her away. I reject your largesse."

Emile kept purring. "Mackenzie was not intimate with the previous woman, my love. His sexual frustration must be...significant."

"Instead of a woman, I'll accept food. I'm jonesing for an aprés-fight snack."

"A snack," said Duane. "Whatever. The girl isn't gonna get her money's worth, anyway. I won't release his chains. She'll have to do her best with a date that can't move."

I said, "There's a moral allegory in there somewhere."

"Mackenzie needs calories, Mr. Chambers," said Meg, my villainous caretaker. "Nutrition."

"The chef's got him some food prepared. Maybe you feed him."

Meg muttered about her medical degree.

"I'm going to Rossi's party," said Duane. "Don't wait up. Nice job, tonight, August. Kinda. Get some sleep. After you've had your fun."

He left. Without a backwards glance. Emile arched an eyebrow and watched him leave.

Meg cut up some fish and an apple with quick strokes that made me think she'd done a surgical rotation. She fed me, talking about the unrest in Naples, and then she went to bed.

My boy Gennaro brought more champagne but Emile ordered it left in the adjoining room. He shot me a thumbs up before going.

I sat and ignored the burning in my right hand and the dull throb in my head. Wondered what day it was. Wondered who the Cowboys would play this Sunday.

Wondered if my grass needed to be cut again before the winter set in.

I refused to think about Kix or Ronnie. Not yet. I'd get out soon. And then...

Voices in the other room. Emile forcing Ernst and the other guards to wait outside.

She appeared at my doorway with another woman. A young girl, maybe twenty. Japanese, dressed in a gossamer white dress.

I said, "Send her away, Emile. Not interested."

Hard to give orders convincingly, arms pinned out and backwards.

Emile smiled lazily. "This is Himari. She bid a fortune for you, Mackenzie."

"Offer a refund. I'm sleepy."

"Himari, please wait in the next room. Do not leave until I return." She spoke to the girl but kept her eyes on me.

Mackenzie August, experiencing trepidation.

Himari made a small bowing motion and left. Emile closed my bedroom door, sealing us in.

She said, "The average champion earns twenty thousand dollars for an hour with a woman. Two years ago, the Prince earned forty. Tonight, an unknown woman bid fifty for you. Fifty thousand, Mackenzie. In order for Himari to win, she was forced to bid fifty-five."

"Aren't the auctions silent?"

"I have my ways."

"You gave Himari the funds," I guessed. "She's a surrogate bidder for you."

"Yes. A way to bid anonymously. Do you know what my husband is doing? Going to an old man party where he'll pick from provided woman and have fun."

"This is revenge."

"Indeed," she said. She stepped out of her heels.

"It won't help."

"Duane thinks he's making a fortune off you tonight. Little does he know, the arrogant and limp old man, he'll be paid with his own money. So tonight I have double the pleasure."

"I have serious doubts about the stability and longevity of your marriage, Emile. You're less chatelaine and more courtesan."

"It was I who suggested you not be given clothes." She lowered to her knees in front of my chair. Placed her hands on my thighs. "As punishment."

"You're a pretty lady. You could go upstairs and find a willing partner."

"Here's some information my husband hasn't told you. Darren Robbins, the American attorney, heard that you were pardoned. He heard that, should you win, you'll be a free man."

Damn it. I'd been hoping he wouldn't learn until I returned to the States.

She slid her hand between my thighs. "You are naive, Mackenzie, if you don't think Darren's already hired someone else to do the job. He is terrified of you."

"As he should be."

"Even if you win, an assassin is waiting to kill you." She smiled, tight and cruel. "You want me."

"I do not."

"But your body says you do."

"If I had more say-so with my body, I would've made better grades in high school. I don't always get my way."

"Like I said, Mackenzie, some women enjoy having a man under her complete control."

"Cute terminology for rape."

"Don't use ugly language. If I free you, do you promise to please me?" she said.

"I do not. I will throw you through the window."

"So you stay in your chains. Entirely immobile. But do not fret. By the end, you will be won over."

"I'm not entirely immobile, Emile."

"Meaning?"

"Meaning I'm going to head butt you."

She frowned and blinked, her sadistic seduction routine hitting unexpected turbulence. "You would not."

"And, if I try hard enough, possibly kick your shin."

"Do not try to resist, American. You belong to me, and your pathetic squirming will be unmanly."

"There'll be nothing pathetic about it. I'm going to head butt you super hard. Possibly render you insensate."

Her hands retracted and rested on my knees. "You wouldn't."

"Would and gonna."

"Why would you do this?"

"I have a theory. You think you like having men under your thumb. Controlling them against your will. But I think you crave like the positive feedback to which you're accustomed. It's a sick game you play, seducing men. Exerting your sex appeal until you get your way. Trying to fill the gaping hole in your ego made by your husband. It makes you feel better to win men over. Prove you still got it. But I'm rejecting you, Emile. No games. And I will hurt you to substantiate it, if you try."

She stuck her hands between my thighs again. The smile returned. "I do not believe you. Even now, as you are being molested against your will, you enjoy it. Your sexual longings must be enormous."

"Perhaps, but not for you."

She stood and slapped me. It was a slow movement and I saw it coming, but I thought it wise to let the crazy lady vent some steam.

"I will use the bracelet."

"Then my body will be no good to you," I said.

"Then I will use shock."

"Could try, but you don't know how, and your husband might find out from the guards."

She said, "Mackenzie, stop being an ass. I get what I want. You are...what is the word, a poker term, in English?"

"Bluffing."

"You are bluffing."

"I'm not bluffing."

She undid the belt at her waist and the robe dress fell in silky waves onto the red carpet. "Look at me."

I nodded encouragingly. "Nice work. You're the poster child for liposuction."

"You want me with every part of your entire body."

"I admit, some part of my mammalian biological instinct is thrilled by you, but I'm telling you No."

"You are scared."

"Mostly I'm tired."

"Enough games." She sat on my lap, maintaining the unwelcome eye contact. She moved the way a lap dancer or prostitute would—enticing and inviting, daring me to resist.

I thumped her on her right cheekbone with my forehead. Hard enough to produce a gasp, and she fell off. Landed hard on the carpet.

Very unladylike, in my opinion.

"That was a warning," I said. "Also my head really hurts and I'd rather not do it harder."

"You hit me!" she cried, holding her face.

"Kinda, yes."

"That will bruise."

"Hope so. Be good for you. Maybe rub some dirt on it."

"I will tell my husband!"

"Do. And he'll wonder how I got close enough, chained like this."

She stood and smacked me again.

It had really been a long day.

"You think we're finished, American? We are not. I will have you and you will regret this." She snatched her robe off the floor.

"Wait."

"Changing your mind, yes? Too late, American. You must beg."

"No, no, it's not that. If there's a cannoli out there, could you wheel it in?"

17

The tailor returned the following day to discuss dinner attire. He was maybe seventy and moved with exaggerated dramatic flourishes, until he wanted to measure me. Then his deft fingers moved quick and precise. He wore a white button-down shirt under a black vest, and he smelled like whiskey.

I said, "You have a gorgeous head of hair. What product should I use to look like you when I'm your age?"

The tailor, whose face looked more etched instead of wrinkled, laughed and winked. "It's all about the breeding, young man. And clearly you have some. But, if you want advice, don't purchase cheap products. Splurge. You're worth it. So is your hair."

"You're British?"

"English. Do not insult me or I'll lampoon you with my needle. Innuendo intended." He held up a pair of leather loafers with severe reference. "I brought Berlutis. Try on these wicked temptresses."

I slipped my bare feet into the soft shoes. Like decadent chocolate for my toes.

Jiminy Christmas.

I said, "I didn't know my feet could be this happy."

Watching from the corner, Ernst snorted.

The tailor said, "As I told you, Berluti. One piece leather, blake stitched by hand. This pair cost three thousand American dollars. The top is alligator, dear boy."

A lesser man would've felt a little woozy.

He said, "Wait until you try on the Valentino jacket I selected for you. You'll simply die. Tapered waist to emphasize these big beautiful shoulders. Like the shoes, handmade here in Italy. Come to think of it, Valentino might be in attendance tomorrow night, the animal."

"Are you the Prince's haberdasher?"

"Of course, O Principe is a dear friend. Sinfully handsome, like yourself, a dream to dress. He only wears Tom Ford."

"Ah. These petty proletarians and their rags."

"His outfit tonight will cost over ten thousand, young man."

"Lipstick on a pig. Am I right?" I said.

"No, Mr. August. You are not. If O Principe was a barn animal, he'd be a stallion."

"Who will you be rooting for?"

"I do not *root*," he said airily.

"Who will you bet on?"

"Not you, I'm afraid. O Principe is lethal."

He stepped closer. Made motions like measuring me. Got his mouth next to my ear and whispered. Not only did he smell like whisky, he sounded like it.

"Listen quick. The blonde girl asked me to pass you this message in secret. Do not give up. She's working to free you."

I moved not a muscle.

The blonde girl...

I wanted to reply but didn't know how.

No words emerged.

...working to free you.

Watching from the corner, Ernst frowned.

The tailor stepped back and said, "That'll do it, beautiful boy. The clothes will be ready soon. And if you're lucky, I'll find something luxurious for your hair."

18

I strode down the posh hallway like a boss, dressed to the nines. Maybe even nine and a half. Did my shackles ruin the effect? I liked to think of them as a fashion statement. In a few months all the cool kids would be wearing them.

I said, "How was partying with Rossi?"

Duane did a shrug. "Rossi. Man never showed. Supposedly hanging out with his new hooker. Just an excuse, though, to hide. Sees assassins around every corner, you know?"

"Try not to let it ruin your vacation."

"Ruin my vacation? I'm making a fortune off you. Just bought this Franck Mueller watch. You had a good time last night?"

"The fight?"

"No. Not the fight. The girl after."

"I already forgot her. I suppose not."

Emile walked behind us, along side Meg. I heard her steps falter.

Small victories.

Meg stayed quiet.

The blonde girl passes you this message. She's working to free you.

My head spun.

Duane was talking. "You guess not. Some Japanese girl, I heard?"

I said, "My date last night, whatever country she's from, was desperate and lonely and broken and she needs a husband who loves her."

Duane laughed through his nose, a soft raspy sound. "Enough sermonizing. Maybe just screw the girl and shut up."

"You like my jacket?"

"Don't give a damn about your jacket, August. Tonight's the last time you gotta play nice. Understand? Get through the meal. Answer the questions. Then you're done. Tomorrow you'll kill the Prince or he'll kill you and it's over. You're free or you're dead. Got it?"

"You and I, Duane. We're in similar situations."

"Similar situations. Me and you. Explain," he said.

"You're running out of time to do the right thing. You've got one more day to take off the chains. If you do, I won't kill you. If you don't, if I have to fight my way to freedom, Duane? I'm going to kill everyone. Including you."

He grabbed my arm and jerked me to a halt. I thought about killing him then. I could break his neck before Ernst shot me. Before Meg could activate the black wrist band. We were inches apart. Child's play to get my wrists around his neck.

But.

It wasn't time yet. My mission wasn't to kill Duane. It was to get home.

I had a son.

I had a wife.

Kinda.

Tools and obstacles.

He held out his hand. Spoke softly. "Ernst, gimme your gun."

Ernst shoved his black SIG into Duane's grip.

Duane raised the pistol and pushed the barrel into my cheekbone. Got his face close to mine.

"You're threatening me," he said.

"I been threatening you all week, Duane. What's new."

"Why should I let you live?"

"Because if you shoot me you're the asshole who killed his own champion. The final fight doesn't happen. The Kings are humiliated."

"You think I care."

"I think you desperately care," I said.

"You don't know shit."

"Your gun isn't scaring me, Duane." That was dishonest. *Huge* lie. His gun terrified me. "Put it away before you hurt yourself."

He pushed the muzzle harder into my cheek. "Doesn't scare you. Maybe. Makes me happy to do this, though, August. You know? Having the time of my got'damn life."

"Good for you. Follow your bliss."

Over his shoulder I saw Ernst's lips part to reveal his teeth. He chuckled. Meg whacked him on the arm.

I'm a riot.

A riot about to be shot in the face if I didn't shut up.

"Doesn't matter," said Duane. "You can't win. The Prince, he's not a man who loses. You're dead tomorrow."

"One way or the other?" I said.

"I won't kill you, August." He lowered the pistol. "Gave you my word. But yeah. You're dead. One way or the other."

"I'm despondent, Duane, at my eminent demise. Can this be my sepulchral attire? I'm bespoke as heck right now."

He didn't answer. Turned and kept walking, pistol in his fist pointed down.

"Seriously. I'd like to wear these shoes in heaven," I said.

19

F errari announced us into the area. The majority of the stadium seating had been removed, making way for formal table and chair settings. Instead of thundering music and lights, polite applause pitter-pattered from the stands. Tonight wasn't about blood, tonight was about money.

Not everyone had received an invitation to the elite dinner, only the most well-heeled. Those in the stands sat around tables with white cloths, waited on by reverent servers. They ate caviar and lobster and drank thousand-dollar bottles of champagne.

Meg had told me tonight was for the billionaires. Italian royalty, Persian sheiks, oil sultans, Singapore gods, and the mafia bosses. Wealthy beyond comprehension.

The cage stood like a tomb at the center. Inside was set another table, heaped with candles and bottles and plates.

While Ferrari chattered, Ernst released my cuffs.

"Don't try it, August," said Duane. "I'll tell'em to use bullets, not electroshock."

Ernst smiled, lips pulling back from white teeth like a

skeleton. "Try, Herr August. You'd be foolish not to. I want to watch you die."

I vant to vatch.

"Mackenzie cannot get far," said Emile. Always watching. "He wears the bracelet. He belongs to us."

Ernst clipped a microphone to my jacket.

Duane whacked me on the back. His party moved to a table near the base of the seating.

I walked up the stairs. Into the cage.

Ferrari stopped chattering. The stadium echoed into stillness, like holding its breath.

The Prince sat at the table, leg crossed. His suit was blue and crisp. He sipped a martini and stared at nothing.

Two specimen under a microscope.

"Why do you wear the black bracelet? You volunteered," I said. My voice felt small. A marble bouncing in an airplane hangar.

My favorite elderly couple sat in the front, their hands clamped around their ears. Food forgotten. They leaned forward, listening and pondering and weighing.

The Prince sucked at his teeth a moment. Said, "A tradition. In the past, all champions wore chains. Now, we wear only the bracelet. Except for the reluctant, such as yourself. The arrogant and the foolish and the prisoners."

He wouldn't look at me. His gregarious smile was absent.

I poured myself a glass of water. The inconsiderate hosts had neglected beer, and champagne tasted like the Executioner looked.

I drank some water and tried a pasta dish. Noodles tossed with white wine and bacon and eggs. A worse combination was unimaginable. And yet...zounds. It tasted as good as my Berluti shoes felt.

"Everyone is listening," I said.

He nodded. Eyes distant. He appeared to have skipped to the stage of the meal where one becomes philosophical.

"Deciding on whom to invest a fortune," I said.

This time his head didn't bother to budge.

"What's the betting line?"

He took a breath. Held it. Slowly released. "Even. We are a coin flip."

"I accept your surrender."

"Never in life," he said and he finished his drink. Wiped his mouth with a thumb and forefinger. Set the martini glass down and refilled it from a stainless steel shaker. Inside, the ice tinkled. The pale green liquid leaked out in oily swirls. "Never in life have I wanted to kill someone as much as I want to kill you, American."

An audible inhalation from the audience. Millions in money swinging to his side. Abhorrence and moral superiority counted for a lot.

I would've bet on him.

"Such sudden hate," I said. "I'm out of touch with the news. Is this about Trump? What'd he do?"

"It is not your President. Italy is in no place to judge a chaotic government." He carefully selected a link of sizzling chorizo and cut it with his fork. Hot juice squirted onto the tablecloth. "Tell me. Do you still think you will escape your captivity?"

"I will."

More noise from our host of onlookers. Murmurs and grumbling.

"You were nearly successful after your fight with the Mexican."

"Nearly."

"You killed the Gurkha, which is hard."

"I've been told that, but I don't remember it."

"Why do you resist?" he asked.

"That answer is obvious."

The chorizo sat on his fork, forgotten. "Yes, but *why*. You are a man of violence. You have the scars. You have the face. The ability. The skill. The anger. The different...mafias, they bring their champion or their prisoners. But you are more than a mere prisoner. Do you understand what I say? I want to know why. You are *more*."

"Maybe if I wasn't actively resisting, I wouldn't be."

"Say that again. But elaborate. This might be your last conversation before I kill you tomorrow."

I made a small twirling motion with my finger. "All of this? It's a sad pastiche of former Roman might. I don't buy it. The Camorra and the Kings and the others, they're a supercilious bunch of lost souls pretending they aren't. Pretending they aren't leading lives of quiet desperation. Consider me an iconoclast. I reject this diorama. And so I resist."

"You intentionally use words I cannot follow. Because you are a proud and obnoxious American."

"I did. You're right. Let me try again. I think this thing is a joke. It's beneath me. If I quit resisting then something inside of me is damaged," I said.

"Damaged if you surrender to this lifestyle."

"Yes."

He scoffed. "You become like me, you mean."

"Maybe. But with better cheekbones."

He did not smile. Which was weird.

The crowd chuckled, listening to a translation.

They got me.

"Perhaps you're right." He swirled his cocktail, a subdued motion. He stared into its emerald depths, no longer the larger-than-life crowd favorite. For a moment, he looked like a boy. "Being an, ahh, opportunist so far has meant that I am alone in the world. And you are not."

Radios squawked simultaneously around the arena. Like an echo. On the belt of every guard who hadn't cranked down the volume. Ferrari's stern security chief put a hand to his ear, listened, and jogged out of the stadium.

"The rabble," said the Prince. "The peasants of Naples are angry. Something lurking beneath has outraged them. They nearly broke through last night."

"How?"

"I do not know. I only listen to the whispers of my attendants. They suspect a saboteur from within. I am weary of it all."

"You weren't this forlorn two days ago."

"Things change, *American*." He growled the word. "The game has lost its shine."

"This isn't a game and it never had a luster."

"That is why you resist," he said. "You do not see the tournament for the opportunity that it is."

"I refuse to become inured to crime."

"Crime leads the way. Crime is life."

"Not to all."

"You have a family."

"I do."

"A son," he said.

"I have one of those."

"You have a wife?"

"Mostly."

"Mostly?" he said.

"It's complex. But she's lovely."

"You do not deserve her, stupid American."

"Hurtful. But possibly correct."

"This meal is over. I will not sit with you at this table one minute longer. The betters will be disappointed, I know, but I can no longer look at your face."

"Yet it's such a nice one."

He smacked the stainless steel cocktail shaker off the table. It hit the mesh metal cage and broke apart. He stood, got his fingers under the nearest tray of food, and flung it upwards in a spray of gory repast.

"Ti odio, americano. Domani muori," he said. His face had gone red.

I picked up a plate of cannoli before he could destroy them.

"I dunno what that means, Prince."

He plucked off his small microphone and dropped it into the carafe of ice water. The speakers crackled and buzzed. Then he took the mic off my jacket and squeezed it between his thumb and forefinger until it broke.

Our hedonistic audience gasped and winced as their headsets issued feedback.

"I hate you, American."

"I deduced," I said.

Ferrari called, "Signori, per favore! Il pubblico deve ascoltare!"

The Prince leaned down, his face close to mine. I heard his teeth grinding. "Tomorrow. If you survive until the third round, I will help you escape. Do you understand?"

"Not at all."

"The first two rounds, I show no mercy. I will kill you. But somehow, if I cannot, then you have earned the reward."

The crowd grew agitated. Ferrari's voice blared from everywhere. We were breaking the rules.

I said, "The reward?"

"Freedom. Your life. Your...wife...and child."

"Why would you help me escape?"

Praetorian guards hurried to the cage.

Ferrari's voice blared in English. "Gentleman, please. Honorable tradition must be observed."

The Prince said, "Because, American, I promised."

He stood and wiped tears from his eyes. Composed himself. Turned and left the cage, marching through the dumbstruck guards.

Ferrari cried, "Principe, dove stai andando?"

The Prince stopped. Set his fist over his heart and spoke in a stentorian voice. "Mala via masta ne."

It was a salute. Most of the audience repeated the phrase by rote.

I could see half of his face from my angle. He smiled and wiped his eyes again. Said, "No. Sei stupido criminale. L'amore apre la strada."

L'amore.

Something about love.

He left the arena. His footsteps echoing.

I grew more and more confused the longer I stayed in Naples.

I took a bite of cannoli.

20

I woke up with an awareness that it wasn't time. I'd only slept a few hours, on the carpet, my arms stretched to either side. Not comfortable.

Ernst released the chains and shackled my wrists together. Guards stood nearby, their electroshock weapons held ready. I watched bleary-eyed.

"What time is it," I said.

"Four in the morning. You will fight now."

"Now?"

He nodded. Indicated I get up. "Yes."

"Go'way, Ernst. Come back in three hours. With coffee."

The four praetorian guards glanced at one another. Should they haul the sleepy and sinfully handsome man to his feet?

In barged Duane. It was too early for barging. He threw fighting shorts at me and started working on his cufflinks. He looked rough, like a cocaine snorter at the end of a bender.

"Get up, August. We're doing this."

"Go'way, Duane Moneybags. Come back in three hours. With coffee. Fight's not 'til tonight."

"Yeah, well, plans change. Rossi says we're doing it now," he said.

"Rossi the Camorra lord."

"Right. Says we're sitting on dynamite. All of Naples about to erupt, but especially the clans. We do the fight now and get the hell out of here. Something's got them spooked. They broke into Vomero. Impossible but they did it. They're here."

"Who is?" I said. Stupidly. I looked out the window. Vomero was dark except for fires burning nearby.

"Mobs. Angry people. Thousands."

"Trouble in paradise. So weird, like people don't enjoy being oppressed."

"Get the fuck up. You got an Italian prince to kill, hear me? I'm betting a lot on you."

I stood. Stretched. Said, "Coffee and breakfast, Duane."

"Not a bad got'damn idea." He stuck his head into the next room. "Someone! Get the chef. Coffee and breakfast. For me and the champion, here."

"You said the Prince is not a man who loses. Now you're betting on me?"

Duane finished with the cufflinks. Pulled at his collar and belt. "I met Rossi last night. Bastard goaded me into it. So don't lose."

"You met Rossi? What'd you think?"

"I hate that son of a bitch."

THE TEATRO DI MONTAGNA was in a state of tumult. That was obvious to people who weren't even keen detectives.

Guards stood at every corner. Cries down the hall. The more furtive residents hurrying to the exits, dragging luggage themselves instead of waiting on porters.

"Everyone leaving?" I said.

"Only the cowards," said Duane with a scoff. "The arena will be full. Trust me."

Our usual procession had swollen. We walked with eight guards, some of which looked antsy—hands at their holster, scanning the hallways, glancing at one another. Emile had lost her patina of confidence. Guests watched us pass. Some of the hotel staff shot me a thumbs up.

"Look, August," said Duane. "You told me you'll get revenge if I don't release you. Kill me. Forget about that. You win this thing, we're both rich. Afterwards I'll get us out of here and we go our separate ways. Alright?"

"Alright? Expound on your proposal."

"I mean, we're square. You win. I get you out of Naples. You keep the money. Live and let live," said Duane.

"Release the cuffs now and we're square."

His raspy voice made a growl. "Can't do it. I let you go, I lose the money. You and me, we need a truce."

"I go into that ring, your life is forfeit."

"Why?" he said. A low scrape of anger. "Tell me that. Why can't we strike a deal? That's how these things work."

"What things? Deals struck by human traffickers? Professional criminals trying to make a fortune? I'm not part of your world, Duane. You shouldn't have brought me here. Our animosity is mortal."

"Unbelievable. Un-fucking-believable. The first ungrateful champion and I gotta bring him. Fine. Forget you, August. We're through." He rubbed his hands together, like cleaning them. "Win or lose, don't look for me after-

wards. I'll keep my word and I won't come looking for you.
But if you come after me, I'll bury your ass."

"You're tiptoeing on the edge of oblivion, Duane, you
just don't know it. Last chance."

He didn't respond. Kept walking.

Something cold and unyielding pressed into my back,
forced me to keep marching. Ernst's SIG pistol.

We neared the indoor arena and the halls became
congested. Hundreds of Neopolitans clotted the passages,
surging towards the stadium. These weren't residents of
Teatro di Montagna. These weren't billionaires. These were
Camorra clansmen. Local soldiers and fighters who'd burst
their way into Vomero and then into the Holy of Holies, the
Theater on the Mountain itself.

Ernst growled in my ear, "They watch the fights online.
Streaming on their phones from the underground. Now
they come to watch you die."

The heat and stench of compacted humanity intensified.

A man in khakis and no shirt was the first to notice us.
He lowered a clear bottle of liquor from his lips. Gaped, like
we were aliens.

"È l'americano! Guarda, è il King! Yankee!"

I knew a little of that. He recognized me.

His friend turned to watch. Then so did others.

"Lo Yankee! Vieni ad uccidere il Camorrista!"

More took up the cry.

Yankee!

Yan-kee, Yan-kee.

Ernst was wrong. They hadn't come to watch me die.
They'd come to cheer for me.

The mass of bodies parted and we passed between the
cheering rabble.

"I am Moses," I said.

Duane, wincing against the noise, looked at me. Shouted, "What?"

"You missed your chance, Moneybags. The end draws nigh."

I put my head down and plowed forward. Kinda fun. Fun and terrifying. The men slapped me on the shoulders. Unseen villains showered us with alcohol. Smelled like Sambuca. The noise and light and heat inclined upwards.

A man wearing a radio found us. Breathless.

"Signori, please! Follow. It is time!" he cried.

The Neapolitan men smashed the lamps and bulbs over our head. The hallway grew dark except for a red glow ahead.

Why do mobs smash things? What inner dam broke inside these lunatics? And why?

Ferrari's voice boomed from everywhere. His normal sensuous and unctuous tone now sounded urgent.

"Ora abbiamo l'evento finale! L'ultimo combattimento. Per favore prendi i tuoi posti!"

We bypassed the small waiting rooms. The horizontally rotating door was up and our river of bodies surged into the arena.

Into hell.

The size of the audience had tripled. Stadium seating overflowed. The floor of the arena was standing room only. Many of the powerful overhead lights were out, and it was obvious why—spectators in the throng fired guns at them. Molten flares were lit and thrown intermittently. Some shot upwards, pausing, and arcing into the unsuspecting crowd below. In the northern seats, an Italian flag was burning and being waved. In the southern seats, so was an American flag.

Italians on both sides were chanting and singing a dirge. It rattled my ears.

"Good Christ," said Duane. "We're going to die."

Ernst laughed. The kind where one's head falls back and the mouth opens wide. A true guffaw. "No. We will not die. You have not been to the European football games? Is always madness."

Somewhere unseen, Ferrari was shouting into his wireless. His head of security charged our way with a cadre of armed guards. They administered powerful electroshocks seemingly at random, winnowing the crowd.

The man with blue flashing devices in his ears glared like this was my fault.

He shouted in Italian.

Meg translated. "Follow him! Mackenzie's fight is about to start!"

"Okay," said Duane. He licked his lips. His eyes were a fraction too wide. "Okay. Ernst, Meg, take Mackenzie. I'm going to the box. These Italian Guidos stink of piss. August, maybe it's not too late. Win this thing and maybe we'll talk."

His normal rasp was hoarse and verging on hysteria.

"And Darren's assassin?" I asked.

"Never mind that. Forget about it. That's got nothing to do with me. Your best chance at staying alive? A truce. Find me after. If you're alive. Which, probably, you won't be."

He turned and grabbed the sleeves of two guards and filtered into the crowd—fleeing the peasants and heading towards the comfortable and air conditioned quarters of the privileged.

The crowd jostled us. Ernst was distracted, and Meg too frightened to function well. Neither had their trigger out.

The moment I'd been waiting for had arrived. The moment to escape. It would almost be easy. Clunk their heads together. Take Ernst's gun and bracelet trigger. Move into the throng.

And yet...

And yet.

There was still Darren's assassin. Here. Watching and waiting. And if I ran, I'd be followed.

Furthermore, the Prince had told me he'd help.

Furthermore, the haberdasher had told me the blonde girl was working to release me.

Something was afoot. And if I ran now, I might be spoiling things.

Part of me wanted to go into the cage. Part of me fed off the crowd's mania and thirst for blood. Some of my inner dams were breaking and I wanted to smash things. Wanted to charge through the crucible. The Prince couldn't finish me in two rounds—I could survive until the third.

Probably.

The functional overhead spotlights found us and my world turned dazzling and brilliant. The mob made a path.

Yan-kee, Yan-kee.

The Prince waited. He looked a little like the Statue of David, but with gloved hands resting through the wire mesh. His torso was long and ridged with muscle. Broad shoulders, trim waist, ramrod back, knotty calves.

"Good luck, American," called Ernst. "Maybe you will make the second round."

Vill make zee second round.

"Stay alive, Mackenzie!" cried Meg the blonde girl. "You can do this!"

The Executioner stood by the door. Despite the mask, I could tell this wasn't the same man. No sleeve of tattoos. And this guy was even taller.

I jumped up the stairs and into the cage. Nobody forced me. I did it volitionally. Temporary bout of insanity.

Mackenzie August, going off the rails.

Deep breaths. Slow the pulse. Think clearly.

I pulled on fighting gloves, which scraped against my electrical burns.

The audience got loud enough to create a localized quake in the Theater on the Mountain, shaking the cage's floor.

The Prince prowled back and forth on his side. Men in his corner clapped and screamed.

In mine, so did Meg.

Ferrari kept jabbering.

The man with flashing Bluetooth ears was circling the cage. Sneering. He carried a pistol now. His men were not above thinning the herd.

More flags began to burn in the stands.

Half of the luxury boxes were empty. Many of the wealthy debutantes had fled, leaving the final fight to the rabble.

Thousands held their hands in the air. Thumbs thrust high.

For me.

I raised my fist. Thumbs up. The audience roared. A sonic embodiment of madness. Hurt my ears.

The Prince met me in the middle of the ring.

"American, you should have fled by now."

"These colors don't run. And waking up this early's got me truculent."

"I will kill you, I am afraid."

We were having to shout and I still barely heard him. Ferrari had finished the introductions, I could tell. Was about to sound the horn.

I shrugged. "I'm also afraid of that."

"But. You reach the third round? You're a free man."

"Why?" I said. Loudly. "Tell me that, I need to know."

He shook his head. Backed away to his corner.

"Roma victa," I said.

The electronic buzzer rang.

Five minutes.

Then five more minutes. I could do this.

21

H e came on in a mixed martial arts fighting stance I recognized. Which meant he'd been trained. Ah nuts. He'd be versed in submission moves. The choke hold most likely. A broken arm or leg wouldn't stop this fight.

I dropped into my forward stance. A defensive crouch. Fists up. He came straight at me. I circled to my right. He was right handed and it made his life harder.

In my periphery I noticed spectators rush the cage. They'd been held back by threat of gunfire but the oncoming crush was too much. Humanity flowed to the base of our platform.

The Prince peppered me with jabs. Easy blocks. I held my palms up, catching them.

He snapped exploratory kicks. I twisted to let them slap harmlessly against the side and back of my thighs.

"You won't get a choke hold," I called.

He grinned. Only a madman would grin during this fight.

"Maybe," he replied. "Maybe not."

He moved in. Impressive combo. Right left right, but I

caught them on my hands and shoulders, and then he was behind me. So quick, and I'd been focused on parrying. I think he planted a foot on the mesh to spring off, got higher on my back.

He went for a grappling move called a rear naked choke hold. Feet around my waist, one arm around my neck, locked in place. It would mean death but I didn't let him. I bunched my shoulders. Caught his right wrist in my right fist, and I pinned his left arm.

"Ahhh," he breathed in my ear. "You are trained, no?"

"Sexy, yes?" I said.

I tossed us both backwards. Landed hard. I had thirty or forty pounds on him and he lost his air.

The onlookers released a throaty roar.

I squirmed enough to get my shoulders and neck onto the mat, which meant safety. Like a good grappler, he tried to get superior position above, but I got my knees up and shoved him away.

Yan-kee, Yan-kee.

It had been a furious thirty seconds. Might've looked a mess to untrained eyes. But to me and the Prince, much had been communicated. Each was facing a skilled combatant. Each had done everything correctly.

He bounced in his corner, reclaiming oxygen.

We met in the middle again. He was quicker and I adjusted, playing defense. He jabbed, a pop from his left hand. I caught and deflected it with my left, a small motion. Another jab, but it was exploratory. The Prince was testing my reflexes—was I a skilled boxer? More jabs. I parried or let them fall ineffectually.

He telegraphed his big combination—squared up so I saw it coming. A jab, uppercut, left hook combo, tight and furious. Lot of power coming through technique. The uppercut missed, the hook caught me a glancing blow.

My counterattack would've killed a lesser man. I move well for a bull, and I drove a right over his shoulder. Caught his jaw and he fell back, my left nearly taking his nose off. He scrambled away, his bell rung. I gave no quarter, attacking like Tyson used to do in his heyday. Thumped his body, hammered his head, which he managed to mostly block, but he would sink like wet sand soon.

The crowd seethed and steamed.

My mistake was I forgot we weren't boxing. I fell into old routines, going for a knockout. The Prince kneed me in the groin, illegal in every other fight I'd ever had. But not at the Gabbia Cremisi.

Holy smokes.

I'd suffered gunshots that hurt less. A cold hollow feeling radiating between my legs, then a wave of hot pain.

I backed off, trying to remain upright. Knock-kneed and hunched wasn't a good look. The crowd roared with laughter and fury.

Neither of us was standing well. Wobbly for different reasons. He shook his head and winced. I got my hands on my knees and tried not to vomit.

The cello and electric guitar wailed and Ferrari called, "Due minuti rimanenti!"

He recovered first, coming my way and shaking out his arms. I forced myself to stand, resulting in a masculine whimper.

Wary of my fists, he tried to get me in a clench. He wanted to outmaneuver me, use his experience on the mat, but I'd spent years cage fighting in Los Angeles and knew enough to stay alive.

Unlike my previous opponents, an insane dervish and an obese juggernaut, the Prince didn't make foolish mistakes. So staying alive was all I did, weathering his storm.

When the alarm sounded, he was clinging to me in a back mount. Boos and cries rained down. More flares burst to life.

Ferrari switched on his wireless and chattered, "Il primo round è completo! Né il combattente ha subito molti danni..."

Gunfire in the audience. Screams. Flashing Bluetooth man bolted that direction.

I panted. "Round over. Leggo and I won't bust your nose."

"Very well, American. You survived." He still hadn't released, talking directly into my ear canal. "But now comes the electricity, no?"

"A shocking development."

"A joke? At this time?"

"When better."

He released and went to his corner.

Meg snaked an arm through and handed me a bottle of water.

"Keep it up, Mackenzie! You're doing great! Anything injured?"

"Everything's injured," I said.

I drank and pushed the bottle back through.

Be nice to sit down. Be nice not to worry about electricity. Get a few more hours of sleep. At home. In America. With my wife.

I had a wife.

Ferrari said dramatically, "E adesso! Quello che hai aspettato. L'elettricità!"

"Back up, Herr August," said Ernst. "The power is turning on."

Zee power!

Simultaneously several men surrounding the cage screamed and jolted backwards. They'd been touching the metal.

Artificial crackling noises issued over the speakers.

"Sports fanatics in Italy are lunatics," I said.

"It's more than that," said Meg. "They think tonight is the start of a revolution."

"Oh good. We'll be martyrs. That's something at least."

"You're their rallying cry, Mackenzie. They're here for you. They might carry you out on their shoulders."

The loud buzzer sounded.

Round two.

Goal—stay away from the power.

The Prince came on. Low.

I saw his move—I knew it before he began. He was ready to end this. He was going to shoot for my feet. Kind of a power dive at my knees, a wrestling move. Drive me backwards. He expected to catch me by surprise.

He shuffled. Side stepped. Grinned.

"Truce?" I said.

"A truce once you are dead, American."

And he shot at my ankles.

I was prepared. I dropped to my knees. My right knee fell onto his left shoulder. Our combined weights and force met at that juncture, a jarring collision. Instead of catching me by surprise and tossing me off balance, his momentum arrested, like a football player trying to tackle a wall, and his shoulder broke.

I felt it give. A dislocation or a tear. Or something. I didn't know much about shoulder joints.

He screamed into the mat. Something withering and accusatory.

I asked, "How do you say 'I bet that hurt' in Italian?"

He tried to shift from under my weight, maybe two hundred and thirty pounds on a good day, but my knees had him pinned hard. Each twist made him wince.

"Why will you help me in round three?" I asked.

"Va' a farti fottere!"

"Was that deeply vulgar?"

"Yes," he said. Panting. Eyes shut.

The audience was rowdy enough that the noise offered us privacy.

I asked again, "Why will you help in round three?"

"I promised to free you."

"Then why are you trying to kill me in round two?"

"I promised to kill you," he said.

"You're a conflicted guy, Prince. I'm unsure how to proceed."

He winced. Ground his teeth and pounded his right hand on the mat.

He said, "You win, American. I know I cannot beat you with one arm. I played the loser's game too long, no? You must kill me."

"Why? This could be the beginning of a beautiful friendship."

"If you don't, they will know. They will suspect treason and kill us both," he said.

"In that case…" I said. I hammered him in the head a few times with both fists. The punches were theatrical, not as vicious as they looked. The crowd enjoyed them. "Why are these Camorra clans here?"

"The whispers. You are rumored to kill Rossi tonight. That is why you were brought, they think."

"I'm flattered. And I might. Who started that whooper?"

"We don't have time for this, foolish American! Kill me or get up."

"Not gonna kill you but we need to make this look good. Hit me as best you can."

He did. Better than I anticipated. I was bent over to hear him and his good fist snaked all the way up to my throat and popped me good.

A disaster.

I fell back. My hand shot out to stop my fall. Meg screamed. My black wristband connected with the mesh cage.

The world went white and hot. Felt like I'd been bit on the hand by a lion. Without a direct connection, the effect was mitigated but hurt like hell.

The black band exploded. Smoked and corkscrewed along the cage wall to the far side. It landed in a sizzling pile of twisted metal.

I regained a shaky defensive stance. Took me a second to remember where I was. The mat tipped and tilted beneath my feet. My arm hurt and I shook it but that increased the pain. The muscles tingled and quivered.

I heard a buzzing somewhere.

Needed water. So thirsty.

The glove on my right hand was on fire. That struck me as significant. But I stared stupidly at the flame a full three seconds before realization dawned and I tugged it off.

Meg and Ernst made noise but they were miles away.

The Prince hit me. A hard right, in the teeth. I staggered and stayed standing.

"Fucking American," he said. "Why can't you die."

My lower lip began to bleed. Blisters were raising on my wrist.

His left shoulder joint pushed at the skin in abnormal spots, and he held the arm to his abdomen. He came again but only had his right arm to battle with. I caught the punch with my forearm, running on instinct. He tried to knee me in the groin but I twisted.

Around we went. He wasn't dazed but operated in extreme pain. I wasn't injured but my judgment was returning slowly. I was engorged with adrenaline and cortisone but had no ability to direct it. We were a mess.

An eternity passed and the buzzer sounded. End of round two.

The speakers issued an artificial sound of the walls powering down.

Men in the crowd began leaping onto the fence. The guards hauled them off or stunned them with electroshock weapons.

Ferrari's voice thundered from everywhere like Mars, the god of war.

I smiled. That was a solid simile. Needed to relay it to Timothy August; he'd enjoy it.

Meg and Ernst waved me over.

"Hey guys," I said. "I don't recommend the electricity."

Meg thrust water at me. I drank some and spilled some down my chest.

Ernst said, "The Italian, his shoulder is broken. Why did you not finish him?"

"I only kill my captors." I handed the water back. "Speaking of, it's time for you two to go."

"Go?"

I held up my wrist. There was no black band.

"Your power is gone. Now so should you be. Before it's too late."

"Why? What's going to happen?"

"The temple pillars will fall."

I hoped. Grandiose words with only a prayer behind them.

I turned my back on Meg and Ernst. Raised my fist to the audience. Thumbs up. Pumped my arm. The crowd reacted like I was an orchestral conductor.

Yan-kee, Yan-kee!

Seams I'd never noticed in the center of the mat opened. Like a trap door. A new section of floor rose in its place, bringing weapons for our use.

There were two hammers and two knives.

The hammers were heavy medieval-looking things. The head was covered with small spikes. One good whack would kill a man.

The knives were Italian cinquedeas. Almost a short sword, broad at the base.

The Prince stood close enough to the weapons that his toes touched them. Arm cradled. He took deep breaths.

"I admit it," he said. I barely heard him over the din. "You are worthy."

"Worthy of freedom?"

"Freedom, yes. And worthy of *her*."

"Her who?"

He used his foot to slide a heavy hammer my way. Keeping my eyes on him, I crouched and rested my forearms on my knees, the hammer between my feet.

He bent to retrieve a hammer and sword. Moved like an old man. Raised up, grimacing. The long knife he shoved under his belt. The hammer he held in his right fist.

"There is another rumor," he said. "There's an assassin. Sent by your countrymen."

"I heard. We're a nation divided."

"I cannot help you with that, American."

"I know."

Ferrari's chatter intensified.

Ernst the German bounty hunter called, "The fence, Herr August. It turns on again."

The Prince nodded to me. Closed his eyes.

"Good luck, American. Who knows. Maybe we meet again one day," he said.

The fence buzzed.

The horn sounded through the speakers, like an alarm.

My mouth bled.

The crowd raged.

And that was when the power in the Teatro di Montagna went out.

PART II

22

"This is torture." Veronica Summers sat on a kitchen stool at the home of Timothy, Mackenzie, and Kix August and Manny Martinez. Her legs were crossed and she drummed her manicured nails on the counter. She glanced at her watch again. She got up, stretched her arms over her head, and said, "I despise waiting. This is absolute torture. Where is he?"

A young prostitute named Ebony sat on the leather sofa, suede knee-high boots crossed at the ankle on the cushions. Ebony looked up from her iPhone and watched Veronica the way a young and unproven actress might watch Sandra Bullock or Meryl Streep. With deep reverence.

She said, "Why's this place so clean?"

"I already answered that, Ebony."

"Why again?"

"Because the men who live here are clean. Fastidious, as one of them would say."

"But it's so nice, like a movie, you know?"

"It's perfect, in my opinion."

"And you're with one of them?" asked Ebony.

Veronica still wore a pencil skirt and gossamer white blouse from work. Her heels rested by the door. She ran a hand through blonde hair that reached past her shoulders, shaking out non-existent tangles. "Yes. I think."

"But you're screwing around."

"It's complicated, Ebony."

"And he ain't gay? That's weird."

"Somehow it's not. I love him. And he loves me, I hope. And we're waiting to be intimate."

"Why?" inquired Ebony.

"I can't remember."

"He let you live here?"

"If I asked."

"He hot?"

"Mackenzie is very attractive, yes," said Veronica.

Timothy August, sitting in a reading chair in the corner, placed a bookmark inside the hardback copy of the recent Jeffrey Deaver novel and closed it. He gave a half smile at the questions. "His mother was foxy."

"Oh," said Ebony. Her attention wandered to and from her phone. "You his dad?"

"We've already been over this, sweetie," said Veronica. "Maybe stop talking. I'm too stressed to listen."

This wasn't an ideal night for Ebony's pimp to threaten her with physical harm, but it had happened anyway. Veronica was new to the prostitute reclamation business and she didn't know what to do with the girl yet, especially because Ebony expressed no desire to quit.

Manny Martinez walked in at midnight. As usual, the man earned a second glance from Veronica. So gorgeous he almost looked feminine, but the breadth of shoulders and the muscles were masculine. She didn't like pretty boys; she liked her men to look fresh from a fight, scarred and fierce.

But it was impossible not to admire the man standing in the doorway.

Ebony gasped and said, "Holy shit, you for real?"

For the moment, Manny ignored her.

Behind him came Marcus Morgan and Sheriff Stackhouse. Marcus wore black wool slacks, a grey shirt, and dark overcoat. His belt buckle and watch and wedding ring all glinted—polished white gold. Sheriff Stackhouse's uniform was jeans and a crisp white button down shirt, collar flicked wide, a tried and true outfit for modestly showing off her eye-popping figure.

Ebony got to her feet and shuffled nervously, unaware this many beautiful adults existed in the entire city.

Manny grabbed Veronica's hand and squeezed. "He's alive."

She released a breath she didn't realize she'd been holding. Holding for hours, it felt. "Where is he?"

Marcus Morgan took note of Timothy and nodded at him. Timothy got to his feet. Marcus said in a deep voice, "Mr. August. This a good place to talk?"

"Absolutely."

"Guy named Darren Robbins nabbed August. I wasn't supposed to find out. Bastard hid it from me."

Stackhouse said, "I pulled traffic camera footage. Mackenzie was loaded into a car this afternoon, outside his office."

"Oh fuck," said Veronica. Her hands slid into her hair and clenched. "This is my fault. Darren put a contract on him?"

"Hundred grand." Marcus went to the kitchen where he knew the scotch was kept. Set out glasses and held up the bottle. Cocked an eyebrow. Manny and Timothy both nodded, so he poured three glasses. Marcus took a slow drink and said, "But the contract got bought out. Duane Chambers stepped in and asked for Mackenzie alive."

"Why?" Veronica lowered onto the stool again and her perfect posture surrendered a few degrees.

"He's being flown to Naples."

Manny went into the kitchen, and from the freezer he took a spiced ice cube purchased at Lucky's, a nearby bar. He dropped the flavored cube into the scotch, swirled, and drank. Set the glass down and wiped his mouth. He glanced at Ebony and said, "Señorita, you want something? Soda? Milk? Apple juice?"

Ebony, standing outside the unhappy huddle around the counter, managed to say, "Um...naw."

Veronica said, "Naples? Why Naples? Manny, what's going on?"

"*Yo no se, reinita.* I'm hearing this part for the first time."

"I did some digging," Marcus said. "Mackenzie's being entered into the Gabbia Cremisi."

Outside on the front porch, standing in the cold air, someone cursed.

Marcus raised his voice. "You two idiots eavesdropping, come do it inside."

Fat Susie and Carlos walked in, a pair of behemoths. Fat Susie was black, dressed in clothes too big to fathom. Carlos was Hispanic, wore a tight red t-shirt with tattoos peeking out from beneath. Bodyguards.

Marcus asked them, "You heard of the Gabbia Cremisi?"

Carlos said, "No place for señor August."

"I've heard of it, too," said Veronica, her voice small. "Darren wanted to go, but he never explained it."

"Someone tell *me* what it is, damn it," said Timothy August. "He's my son."

Marcus said, "It's a gladiatorial tournament, kinda. Never been. A Camorra fight to the death. Big deal."

"What's the Camorra?"

"Organized crime in Italy, Señor August. But not so organized," said Manny.

Timothy looked at the faces and judged their severity and asked, "Is the Camorra the boss of the District Kings?"

Marcus said, "Nah. The Kings be a power unto themselves. Though newer, they belong in the same sentence as the Sicilian Mafia or Cosa Nostra, the Brothers Circle in Russia, the Yakuza, Triads, the major players. Anyway, they all gather for the Gabbia Cremisi. A fight to the death. Each send a champion to win, or a prisoner to be executed. Kings never gone before. Duane, he a minor King. On the Board of Directors. Be my guess, he wanted to go so he bought Mack's contract."

"What if Mackenzie doesn't agree to fight?" asked Timothy.

Carlos answered, "Don't got a choice."

"Carlos, you been?" asked Marcus.

"Ten years ago, working for hombre in *Mejico*."

"That's absurd," said Veronica. "Darren never mentioned it's a blood sport. Gabbia Cremisi translates as Crimson Cage. How is there no outcry about this atrocity? It's essentially a human version of a dog fighting?"

"Essentially." Marcus nodded.

Carlos said, "Tournament lasts a week. He wins, he fight the next guy."

"Certainly the tournament is not a televised event," said Veronica. "It can't be public knowledge."

"Nah, but it ain't a secret. Naples is a different type of city," said Marcus. "Gotta know that to understand. It's like an annual party for the criminally wealthy. Naples be a place where anything goes, you got enough scratch."

Veronica said, "Marcus, you've never been?"

"Not a big fan of violence. Avoid it when possible."

"But you're invited."

"More or less."

Manny and Veronica shared a look. A glance that asked the question—*are you in?* Searched the other's eyes. *Of course I am.*

Veronica pulled her purse close and took out her iPhone. "I'll book a flight."

"And I'm feeling feverish" said Manny. "Might call in sick a couple days."

Marcus placed a large hand on Veronica's phone. "Book a flight to Naples?"

"Obviously."

"To watch the Gabbia Cremisi?"

"To bring Mackenzie home," she said, a trace of anger and hurt between the syllables.

"And I am going to kill all the Camorra," said Manny.

"I get it," said Marcus. "I ain't happy either. But you two be Bonnie and Clyde against the entire mafia. That's a machine can't be beat."

"Pack your bags, Marcus," said Veronica. "You're going too. I need a way in. You're my date."

Even though nothing about him seemed to move, Marcus expressed displeasure. A muscle in his jaw bunched.

She said, "Marcus, you remember the poker game."

"I do."

"Mackenzie went there. For me. Knowing full well he could be killed. He's on his way to Naples because of *me*. I won't sit here and hope. This world isn't enough for me without him in it. He's the best of us. And I *just* got him and I can't lose him."

Marcus poured another glass of scotch and immediately drank it. Set the glass down and picked up the bottle again. He didn't pour, though. Just held it.

Manny said, "Señor, you saved Mack's life in that train yard. Said you liked this world better with him in it."

"I remember."

"Nothing's changed. We need him back."

"We can't bust him out, Manny."

"Mack, he is not like other men. He might escape without our help."

Marcus rumbled, "You two kids be young and carefree. Still babies. Me? I got a wife. Got a kid. I know I'm in the underworld, but I stay on the safe side."

"Marcus, I need you. Just get me in," said Veronica. She grasped Marcus's hand with both of hers. "Nothing dangerous about that. Please."

Manny grinned to himself. No man, not even happily married Marcus Morgan, was impervious to the powers of Veronica Summers.

Marcus said, "And then what."

"I'm not sure. This is happening quickly. I need more information."

He asked, "What about Kix?"

Sheriff Stackhouse elbowed Timothy August and she said, "My gorgeous boyfriend and I will watch him, naturally. You go get Mackenzie."

"Damn it," said Marcus. "Wednesday was gonna be nice. Got a tee time at the lake, one more round before it get too cold. Mackenzie still being a pain in my ass. Sure you want to do this?"

"Of course. He's my husband."

Manny made a gasping sound. "*Tu marido?*"

Timothy stood a little straighter. "Husband? Beg your pardon?"

"Hold up," said Ebony watching this from beyond the huddle. "This guy, he's you husband, but you ain't screwing?"

Veronica winced. "Oh right, I forgot about Ebony. Her pimp threatened to kill her. Can she stay here for a day? Maybe two?"

"Um, well..." said Timothy.

Stackhouse grinned. "Absolutely. That's what the sheriff is for."

"You the sheriff? Hold up," said Ebony again.

23

Veronica raised hell and fury, and found several jets but no pilots at the Roanoke airport. Instead she and Manny and Carlos and Marcus raced to Dulles in Marcus's black Lexus LS, making the trip in three hours because Manny drove. He played Sinatra and podcasts about economics the whole way.

"Sinatra, he's the king," said Manny. "Me and him, fine Americans."

En route, between calls to the airport, Veronica moved money around bank accounts using her phone in the backseat.

She said, "Private flights are absurd. A year ago this would've bankrupted me. Good thing I shot my father."

Manny laughed as he rocketed past an eighteen-wheeler. "Inheritance, a beautiful thing."

"I'll pay half," said Marcus, working on his laptop from the passenger seat. "This trip gonna cost more than you think."

An associate of Marcus's met them at the international airport's parking lot at four in the morning. He wordlessly set a black backpack on the trunk of the Lexus. Marcus zipped it open while Veronica and Manny shivered and stamped. Inside, he found four burner passports, four international phones, stacks of euros, and two new credit cards registered to each passport.

Marcus nodded to himself. Set a small diamond into the man's hand. The diamond's culet glinted red. The man turned and walked away without a word, shoes echoing off the concrete ceiling.

Veronica asked, "Who was that?"

"One of the nameless dudes keep this whole show running smooth."

"You gave him aurum? The red diamond?"

"Yep. A currency only us lowlifes use."

"One of Darren's buddies offered me a fistful of the red diamonds to marry him," she said.

Marcus paused, mid-zip. "A fistful?"

"Should I have been flattered?"

"Make you one of the most powerful women in the American underworld."

Manny made an appreciative grunt. "Maybe I marry him."

Thirty minutes later they bypassed security and boarded an HA-420 HondaJet. The private jet was not ideal—smaller and slower than what they'd prefer, but last-minute options were limited this early.

At 5:15 a.m., almost exactly twelve hours after Mackenzie had taken off from Reagan National airport, they were wheels-up and pursuing him across the Atlantic.

24

—————

Veronica woke as they refueled in Bermuda, an extra and necessary stop for their smaller private jet, a stop Duane's Gulfstream didn't have to make. It was noon, local time. Marcus quietly typed on his MacBook Air. Carlos and his biceps took up two seats across from them. Manny was asleep next to her, beautiful in repose. She took his hand and squeezed. It wasn't sexual or romantic, or even friendly. It was familial and she needed it.

She woke again in Portugal, this time for good.

The stewardess, unable to stand fully upright, brought them fruit and champagne. She tried and failed to not ogle Manny, whose pale blue shirt was only half buttoned.

Veronica noted it was Burberry and probably cost three hundred dollars. There was more to Manny than carefree Hispanic marshal, she knew, and some time in the future, on a calm day, she would pry.

She held a crystal bowl in one hand, a dainty fork in the other. She speared a pineapple bit. "Tell me about the tournament."

"I been doing research," Marcus said. "Kings never been,

so I don't know everything. The fights are an excuse for the mafia bosses to drink and gamble and fuck and buy product, I know that."

"Product?"

"Girls, ice, guns, security, luxury cars, yachts. You want it, Naples can provide it."

Manny yawned and stretched. Finished his champagne in one swallow and the stewardess immediately refilled it. "The Kings, they do not attend. *Porque?*"

"Got something to do with old and new money. The Kings are fairly new. Started taking over power from the Sicilians in the eighties, everywhere but New York City. Some of the more powerful Kings, they ain't secure in they manhood yet. New money. Worried about hobnobbing with the world's biggest swinging dicks. The Russians or the Colombian or the Yakuza, that's old money. Generational billionaires. The Kings don't wanna swim with bigger fishes."

"Tell me about the tournament," she said again.

Carlos responded. "Eight contestants paired off. Four fights, first night. Winners fight again two nights later."

"A fight to the death?"

"*Sí.*"

Veronica said, "I cannot imagine Mackenzie being forced into the ring and killing a man."

"*Simon,*" said Manny. "But imagine him losing? No way, Jose."

"What if we don't release him in time? What will Mackenzie do?"

"Better question," said Marcus. "Is how you plan to release him?"

"I have no idea."

25

Their trip took four hours longer than Duane's. They landed at the Naples international airport instead of the small private strip. An associate of Marcus's welcomed them, took them around customs, and delivered a rental Fiat. The four of them, stiff and tired and grouchy, squeezed in, closed their car doors, and cranked the air conditioning.

"Look at this," said Manny, slapping the steering wheel. "Ay dios mio, what junk. See, this is what's great about America. We have real cars."

"Have you secured tickets into the Gabbia Cremisi?" Veronica asked Marcus.

"No. Ain't so easy. Teatro di Montagna is booked solid and you gotta be a resident of the hotel to attend the fights."

"Translates as Theater of the Mountain?" she asked.

"Something like that. Big damn place, apparently. We on standby."

"Standby is unacceptable."

"I got us rooms at the hotel next door. These stupid motherfuckers kill each other with some regularity, so I hear. My source expects a room to come open soon," said

Marcus. He entered the name of the hotel on his phone and directions appeared. Manny glanced at them, nodded, and eased the car out of the parking lot, muttering about driving a toy car.

"Your source? Can't you tell them that you're with the Kings?"

"Could, but then Duane find out. Be an issue. Need to stay hidden from him. For a while."

"So we aren't here as Americans," she said.

"Nope. We here because of Manny. He a rich-ass investor from the Caribbean and I be his best friend from South Africa. We're rooting for the Zeta champion. Carlos be Manny's walk-around guy. We just hoping nobody recognize Carlos."

Manny nodded approval.

Veronica said, "And me?"

"Arm candy from Switzerland. To put it politely," said Marcus.

"My alias is that I'm a girlfriend."

"Keep in mind, these people ain't as sensitive and woke as us. This still a man's world."

"Not for much longer," she said. "I might kill them all."

Rioters swarmed their car at an intersection, slapping their hands against the windshield and windows. At the next, they dumped soda bottles on the roof. Furious Neapolitans shouted through their tinted windows.

"The fuck they doing," said Marcus.

Manny laid his .357 sideways across his lap. "Losing your deposit, amigo."

Veronica translated as best she could. "Something about crime and a man named Rossi...and the tournament. I don't understand some of the local lingo."

"It's the Camorra and their amateurish clan wars. You want criminals running the city? No you don't. They make a mess."

Due to frequent stops and reroutes, their trip up Vomero mountain took three hours. Even with Siri constantly correcting them they got lost in the maze of tight streets.

"All these buildings, they look the same," complained Manny. "Cities in America way better than this."

They arrived at the underwhelming hotel at midnight, local time. Went to bed exhausted.

27

They woke up the same way—exhausted. Veronica had no idea what time it was on the East Coast.

Coffee o'clock, she knew that.

They drank *caffè* and ate *fette biscottate* in a shady palazzo in front of their hotel. This high in Vomero the air no longer stank of sewage. They listened to competing minstrels on the far street corners and inhaled the scent of sizzling sausages.

"According to my sources," said Marcus Morgan, reading off his phone. "This part of the city is called Magliari. Means cheating merchants. It's a kangaroo court for the Camorristi. Summers, what the hell is a kangaroo court?"

"Means anything goes," she said, dipping a corner of her bread into a mug of coffee. "No one is really in charge, and those who try are incompetent clowns."

Manny nodded appreciatively.

Marcus continued, "No police in this part of the city. It's the wild west. And *that* is the Teatro di Montagna."

He pointed down their street. At the far end, seven

blocks removed, an enormous structure glimmered in unbroken sunlight.

"That's the hotel?" said Veronica. "I thought it was a royal palace. It looks as though the Artist formerly known as Prince designed it on a Bill Gates budget."

Carlos said, "The tournament. It used to be different. In Secondigilano."

"That hotel, *ay caramba*," said Manny, nodding his head down the street. "We can walk in?"

"Not recommended. One of the most heavily guarded places on planet Earth at the moment," said Marcus. "By eight powerful mafias. Without a reservation? We be escorted out pronto."

"No rooms have come available?" said Veronica.

"Not yet."

"Soon," said Manny and he finished his coffee, drunk with heavy whipping cream and butter. "I got a good feeling, *migos*."

"First things first," said Marcus. "We need to look the part."

"Clothes," said Ronnie. "Yes. I brought nothing befitting that hotel."

They navigated the crowds on Pavone Vicolo, which Veronica told them translated as Peacock Alley. They passed wine shops, bakeries, upper crust cocaine dealers, small grocers, brothels, casinos, banks, and everything else.

Veronica made a small gasping sound and hurried to the glass display window of a couture boutique. "Omigosh. It's a Lela Rose."

Manny followed her, hands in his pocket. "Huh?"

"It's the most beautiful thing I've ever seen," said Veronica reverently, resisting the urge to place her fingers on the glass between her and the blue evening gown.

"It's a blue dress, señorita. You have at least one, I seen you wear it."

"This is a Lela Rose, Manny. Just *look*. Off the shoulder neckline, a-line cut, fold-over bodice, and—"

"And Italian materials, my love," said a man hurrying from the storefront's open door. He looked maybe seventy, a hard etched face, wore a vest, and sported a gorgeous head of silver hair. He took Veronica's hand and kissed it twice. He smelled like whiskey. "You two are the most beautiful people I have ever witnessed. Did Valentino send you?"

Veronica smiled. "Only in my fondest dreams would I be sent by Valentino. We're mere patrons. You're English!"

"I am, and with Her Majesty's blessing I would arrange a ménage à trios with both of you two ravishing creatures if I had time. You need clothes."

"We do."

"Come into my store this instant so I can get my hands on you. You *must*," he said. He took Manny's hand too and drew them into his place of commerce, called Sa Majesté.

Veronica was breathless at the designers she saw waiting on mannequins.

"Who are you, I must know," said the proprietor and haberdasher. He ran his hands around Manny's neck and then across the shoulders, whispering to himself. Then he did the same to Veronica's waist and bust. The tailor's young assistant listened attentively to the man's mutterings and made notes on a pad. "I must know, tell me everything, and I will dress you like the Maharaja and concubine you are."

"We...ah..." said Manny. He screwed up his face in thought. "I forget. I'm from South Africa, maybe."

The tailor smiled a wicked smile and said, "That, my love, is balderdash."

Their voices sounded hushed, the noise soaked by the stacks of cloth.

Marcus, standing at the doorway, uncrossed his arms. He made a noise, somewhere between a sigh and a grunt. He set two stacks of Euros on the marble counter, and then deliberately placed a red-tipped diamond on top. "We need to look good," he said. "And we from *nowhere*. This the place for us?"

"Indeed, indeed." The tailor gave them a slow nod. "Say no more, my black pillar of strength and sex. I dress the champions myself, for the second fight, so I can handle you." His assistant whisked away the money and diamond, and vanished into the back room. "Are you remaining for the entirety of the week?"

"Hope not."

"What a bizarre answer! You four are trouble and I love it," said the man. He was rubbing his thumb and forefinger across his chin, pinching at it. "You won't blend in, even if I dress you in rags. What's your *story*?"

"Manny, he's rich and here to bet on the fights. From the Caribbean. I be equally rich, from South Africa. Carlos, behind me, the muscle."

Veronica said, "And I am sexual recreation."

"My god, and you're an absolute Lamborghini, I'm positive." He clucked his tongue a few times, running his eyes around the store, cluttered with fashion, dripping with excess. "Okay. How soon?"

"Today."

"Today? Go to hell this instant, that absolutely cannot be."

"Must be," said Marcus.

"Damn you, sir," said the tailor. "I was going to wrap this

woman in a couture bandage dress so taut the men would be coming at her with scissors."

Veronica watched him with eyes wide and hopeful, to the extent the tailor thought about kissing her on the lips.

"No time," said Marcus. "Tight schedule."

"I need a jacket," said Manny. "To hide, ahhh, weaponry."

The man scoffed and waved his hand. "Obviously, beautiful boy. Okay. If it absolutely *must* be today..."

"Must."

The tailor's assistant returned, pen and pad ready.

The haberdasher said, "Off-the-rack it is, and I shall not sleep again. Never in my life have I had such bodies wander innocently into my jaws. Small modifications are a necessity and you cannot, *cannot*, deny me that. Here's what I propose." He waved at Carlos in the doorway. "Pierre Balmain for the muscle, nothing fancy, stretchy distressed jeans and two tees. Trendy enough to pass the muster. Her Majesty preserve us, those biceps. For you well-heeled boys..." He sucked at his front teeth. "You look good in black. Tom Ford all the way for the South African, then, and for *you*..." He unbuttoned Manny's shirt far enough to place his hand flat on Manny's chest. "You're a boxer? I am overcome. Nothing but form-fitting Armani and Cucinelli, or I'm not worth my needles. Yes? Yes. You'll both need two casual shirts, two pairs of slacks, and a jacket. Tuxedos are not good enough for you, understand?"

Marcus wondered if he'd be required to expend more resources than he wished on clothes, but the tailor seemed to read his mind.

"This is all covered, black beauty. Never fret. You gods and goddess simply tell the wealthy aristocrats and their whores where you got the fabrics and we're even, yes? Yes.

And now *you*, my blonde girl," he said and he started unbuttoning Veronica's shirt with deft fingers. "So slim and yet so bouncy. How do you feel about Gucci and our pal Valentino and plunging necklines and slip dresses?"

"I think I might cry," she said.

"Good. I want to watch. Now let's get you naked."

28

L ater, Manny strode into a gun shop named Lo Sparatutto Felice. The heady bite of fired gunpowder hung thick and the air was pleasantly greased with expensive oil. The floor was polished cement and weaponry decorated every inch of the walls. Mostly small arms, but a display column on the right contained backlit handheld surface-to-air missile launchers and anti-personnel RPGs.

Two bald and elderly gentlemen were bent over a disassembled assault rifle, lovingly polishing and oiling every inch.

They looked up and said, "Benvenuto e buon giorno, giovane signore."

Manny grinned. "Habla español?"

One of the old men (they were interchangeable and indistinguishable, possibly twins) winced and shrugged, his motions slow.

"Speak English?" asked Manny.

"Ah, yes sir."

Manny set his heavy .357 magnum on the steel counter

and said, "This is the love of my life, señors. But for the next few days I need smaller."

The man smiled, crinkling his eyes. He had a gentle grandfatherly way of speaking. "Very good. Of course, sir. For what occasion?"

"An indoor party. Party-goers will be wearing vests, my guess."

"Guards. How many?"

"Mucho."

The gunsmith affectionately set down the stock he'd been holding. "Here to watch the tournament, then."

"Here for a friend. Save a life."

"Not to take?"

"Only when necessary. But, friendly old man, it will be necessary."

"You are a professional, sir?"

Manny shrugged and waffled his hand. "More than amateur. And I need to blend in."

"A handgun."

"Two, por favor."

"Preference?" the elderly man asked.

"You have Beretta M9?"

"Of course, sir. The *Polizia di Stato* use the Beretta 92FS."

"From Italy."

"Yes, but if I may make a suggestion?" the man said. He and his counterpart spoke briefly in Italian, and he wiped his hands on a white cloth. "The new Beretta A3...how do you say in English...update? The update has a seventeen-round magazine and a thinner grip. Easier to conceal, sir."

"Perfecto."

"And your other choice?"

Manny said, "Something quiet."

"Suppressed."

"Sí."

"How many rounds will be fired suppressed?"

Manny made a happy humming noise. "Good question. Not many. One magazine?"

"Indoor."

"Probably."

"Your aim is good?"

Manny grinned. "Better than good."

"Subsonic ammunition, then. I have specially made cartridges for the HK-23 and I think you'll be pleased. Would you care to try them on our range, sir?"

"We both would," said Marcus Morgan, walking in with a new gray shirt and black sports jacket combo by Tom Ford. Though unwilling to admit it, he thought he looked sexy as hell. Especially with the silver Versace aviator sunglasses. He laid a stack of euros and a red-tipped aurum next to Manny's .357.

The old man's face relaxed and brightened at the same time. "Ah. I see. Very good, sirs."

Manny said, "Where's Ronnie?"

"Trying on every damn outfit in Italy. Carlos on duty."

"I bet he enjoying that show."

"We both were. S'why I had to leave. My head about explode," said Marcus.

"My señorita heats up the room."

"Ain't particularly modest, neither. Your señorita?"

"Mack's. But I call dibs, he gets killed. You know, because of Kix."

Manny and Marcus followed the gunsmith behind the wall to a padded firing range. He tottered into a cage of shelves to find the promised handguns.

Marcus picked up a heavy set of protective earmuffs. "Can't believe I'm buying illegal handguns with a fucking federal marshal."

"Right? Life is beautiful, mijo. How many diamonds you think that bazooka cost?"

29

The tailor finished bringing Veronica clothes and marking alterations. He set two assistants to sewing, and he sat beside her on a straight-backed Benetti chair while she tried on necklaces. He drank whiskey and languidly gushed compliments, like a man basking in post-coital afterglow.

He said, "You say you're from Switzerland, darling."

She arched an eyebrow at him but didn't answer.

"But I bet," he said and gave her a conspiratorial smile. "You're here to root for the American."

She shrugged a shoulder, a move she knew drove the boys wild. The tailor, forty years her elder and deeply gay, admired the motion.

He said, "Surely you were there last night, at the drawing."

"I wasn't. We only just landed."

"Good hell, my bosomy plaything, but you heard what he did?"

Veronica's pulse quickened. She turned her gaze back to

the mirror and mastered her emotions. Something she was good at.

She said, "I haven't heard. Tell me?"

"I did not attend, you understand. I hear second hand. But apparently the American is aggressively handsome and monstrous. He insulted the infamous Ferrari, who is the master of ceremonies, of course. He threatened to kill all the guests and destroy the hotel. Refused to be tattooed. And drove a fork into the eye socket of the Yakuza champion. So the story goes, four guards are not enough to subdue him, the sexy animal."

Veronica peered hard into the mirror, forcing back a smile and a flood of tears.

"And," said the tailor. "He did it all without breaking a sweat, they say. Very James Bond."

Veronica bit her lip and closed her eyes.

The tailor's story was the most Mackenzie August thing she'd ever heard and her heart threatened to burst.

He said, "You *are* here for the American."

"If what you say is true, who wouldn't be?"

"If he wins tonight, perhaps you should bid on him. Could be the most unforgettable hour of your life."

"Bid on him?" asked Veronica. "You mean, for sex? You're joking."

"Oh my love," chuckled the tailor. "Welcome to Naples."

She returned to the palazzo at the pre-determined time for a late lunch. She carried five bags and the promise that the rest of the group's clothing would be ready by dinner.

Marcus sat beside her and drank coffee, checking his phone in a state of discontent.

"Where's Carlos?" he said.

"Poor Carlos was bored to tears so I released him. Any news on a room at the Teatro di Montagna?"

"Still waiting. Apparently this year is less bloody than usual so far."

"If there's no room available for us by dinner, I'll get myself invited and wait for you inside," she said. She examined the menu without an appetite, her thoughts entirely occupied by her husband, locked away in the impenetrable fortress. "What time is the fight?"

"Dunno. Tonight. How you gonna get yourself invited?"

"Promiscuity. Or at least the promise of it. Men are idiots, Marcus," she said.

"I'm aware."

Veronica related the story about Mackenzie at last night's drawing. Marcus listened without comment but she noted the muscles flexing and bunching in his arms on the table. At the end, finally, he said, "Fucking Duane Chambers. Not happy with that man."

Carlos returned an hour later, looking like a new species in his thousand-dollar outfit. Muscle but with style. "The city? I have been learning. It is a war zone," he said.

"A war zone."

"The Camorra. They are angry. But at each other."

Veronica said, "Infighting within the ranks?"

"The Camorra ain't like the Kings," said Marcus. "No hierarchy, strict or loose. Buncha clans, buncha shifting alliances. Whoever got the most power? He's in charge till someone pops him."

"Man name Rossi," said Carlos. "He in charge. Today. But the man, he is hated. Will be war soon, señor. Already the fighters talk."

"Talk to you?"

"Sí. I know people here. Worked in Naples ten years ago. I say I hate Rossi. They ask me to fight." He held up his burner cellphone, vibrating incessantly with incoming texts. "I'm on group message. Ay dios mio."

"Handy contacts," mused Marcus.

Manny reappeared an hour later. He wore designer jeans and a cashmere sports jacket with Givenchy metal sunglasses. Nearby men and women gaped at him as he ordered a coffee and sat down.

Veronica caught the flash of a pistol carried in a shoulder holster. The tailor would weep if he saw the Armani shirt worn under a gun.

He stirred his fancy powder into the coffee, sipped, and said, "We got a room at the mountain hotel."

"The theater on the mountain," corrected Veronica. "How do you know?"

"Have it on good authority a room opened."

Marcus grinned. "Good authority."

He took more coffee. "A Japanese man staying there, he died. Nasty *coño*, needed killing." Though he'd been living in America most of his life, Manny still stumbled through words beginning with an S and another consonant. He pronounced it, "estaying."

Veronica said, "Needed killing? You shot him?"

"Found him abusing a whore, mamasita. Had to. Best of all, hombre had three diamonds in his pocket," he said and he held up a small pouch dangling from his pointer finger. "The red kind."

"Stealing aurum," said Marcus. "A much bigger offense than killing a man."

"So maybe I don't tell nobody. No way to track them, sí?"

"Correct. Decentralized. You got'em, they yours. Like bearer bonds."

"I sent his body to the hotel, because manners make the man. S'what Mack says."

"Sound like the profoundly stupid shit he says." Marcus stood. "Can't believe it, but I miss him. Almost dinner. Let's go."

30

Although the Teatro di Montagna's lobby was mostly deserted, Veronica and Manny caused a quiet and dignified stir as they entered. Manny walked with the casual swagger that originates from confidence and athleticism and carelessness. Veronica moved with a sensuous cat-walk that comes from strong long legs and heels. She wore an embroidered silk mini-shift dress, the color of ivory, perfect for a lady of leisure walking in from shopping. She wished her legs were a little darker to offset the ivory, but it was November and the sun had been poor in Virginia. Carlos and valet boys carried their luggage.

She did her best to act as if twenty-thousand-dollar brocade sofas and soaring cathedral ceilings with travertine arches was nothing special. The tiger lounging near the three-tiered fountain was a little much, though.

She and Manny washed their hands with lemongrass-scented warm towels and accepted champagne aperitifs from the concierge's assistant.

Manny checked in at the marble reception desk and declared he would be taking the room that just opened. The

severe reception clerk examined him and Veronica, and
Marcus, and then Carlos.

"It's a small room, I'm afraid, Señor Garcia," he said,
using the name from Manny's passport. "Not a suite. A mere
two beds."

Veronica set her crystal champagne flute on the counter.
"È un onore soggiornare in qualsiasi stanza disponibile nel
tuo hotel di lusso. E inoltre, sono più intraprendente di
quanto sembri, signore."

*It's an honor to stay in any available room at your fine hotel.
And also, I am more adaptable than I appear, sir.*

The man, undone by Veronica's wink and her perfect
Italian, blushed and nodded his head. He said, "Sì signora,
molto bene. E ti avviserò se si apre una stanza più adatta."

Veronica translated for Manny. "We're taking it, and he'll
notify us if a more suitable room opens."

Manny said, "Tell him that's perfect."

"He speaks English, doll."

"Oh yes."

Ronnie told the attendant, "Anche se vengo dalla
Svizzera, mi piacerebbe incontrare il campione americano.
È possibile? Dove rimane?"

*Although I am from Switzerland, I would like to meet the
American champion. Is that possible? Where does he stay?*

He replied, "Mi dispiace, signorina. I campioni sono
nascosti dietro le porte sorvegliate. Una visita è
impossibile."

*I am sorry, miss. The champions are hidden behind guarded
doors. A visit is impossible.*

Manny caught the gist. He thought about pulling a gun
and making demands, but the lobby was well guarded and
dozens more could be called for. The time for war was later.

Veronica began a polite plea but he interrupted her,

insisting, "Se ti sbrighi puoi ordinare la cena, cambiare e avere ancora tempo per guardare il combattimento. Ma devi essere veloce. L'ora si avvicina!"

If you hurry you can order dinner, change, and still have time to watch the fight. But you must be quick. The hour approaches.

31

F inding Mackenzie before the first fight would be impossible. Veronica knew it immediately, as she got lost simply making their way to the room. Not all elevators went to all floors, random hallways were barred, and the lounges, salons, and restaurants seemed haphazardly thrown in with the guest quarters. She knew there must be a method to the madness but it felt like a jumbled ten-floor casino, much of which was hidden intentionally.

But oh, what a casino. For a woman who usually suppressed her delight in traveling, the Teatro di Montagna was methadone. She wanted to examine the teak floors and oriental rugs, and try the furniture in every nook they passed, each with steaming samovars. Such perfect settee and jardiniere arrangements were impossible.

Their room was clearly one of those the architect shoe-horned in to maximize income—an awkward and inefficient space. Honeymooners might call it cozy and romantic.

Veronica said, "It's darling and quaint."

Marcus grumbled, "Fucking tiny."

The porters hung up bags full of clothing delivered by the tailor and they left.

"We here," said Marcus, looking at the solemn group. "Anybody got a bright idea?"

"We can't release Mackenzie before the first fight," said Veronica. "This is much more sophisticated and elaborate than I imagined."

"Could try," said Marcus. "But got no real chance. We all be dead. And I ain't about that."

Manny nodded. "Agree. Mack, he wins tonight. We bust him out tomorrow."

"You think he will?" asked Veronica.

"I know it, mamita."

"Me too," she said. "He can be a shockingly terrifying man, when he chooses."

"An issue," said Marcus, holding up two golden slips of paper. "This room provides two tickets to tonight's festivities. But we got four people here."

"I'm going," said Veronica. "Full disclosure."

"Obvious. Manny?"

"Hashtag me too, señor."

"Carlos and me, we'll get drinks at a bar. Maybe tag along behind the fighters as they come back," said Marcus.

"Perfect. In the meantime, I'm commandeering the lady's room for the next sixty minutes. Minimum."

Manny jerked a thumb at himself. "Us fine gentlemen, we'll scout the other women's attire." He pronounced it, "ehscout," a mispronunciation that somehow sounded sensuous out of his lips, Ronnie thought. "Report on how formal the women are dressing."

"Sometimes, Manny, you're surprisingly thoughtful."

"Yeah, it's weird," said Marcus. "I seen you shoving your

gun into kids' mouths before, but then you got this sensitive side."

"Not a kid, hombre," said Manny. "He was a teenager. Big difference. Vamos!"

Despite Veronica's best efforts they still missed the first fight. It had been a slaughter under five minutes.

An usher escorted them to their seats, high above the cage, near the cupola. The cheap section, though that was a relative term. The higher they went, the louder and more bloodthirsty the fans. An eclectic mix of the crazy rich below, closer to the action, and the bourgeoisie above. The nosebleeds were for the merely rich, not the wealthy. And high over all, the ring of honor. The suites had open-air seating and glass floors, letting the mafia bosses and the billionaires look directly down on the action.

Manny and Veronica had seats next to the aisle. One of the servers bowed politely and asked, "Vorresti una bevanda?"

Would you care for a beverage?

Veronica said, "No. Grazie."

He smiled and placed a small radio in their hands. The radio had two dials—one for volume and the other for channels. Manny inserted the earpiece and toyed with it.

He told Veronica, "Translations. English, and Italian, and Spanish, and...others that don't matter."

The announcer's voice boomed out of speakers, drowning out the violins and cellos.

Veronica gripped Manny's hand and shut her eyes.

The next fight was between the Russian and Colombian. Veronica kept her eyes closed during the first round, but a burst of electricity announced the second and she couldn't help herself. Would these men actually hurl each other into the cage?

"This is barbaric," she told Manny but no one heard. Manny was cheering as loudly as the rest.

For the final round, weapons raised from the floor. Short sword and a shield for each.

The combatants began losing body parts and Veronica placed a trembling hand over her mouth and shut her eyes again.

Poor sweet Mackenzie.

She would kill Darren Robbins herself.

Finally, after an eternity, the crowd roared. The Colombian had given up the ghost. The Russians helped their champion limp away and the dead Colombian was dragged off to the tune of a mournful dirge.

"Holy fuck," she moaned. "Where are the vomit bags."

The voice came over the speakers again, rattling her teeth. She heard the name Mackenzie and she gripped Manny harder to keep from falling.

The crowd began a chant.

"Yan-kee! Yan-kee!"

Mackenzie appeared, walking within a guarded retinue. He wore red, white, and blue fighting shorts; no shirt. He moved around easily, loose and ready.

"There he is, Manny, do you see?" she cried.

He towered over his opponent, a fighter from the Zetas. The Mexican looked strong and wiry but Mackenzie was a weapon of war. His shoulders were beefy, his chest thick, arms made of rock. He wore muscle like armor.

Veronica never loved anyone or anything as much as she loved him in that moment. Tears spilled freely down her cheeks.

"What'll he do?" she shouted into Manny's ear. "I know Mackenzie, he would never kill that tiny man."

Manny shook his head. His eyes were hard and muscles in his jaw kept bunching.

Mackenzie did something that caught the attention of the entire arena. He looked at the suites above and stuck up his thumb.

"What is that, what's he doing," Veronica asked no one in particular. Then, "What's that on his back? Is that...did he get a *tattoo*?"

"*Simon*, looks like."

"What's it say? King? ...I kinda like it."

The round began and Mackenzie played defense. So did the Mexican.

Veronica joined in the cheers.

After a minute, the Mexican kicked Mackenzie in the head and they both went to the mat. Veronica couldn't see over the raging fans so she stepped into the aisle.

"The Mexican is biting him!" she shouted, going up even higher on her tiptoes. "That little piece of shit is insane!"

Mackenzie threw him off and stood. It looked to Veronica like Mackenzie was trying to talk to the Zeta champion.

A server was ascending the stairs and Veronica grabbed him for support. The young man took a second glance at Veronica, stunning in her strapless red minidress, and decided he liked the arrangement.

Within the cage, Mackenzie stuck his thumb up again.

"What is that?" she called. "What's he doing with his hand?"

The young man she clung to didn't know.

A lady in front of them, a classy Chinese woman wearing a cheongsam the color of midnight, turned and explained in her best English, "He fight for the Kings. The

American, he been told he be killed even if he win. We think he refuse to fight!"

"Oh my god," said Veronica.

"Yes we think too!"

"He's pointing his fist at the suites," Veronica shouted at Manny. "At Duane, I bet, that asshole."

Manny said, "Makes sense. Mack is bartering with Duane. Maybe won't fight until Duane give him thumbs up?"

Half of the audience was now pumping their thumbs into the air.

The pretty Chinese woman said, "I love you dress. Where did get it?"

Below, Mackenzie got to his knees and closed his eyes.

"Oh shit," said Veronica. "What the hell's he doing?"

The man (Indonesian maybe?) in front of Manny had been casting a leery eye at Veronica. He turned and politely whispered to Manny, "She is with you?"

"Yes, my...I forget. Girlfriend, maybe?"

"She is for sale?"

Manny laughed and clapped the man on the shoulder. "You can try. But also I might shoot you in the...groin, I think, is the English word, sí? You know the word groin?"

The Mexican suddenly leapt on Mackenzie and began choking him. The crowd roared as Mackenzie was bent backwards.

"Oh merda," Manny groaned. He laced his hands into his hair.

"What's he doing!"

"He dying," said the Chinese woman, still fingering Veronica's dress.

Veronica screamed until she and Mackenzie were both

red in the face. The server holding onto her joined the screaming.

"Get up!"

Yan-kee, yan-kee!

Mackenzie kept pumping his fist, thumb upwards. So did the rest of the crowd.

There! She found the American suite, above the red, white and blue section. A man paced back and forth. She didn't know what Duane looked like, but she assumed that was him. A woman swatted at him with her clutch purse. Most of the crowd was waving their thumb at him. She and Manny were in the seats dominated by the Triads, across the stadium.

Finally, as Veronica ran short on oxygen, Duane stuck his thumb into the air.

Quick as a wink, Mackenzie escaped and regained his feet.

"I'm going to pass out," said Veronica, who genuinely felt lightheaded. The young server put his arm around her waist.

Time was almost up in the round.

Mackenzie cornered the Mexican and threw a vicious combination of punches and the man fell. Every section except the Zeta's erupted. Mackenzie returned to his corner and sat down.

"What he do," shouted the Chinese woman. "Kill him!"

He won't, thought Veronica.

No chance, not Mackenzie.

The voice came through the speakers again, declaring the American the winner. Veronica's eyes widened as the Executioner hefted his axe and entered the cage.

"But you tell me," said the pretty Chinese woman. "Where you get dress?"

32

Twenty minutes later, they met at a bar called Sangue e Tonico on the fourth floor. The fights had been broadcast on flat screens for those without tickets, and Marcus Morgan had watched with professional concern and Carlos had left finger print indentions in the standing wooden table.

Manny and Veronica joined them, a bit shell-shocked, and called for drinks.

"I cannot believe such a brutal and savage spectacle exists. Is the Italian court system non-existent?" said Veronica, and she drained half her white wine.

"Exists. And on the take."

She said, "Our gang of renegades should invade Darren Robbins's house and take turns shooting him."

Manny raised his glass to her. "My kinda woman."

"Mack was taken to the second floor," reported Marcus. "Into an unmarked and guarded hallway. Couldn't follow past."

"He see you?"

"Nope."

Carlos set down his beer, still sweating from watching Mackenzie. "Hard to fight our way in."

"More like impossible," said Marcus. "Dunno where in the fucking hallway they took him. Take time. We find him, be hard to fight back out. Need more information."

"Imma get into that hallway," said Manny. "Do some reconnaissance."

"How?"

"The hotel employees." He indicated two guys passing the bar. Young men wearing black shirts and crimson vests. "Some be Hispanic. Imma take the uniform and wear it with pride, *migos*."

Manny's phone was laying flat on the table and it beeped. Incoming text message. He glanced at it and grinned.

"Just made fifty grand. Drinks on your favorite Spic."

Marcus said, "Fifty grand ain't chump change. How you manage that?"

"I bet on big Mack. He was getting great odds yesterday." He shrugged and waggled the phone proudly. "Bet twenty, my entire savings, end up with fifty. So easy even a Puerto Rican can do it."

Veronica finished the wine and set the glass down with conviction. "You just reminded me. I was told we could bid on the winners."

"Bid on them?"

"The winners are put up for auction. Like a stud horse. For one hour." She stood. "I'm going to win Mackenzie."

Marcus stood. "I'll help you bid."

"Duane might be there, and he'll recognize you," she said.

"Hm."

"I got this."

Manny tossed back his gin and tonic. Wiped his mouth. "Imma get my hands on a uniform. Break into the hallway."

"Me and Carlos," said Marcus. "We'll be nearby, case we gotta shoot our way out. Carlos is ready to die, need be."

He grinned. Carlos nodded.

Veronica followed a crowd of glamorous women and their wealthy bloated husbands to the fifth floor, where she discovered something of a betting hub. A central bar formed the eye of the hurricane, serving drinks in all directions. The patrons gossiped and pointed at screens over the bar and on the outside wall.

Four umbrella pine trees rose above the bar in travertine planters, fed sunlight from a system of mirrors and skylights. Historic Gabbia Cremisi weapons were displayed in glimmering vitrines. The bar's color theme was rose and ivory.

Two hotel staff members walked past, carrying a man on a stretcher, and two others were quickly cleaning up blood from the carpet. A stern man wearing two flashing Bluetooth earpieces stood with a cadre of guards, dispersing the angry clans.

Clearly the man on the stretcher had just been shot and killed. Veronica tried to shrug it off, because the rest of the room struck her as nonplussed. The juxtaposition between the sudden cruel violence and the laissez-faire attitude of the patrons was disorienting.

Just another day in the life of a mafia boss.

The pretty Chinese woman from earlier hurried to her and said, "It you!"

Two of her friends joined, huddled around Veronica.

"You see," said the woman. "Look right here. This the dress I told you."

The women, lovely and beautiful all of them, their dark

hair luxurious beyond belief, caressed Veronica and her red minidress.

"Thank you. I adore your cheongsam," said Veronica, indicating their traditional high-necked, short-sleeved formal dresses. "Where did—"

"You know we did?" said the woman. "We call him. We call the man, you say."

"You did? The tailor at Sa Majesté a few blocks away? That was fast."

"You know we did? We ask for it all!" She laughed and so did her friends, an unusual high cackling. "We say we take everything!"

She pronounced it, "errytheeen!"

Veronica, a sucker for enthusiasm and gorgeous dresses, laughed with them. If they practiced law, these women would be her sisters.

She asked, "I'd like to bid on the winners. Do you know how? Is that horrible of me?"

"No, not horrible," said one of the lady's friends. "We fuck too! Don' bid on Riku! He Japan!"

"We bid America! We love him also!"

Veronica nodded, flustered. Said, "How do I—"

"Phone number on screen! We love you, so pretty!"

Then, like the winds shifted, they turned and hurried back to the bar. Short-stepping in heels, cackling.

"Phone number," said Veronica, walking around the bar. She found a screen with Mackenzie's photograph and video from tonight's fight. There was a phone number with instructions. She had to text in her bid.

She looked at her phone and a blush burned her cheeks.

Considering her history, she thought, how on earth could this embarrass her?

As she toggled her phone, someone across the bar

screamed. She jumped and automatically clutched her purse and phone to her chest.

A man (maybe Russian?) lay on the ground, a knife protruding from his shoulder. Above him stood another man (maybe Colombian?).

The angry man with flashing Bluetooth headsets swooped in with his cadre of enforcers to intercept the violence.

Veronica didn't get to see the conclusion because a gentleman (maybe Italian?) in a tuxedo placed himself directly in her line of sight. A handsome guy, if a bit on the heavy and puckered side. Too much gel in the hair, too much entitlement in the smirk.

He held a drink out to her. "Too many criminals in the room, no?"

She stared at the drink but didn't take it. "Too many criminals, not enough lawyers."

"You are bidding on a champion?"

"Maybe."

"I'm Antonio," he said, still offering the drink. "And you need not bid for me. I am here, *mi amore*, and I am yours."

"Oh..." she said, trying to see around him. The Russians and Colombians seemed exceptionally unhappy with each other, shouting with guns drawn.

"From the moment I saw you," he said.

"Thank you, Antonio. But I decline."

Another man (Chinese? With the Triads?) joined Antonio, also offering a drink to Veronica, and made essentially the same proposal, irking the Italian gentlemen. Veronica maneuvered enough to get a glimpse of the phone number for Mackenzie. She backed away from the bar, entering the number as quickly as she could as her two suitors argued.

She pressed Send and received a text response immediately.

>> **BID AMOUNT FOR MACKENZIE AUGUST -
AMERICAN CHAMPION**

"Shit," she said to herself. How much? Not the foggiest.
A grand? Two grand? Three?

"Bid high," said a voice at her ear. She turned. Another
Italian man, this one older and losing his hair. Smelled
good, though.

"You think?"

"The recent average? Twenty thousand euros," he said.

Veronica's jaw dropped. "You're kidding."

"Not to a woman as *bellissimo* as you." He was also
offering a drink, but Veronica didn't notice.

"I never charged a fourth that much," she muttered to
herself.

She punched in a number.

30,000

And gulped.

Mackenzie was worth it.

Or, she thought, he better be.

>> **GRAZIE. BID RECEIVED.**

The gentleman was standing so close to her that his
pelvis rubbed against her hip, and he did his best to look
down her dress.

"Perhaps," he said. "We could talk in my room, no?"

"Flattering, but my heart is set on a champion."

"I saw your bid. I can pay that much."

"For me."

"For you," he said.

"Damn it, I've been undercharging. You mob guys are
loaded. Good for you."

"So—"

"Also, no. Hell no," said Veronica. She moved away, finding a spot at the bar. Caught a glimpse of herself in the mirror.

No wonder the sweaty mafia men were after her—she looked perfect, in her professional and critical opinion. Amazing what money can do. She wished Mackenzie could see her...

Should she bid more? Maybe. He seemed a crowd favorite.

She punched more numbers into her phone.

35,000

>> GRAZIE. BID RECEIVED.

There was a digital clock counting down on the screen. Three more minutes.

Ugh. Forever.

She ordered a sauvignon blanc. The swarthy bartender set a wine glass in front of her and said, "For the lady? Free."

"Thank you." She sipped. Exquisite. The Teatro di Montagna was serving bottles of wine in the hundreds. Maybe higher. "How much do you think I should bid on a popular champion?"

The man, perhaps a few years younger than her, winked. "Signorina, for me? You pay nothing."

"Never mind, god," she said with a groan.

The Colombians and Russians were still shouting on the far side of the bar. Her favorite Chinese ladies cackled at their phones, punching numbers and sloshing champagne. Girls across the room, girls she recognized as prostitutes, were capturing the drunk and hungry men like shooting prurient fish in a barrel. She spied more men being carried on stretchers through a salon down the hall.

"This place better have excellent in-house counsel," she

muttered into her glass. "Unless those are judges walking away with the girls."

At 11:40, the timer hit zero and her phone buzzed.

>> THANK YOU FOR BIDDING ON THE AMERICAN CHAMPION. UNFORTUNATELY YOU WERE OUTBID. GRAZIE.

She stared. And stared. Couldn't move. "Fuck."

Someone wealthier than her had just bid an astronomical amount for the right to have sex with her husband.

The woman had good taste. And if Veronica ever found out who she was, she'd drown the slut.

She drank half her wine, hoping Manny was having better luck.

AT 11:45, Manny finally found a hotel employee his size. A room serviceman walked down a guest hallway carrying a bucket of ice and chilled champagne, and Manny hung back ten feet. The man stopped at 3014 and let himself with a keycard.

Without breaking stride, Manny followed.

The man saw him and smiled ingratiatingly. "Ah, Signore, hai ordinato lo champagne? Posso mettere—"

The lavish suite was empty so Manny pulled his new Beretta and pressed the nozzle hard into the man's nose.

"Amigo," said Manny. "Take off your pants."

To the serviceman's credit, he acted as though accustomed to absurdities at the Teatro di Montagna. He obeyed Manny's requests with polite acquiescence, and in five minutes was handcuffed to the bed, wearing only his boxer shorts.

"Here's how this goes," said Manny, straightening the

crimson vest over the black shirt, and inspecting his reflection. "I'm leaving. But I'll come back and release you. If you are not here..." He referenced the name tag on his vest. "*Niccolo*, then I find you and sodomize you with my pistol."

"Yes sir," said the man, gravely.

"You know what that means? Sodomize?"

"No sir."

"Stick my gun in your butt. Maybe I pull the trigger. So you stay here. Sí?"

"Yes sir. Very good."

"I'll come back and release you, and buy you a drink. To apologize." He picked up the bucket and popped a piece of gum into his mouth. "I'm taking the champagne."

"As you like."

"Wish me luck, hombre."

"Good luck, sir."

Manny strode to the second floor, following Marcus's directions to the unmarked guarded door. Withdrawing the guest serviceman's identification from the vest pocket, he flashed it but the two bored sentries didn't spare him a second glance and he went straight through.

Once inside, Manny slowed. He took out the piece of gum he'd been chewing and pressed it underneath the cold champagne bottle. The moisture ruined the adhesion so he wiped it with a hand towel and tried again. Two handcuff keys were in his pocket, on a small ring. He separated them and forced one into the gum and, satisfied, replaced the bottle into the ice.

He turned a corner and nearly collided with a small metal pushcart, guided by a young boy. The boy smiled shyly at him and said, "Mi scusi, signore."

"You speak English?"

"A little."

Manny stood at a hallway T-junction. Armed guards patrolled all three directions. He lowered his voice. "Which way to the American?"

The boy laughed. "I go there too! We both bring champagne."

Manny pointed at the boy's cart. "That champagne is for Mack?"

"Mackenzie the King! Mackenzie the Yankee! Yes, signore."

"Here," said Manny. He picked up the ice bucket from the cart and replaced it with his own. "The kitchen made a mistake. You deliver mine. I'll return yours."

"Good idea," said the boy. He smiled so big Manny thought about adopting him. "My bottle of champagne is no good. I was worried."

"Why?"

"I think the Mexicans poisoned it. Revenge for beating their champion."

"That happens?"

"Of course. You are new, no?"

Manny nodded. "I am new. You go, I'll follow."

The boy turned left and then right down the opulent hallways, stopped at a door with an American flag placard. He knocked and tall bearded man opened.

"Champagne," the boy said. "A gift from the hotel. For the American."

"Ja," said the man. He irritably jerked his head in. "Come in with it, then."

Come in viz it, zen.

Manny angled himself enough to peer inside the room. White walls, white couches, floor the color of wine. No Mackenzie. A guard sat on a chair, his feet up.

Two guards only? Like winning the lottery.

Manny's hand dropped to his side. The HK-23 was clipped to his belt, under the vest. The barrel and attached suppressor pointed upwards along his spine.

Two guards only...

A radio squawk echoed down the hall. A roving sentry. Big guy, buzz cut, walking with his Beretta ARX held in both hands, pointed at the ground. Impressive assault rifle. He wasn't a fat Italian guard with his feet up. This guy meant business. Special forces. He looked Asian, but maybe not far East?

Asians all looked the same, Manny thought, very unlike Hispanics.

The man regarded Manny with the hostility all professional badass guards possessed and turned his direction.

Change of plans—deal with the frowny roving sentry, and *then* bust into Mack's room.

The young Italian boy returned and shot Manny a thumbs up. The German closed the door. Still the sentry came on.

Manny's pulse went from 60 beats per minute to 64.

The man asked Manny, "Sei nuovo?"

Manny didn't know Italian but nuovo sounded like nuevo, the Spanish word for new. He grinned and nodded.

"Sì," he said, shoving as much Italian into the syllable as possible. It was one of the few Italian words he knew.

The man looked at the boy. "Gennaro, chi è questo straniero? Non lo riconosco."

The man's Italian was clipped. Formal, not his first language.

Manny said, "You speak Italian with a British accent, señor."

The sentry, clearly startled, turned his baleful eyes back on Manny. "And you speak English."

"I do, though us Hispanics sound better in English than you ugly British."

"I'm not British and you don't work here, *amigo*."

Manny snapped his finger. "Ay dios mio, you're a Gurkha. Good for you."

A Gurkha was a member of the British special forces group comprised entirely of elite Nepalese super fighters. Gurkhas were some of the world's best. Manny knew enough to take the man seriously.

Shame if he had to kill him.

The man said, "Who are you."

Manny tapped his name tag. "You can't read, Gurkha? Name's...errr, Ricky?"

"Tag says Niccolo."

Manny did a shrug. "Same thing. Italian names all sound alike."

Gennaro laughed.

"You don't work here," the man said again.

"Are Gurkhas usually this rude, bebé? No manners in the special forces. You notice these hallways don't have security cameras?"

"Last thing rich people want," said the giant Gurkha. "Is their behavior recorded." His hand went to the radio on his shoulder, most likely to call for clarification about the smart-ass guest serviceman in the champion hallway. "Wait here."

"What is this?" said a new voice. A beautiful woman walking towards them, wearing a green evening dress. Or, wearing most of it; her breasts were about to spill out. "Is something wrong with the American champion?"

"No, signora," said Manny.

The man nodded deferentially to her. "No, Mrs. Chambers."

The woman stopped between them. Smelled like ten-thousand-dollar perfume.

Mrs. Chambers, the Gurkha called her. Duane's wife. She'd been on the plane with Mackenzie.

Gennaro smiled, looking on.

She said, "You two men work for the hotel?"

Manny said, "Only until you make me a better offer, mamita."

He was maintaining eye contact with her and smiling, something he knew caused occasional and temporary insanity with women his age. Or older. Or younger.

The Gurkha said, "I work directly for Signore Rossi, Mrs. Chambers. And I have my doubts about this man."

"You work for Rossi?" said Manny and he made a tsk'ing noise. "Mercenary working for an evil man? Makes you evil too."

"You're about to find out," said the man. "Just how evil I am."

Mrs. Chambers took a slow breath and said, "If I ordered you two to go into my bedroom and undress, are you compelled to obey? I'd settle for one, but I'd prefer both."

"Your wish, my command," said Manny.

"I am on duty," said the Gurkha. "And I will not leave my post. Ma'am."

Manny scoffed. "Coward. You would not know what to do with a woman like this anyway." He nodded his head at the hulking sentry and told Mrs. Chambers, "He's a Gurkha. Had his penis cut off for the sake of Her Majesty."

The little boy named Gennaro gasped.

The man said, "We...? No, that's untrue."

"Prove it."

"What?"

"Right now," said Manny. "Prove it. Drop them pants."

"All kinds of bad things are about to happen to you, *Niccolo*."

"Wait here," said the woman. "I need to check on my champion. And then the three of us, we're going to my private suite."

She strode past them, giving Manny an especially smoky stare down. She went to the American door and opened it.

Manny told the fuming sentry, "Go patrol somewhere else, Bruce Banner. I want this one."

"You don't work here," the man said in his disorienting British accent. "And that makes you a dead man."

"Go on, big guy. Keep walking, I don't share."

At that moment, Mackenzie crashed through the door, his hand around Mrs. Chambers's throat. Manny was too stunned to move. She kissed him on the mouth and whispered, "You may not leave yet." Mackenzie began to deflate like a balloon. His knees went out and the rest followed.

"Guards?" Mrs. Chambers called. "Some help, *s'il vous plaît*."

Manny reached her first. He grabbed his friend by the arm. For a minute, Mack looked as though he recognized him.

"What is...what is happening to him?" asked Manny. "What'd you do?"

"I have taken back what's mine."

The Gurkha reached them. Growled, "This fucking prisoner keeps trying to escape." He raised his fist, ready to break Mack's face.

Manny caught the Gurkha's wrist. Held it in an iron grip. He whispered, quiet as death, "No, señor Gurkha. You are finished."

Their faces were inches apart. Eyes locked.

The man said in a growl, "You definitely don't work here, Spic."

Guards came running. A lot of them.

The Gurkha understood Manny was more than a serviceman. He tried jerking his hand free, tried bringing his assault rifle up, but Manny was too quick—his free hand produced a five-inch fixed blade from his belt, a SEAL Pup. Manny delivered two short savage punches—burying the steel under the man's ribs, into the lung, and thrusting over the hip bone, ripping the lower internal organs. Immediate and irreparable damage.

The man had less than five minutes, his spleen spilling poison into the destroyed kidneys and liver and pancreas.

Just as quick, Manny's knife disappeared. Surgical destruction in less than a second.

No one noticed the Gurkha's silent agony and collapse, because too many guards were arriving, too much mayhem. The Gurkha and Mackenzie huddled on the floor, struggling to stay awake.

Manny cursed quietly. Be hard to carry Mack *and* fight his way out...

Not hard. Impossible.

He turned and hurried Gennaro before him, down the hall. "Come on, mijo. This is no place for you."

More guards sprinted their way, ignoring the hotel staff.

Manny's jaw was set, his eyes hard like diamond, his heart burning. So close. The key had worked, but Chambers had some other method of controlling Mackenzie.

He was beginning to hate this hotel.

33

A hotel reception clerk and two porters arrived at Manny's door at one in the morning, as he and Veronica returned to their room, defeated.

The clerk nodded politely to Manny and said, "Señor Garcia, it has been a bloody night. We've lost twenty-six guests so far, and therefore we have a more appropriate room for you."

"Twenty-six?"

"A common occurrence when housing many of the world's most...passionate guests." He leaned closer, as if sharing confidential information. "Which is why we require payment upfront, sir. May we move you to your new accommodations? It is only around the corner."

Twenty minutes later the four insurgents settled into a much larger suite, with two bathrooms and two bedrooms and a mattress for all. Despite Veronica wearing a relatively modest nightie, each time the men glanced at her their spines naturally straightened and their shoulders pushed back, an involuntary response at being in the same room with a sun goddess.

She set her toothbrush down, came out of the bathroom, perfect teeth sparkling, and said for the third time, "How confident are you that Mackenzie did not have enough time to be seduced and coerced into sex before his escape attempt?"

Manny grinned in the doorway, where he was using a washcloth to clean his knife. He was bare chested, in the process of changing shirts. He had nothing on Mackenzie, Veronica thought to herself. But still. The man was not unpleasant to look at.

"I was with big Mack in Los Angeles, señorita. Even during his wild years, his single years, if he was with a girl? He was faithful," said Manny. "Trust me. He didn't...*follarla* the girl."

"*Follarla* means screw?"

"Close enough."

"I have no right to be jealous," she said, rubbing the flat of her hand along her neck. "But I am. He's the only thing in my life worth being jealous of."

Typing on his laptop and yawning from his bed in the next room, Marcus asked Manny, "The hell happened to you in Los Angeles, marshal? Why'd you move here and start hanging out with August?"

"A long story," said Manny. "None of it good. I never met a good man, 'til Mack. Being around him, it helps."

"I know the feeling." Veronica went to her heirloom bed and slid under the covers. "We'll get him back. Right, Manny?"

"No doubt. My bet, soon enough he'll get out without our help. Almost did tonight." He finished with the knife and slid it into a hidden slot along the belt line. "What about you, *pana*? The hell happened to you in that train yard last year? Why didn't you kill Mack?"

Marcus stopped typing. Leaned back against the wooden bed frame and removed his reading glasses and sighed.

"Should have. I be a dead man, the Kings knew the truth. But I think, when I looked at him, I saw myself, if I'd grown up with parents. A man with violence in him, but... tryna do right. Because that's a hard thing, fighting against the desire to hurt. And August's got the fight. But he's a good dad, a good man, a believer in the Almighty, and I couldn't pull the trigger. Maybe August is authentically the man that I'm pretending to be. You know?"

Carlos was almost asleep. He mumbled, "Didn't know you could talk so much, *jefe*."

"Still waters run deep, boy. Tomorrow, Carlos and I gonna find out more about the anti-Rossi sentiment in Naples. We wanna crack this fortress? Might need to coordinate with the local militia. Loyalty can be bought with enough ice," said Marcus, and he slid his reading glasses back onto his nose. They were, of course, black and silver.

Veronica yawned and stretched. "I'm going sunbathing tomorrow. There's usually gossip at the pool and I need to discover the dirt on the black bracelet he wears."

Manny pulled a t-shirt on, clipped the Beretta pistol to his belt, and shrugged into his sports jacket. A more dashing figure would be hard to find.

Veronica asked, "Going somewhere, handsome?"

"Out. Wanna go?"

"Absolutely not. I'll be asleep in seconds."

He grinned and gave them a quick salute. "The night is young. I'm loaded and the casino might still be open."

34

Veronica woke and found herself lying next to Manny. She hadn't heard him return last night, yet here he was—on the bed with her. He'd fallen asleep on top of the covers, still dressed, a crime considering the value of his clothing. His mouth hung open half an inch and he breathed slowly and deep, creating a faint rattle. She slid out of the covers and went to the ladies room. Only when she returned did she notice the cargo Manny had returned with.

Lying on the floor between the two queen beds was an ugly machine gun, a rocket launcher, and two backpacks. One backpack was full of cash in euros. Sticking out of the second backpack was what appeared to be four rockets.

Her eyebrows lifted. The casinos in Naples paid out differently than those in Vegas. Did this hotel have *any* rules?

She tiptoed around the ordnance like it might blow, and she picked up a phone and ordered room service.

"Portami due di tutto," she said.

Bring me two of everything.

Soon, guest servicemen wheeled in four carts of prima

colazione—caffè latte, biscuits and butter, cornetto, bacon, eggs, fette biscottate, and a fruit salad. She helped herself to coffee and bacon and invaded Manny's bed to eat, since he still occupied hers.

Marcus returned from wherever he'd been. Without speaking he crouched between the two beds and picked up the rocket launcher, inspected it, and set it down. Did the same thing with the machine gun, and then he opened the first backpack farther.

Manny rolled over, yawned, and sat up, instantly awake.

"The rich gamblers at the casinos in Naples?" he said. "They have no idea how to play a hand of poker."

"Three more diamonds here," said Marcus, holding the red-tipped jewels in his palm. "You steal more aurum?"

"Steal? You offend me, señor," said Manny. "They were given to me."

"By a dead guy?"

"By a guy who needed killing."

"Rumor in the hallways, the American champion killed a Gurkha last night," said Marcus, standing up with a slight grunt. "That you?"

"Again, *migo*, a guy who needed to be dead."

"Six aurum you taken since you arrived. And killed a mafia special forces soldier," said Marcus. "By now, you a wanted man."

Manny rolled out of bed and took off his fortune in wrinkled fashionable clothing. Veronica didn't watch. Much. He said, "Always been a wanted man. Otherwise, what fun would life be? I live with inexhaustible joie de vivre."

"August teach you that?"

"Of course."

Veronica smiled. "Sounds like him. Don't you love watching his lips as he speaks?"

Manny and Marcus looked at her. Didn't answer.

"Oh," she said. "No? That's just me?"

SHE AND MANNY found the pool on the roof of the eastern wing. Most of the patrons sat on chairs in the shade under a portico, their feet set in a shallow cool stream intended just for that. The younger and more athletic guests lay in the hot sun.

Veronica chose a chair near a small pool inlaid with smooth river pebbles, set on either side with tuberose planters. Manny tried to take the chair next to hers but she shooed him several chairs down.

"I need information," she explained. "Which is easier to do when single."

She slid Dior sunglasses into her hair and let the cover-up slip from her shoulders. She wore a string bikini, the color of saffron. The top was decorated with aqua blue polka dots and the bottom tied at the hips.

Wearing that, Manny thought, she'll get all the information she needs. Looked too small.

Two pool attendants came running. They smoothed out the towel for her on the luxury chair bed, adjusted the chair's reclining back, and opened her umbrella. Offered to help with suntan lotion. The more fortunate of the two was tasked with fetching her a chilled white wine at a bar inside the portico.

Manny laid out his own blanket and no one offered to get him a drink for several minutes.

Over the next hour, rich and powerful denizens of the Teatro di Montagna flowed by. So many men brought Veronica drinks that she began placing them behind her chair, barely touched.

She was good, Manny thought as he watched her charm all suitors. The way she smiled and used her hair and turned her body, you'd never guess she had a law degree from William & Mary, graduating Order of the Coif.

He'd learned from Mack that she'd been forced into prostitution by her father and fiancé. Witnessing the men salivate over her, he understood—what lonely man wouldn't pay a fortune?

He ordered lunch, finished, grew bored, and got up to walk the shallow pool. The smooth river stones massaged his feet and he fondly reminisced over the previous night's victories. Manny was a man unafraid to part fools from their money.

Veronica found herself alone, finally, and joined him. As she arrived, as if waiting, her favorite fabulous Chinese women came quick-stepping in her direction.

Veronica smiled at them but they were more interested in Manny. Each woman grabbed him by the ears and kissed him on the mouth.

"You know we did?" a woman asked Veronica between high-pitched bouts of laughter. "We go casino with Manuel!"

Somehow he managed to fit his arms around all three women and they walked up and down the wading pool, laughing and talking. Veronica bit her lip to keep from laughing when Manny caught her eye. It had been quite the night, and she blushed listening to the sordid details. When the party broke, they each kissed Manny again and petted Veronica.

"We love you, so pretty!"

Then they were gone, like a tornado evaporating.

"I like your friends," she told Manny.

"Billionaires," he said. "From Singapore. Three single señoritas who love watching men kill one another."

"Billionaires? Really?"

"So they say. I took a fortune from them at the card table and they only laughed. They rented a room at the casino for their own private party. Some wild women."

"Is Duane at the pool? Do you know what he looks like?"

"Never met the man. His wife isn't here."

"She's the woman in the hallway who captured Mackenzie," said Veronica.

"Yes."

"I gleaned some information about the black bracelet. It's activated by remote control, delivering a powerful sedative. High-tech handcuffs."

"A handcuff from hell, ask me."

"I've lost track of the human rights violations at this hotel. And another piece of juicy gossip..." She pointed surreptitiously at a saloon over the bar, a shady area with fans and gauzy flowing curtains. "That's the VIP lounge. The holy of holies, home of the 'It' crowd. Well guarded. And I'm going up."

"How you doing that?"

"Easy." She smiled and reached a hand behind her back and undid the knot of her bikini top.

Manny gulped. "Don't think this is a pool for nude sunbathing, *mami*."

"It is now." She raised her arms and drew the strings over her head and laid the bikini top in Manny's hand. "Be careful, please, Manny. This suit cost five hundred dollars."

"Don't see how," he said, keeping his eyes firmly fixed on her Dior sunglasses. "Like you're wearing napkins. I think maybe you should start sporting one-pieces. Or scuba diving equipment."

"Also." She took off the glasses and gave them over. "These too."

"Why?"

"Men are idiots. They get scared by women wearing them. Isn't that silly. Wish me luck." She slowly cat-walked to the deeper pool and waded in, up to her thighs.

"*Simon*," Manny said to himself, his throat a little dry. "So silly."

Veronica strolled topless through the water, letting her fingers graze the surface, moving her hips in a swiveling motion. She had all the subtly of fireworks. Poolside conversation died down and necks craned. Was this some angel descended from the sun? Sól herself, perhaps?

Manny wished he'd brought a gun—first gringo touches her gets shot.

He examined her waist and then his own. It wasn't often someone else made him feel insecure about his midsection. Did she ever eat?

One of the beautiful Chinese women hurried to Manny and whispered in his ear.

"Pretty lady, she friend yours?"

Manny nodded. "Sí, we're amigos."

"She have surgery? How she look like that?"

"Surgery?"

"You know!"

"You mean...?"

"Yeah, you know? How she do? Real? Fake?"

Manny pressed the heels of his hands into his eyes. Made a sighing sound. This had grown weird. "I don't know. You ask her, not me, mamasita."

"No, can not! So pretty!"

It didn't take Veronica long to get the attention she needed. Manny watched as the tournament's ring master,

Ferrari himself, silver hair glinting with sunlight, came down from the private lounge and beckoned for Veronica.

She shook her head and waved for him to get into the pool, a playful move.

Girl's a pro.

Ferrari blushed and said something in Italian. He took off his loafers and waded down the ramp to his ankles, holding his linen pants up. He and Veronica spoke and laughed, and a moment later she was walking up the stairs to the private lounge.

Now that the sun goddess was out of sight, a few other girls followed her example, disrobing and getting into the water. If any rule about it had existed, it had been shattered by a woman daring them to resist.

Veronica Summers, trend setter.

Hopefully, thought Manny, not to her detriment.

35

That night, Manny, Carlos, and Marcus sat at the central hub on the fifth floor of Teatro di Montagna, alternating glances between the television and the updating betting lines. On screen was a live feed from the rooftop—Mackenzie was being forced to sit on a floating platform inside the pool on the roof with the other three remaining champions.

The throbbing music couldn't be heard from inside the air-conditioned and cushy bar and the three men preferred it that way at the moment.

Marcus took a sip of Macallan scotch, and with his other hand he kept the radio's earpiece firmly pressed into his ear. Manny drank limoncello.

Mackenzie pumped straight into their ear canals through the radio, saying, "And then there were four."

Another voice replied in a thick Italian accent, "Ah, the American Yankee. Good of you to join."

"The hell is going on?" asked Mackenzie.

Safe on his barstool, Marcus murmured, "That's the

Prince. Even I heard of him. International hitman for the
Camorra. Does this shit for fun."

Carlos made a humming noise somewhere deep in his
thick chest. "The Prince. Killed El Salvador's don, last year."

"This is bullshit," said Marcus. "Us sitting here. Hiding.
And the man we came to get in the same damn building."

"Sly like serpents, though," said Manny.

The feed on the screen switched to a better view of
Mackenzie drinking a beer, and Manny pointed at a bar in
the background. "There. The lounge is above that bar. See?
That's where Veronica is."

"By herself," said Marcus. "With the richest and most
dangerous perverts on the planet."

"You're angry tonight, amigo."

"Tired of sitting."

The four of them had hotly debated Veronica's acceptance
of Ferrari's invitation for tonight's Bunga Bunga party. She'd
eventually resorted to aggressive profanity, insisting Mackenzie
was worth the risk, and stormed out, carrying her high heels
and wearing a leather skirt and a scandalously tiny top called a
bralette that was "fashionable as fuck, you backwards idiots."

Manny drained his glass and waved for another. Though
it wasn't hot, he wiped his forehead with a napkin.

Something happened to Veronica in that lounge, Mack
would kill him. Maybe twice.

One of the bartenders set another glass of the lemon
liquor in front of him and said, "You have the bar to your-
selves, signori. You don't fashion a dip?" He nodded at one
of the screens where partiers were jumping into the pool,
splashing the floating platform.

The truth was, they didn't want to be seen by Duane or
anyone with him, whom they knew would be in attendance.

Manny, acting as the frontman to their entourage said, "I do not swim with petty rabble-rousers, mijo."

"Very good, signore. Any money on the line tomorrow night?" asked the man.

Manny drained half the glass. "Betting it all on the American."

Marcus said, "You ain't getting odds. Even money at the moment."

"Easiest double up I ever made. The American, tough gringo. He won't lose."

The bartender bowed and moved to wash glasses.

On the bar, Carlos's phone buzzed incessantly.

He glanced at it and said, "Gonna be trouble tomorrow, Señor Morgan. The clans say Rossi is here."

"What's their plan?"

"The clans, they're too unorganized. They don't have a plan. They love Mackenzie, though. Say he's here to kill the Prince and then kill Rossi."

"Hmmm," said Marcus. "Maybe they're right."

In their ears, the Prince was addressing Mackenzie. He said, "Then it is you who are playing the loser's game, my American friend."

36

The three men were pacing their room when Veronica finally returned at midnight. She stepped quickly in and closed the door. Leaned against it and took a deep breath.

Smiled. "That was close."

"Qué?" said Manny. "What was close?"

"Rossi sent men to follow me."

Manny's hand reflexively settled on the butt of his Beretta at his hip. "Why?"

"Because, Manny, he wants sexual congress and I slipped away when he wasn't looking. He doesn't know my name or my room number so he issued his stooges, but I eluded them, because I am mistress of sneakiness. There are very few cameras."

Manny and Carlos and Marcus all glanced at one another.

Marcus spoke. "Ronnie—"

"I stayed with Rossi for two hours. He sat removed and mostly listened to the other heads of the mafia. He's rigging the fight against Mackenzie tomorrow and betting a fortune on the champion from Japan." She went into the bathroom long enough to change into her nightie. "The Executioner has been ordered not to stop the fight, especially if the Yakuza champion breaks the rules. Plus, the head of the Yakuza is a man named Haruto and he's planting an assassin in the crowd from Japan to take shots at Mackenzie if he's winning."

Manny said, "But if—"

"There's more," said Veronica. She took the glass of white wine out of Manny's hand and drained it. Wiped her mouth with the back of her hand, somehow making it look good. She went into the bathroom and the water started running. "I overheard the bosses talking. If Mackenzie wins the tournament, he'll be killed anyway. Duane agreed not to, but Darren found out and hired an assassin to do the job. Supposedly the hitman is already here."

Marcus took off his reading glasses and rubbed his eyes. "Then we can't let Mackenzie reach the fight tomorrow."

"Intercept him as they walk to the arena," agreed Manny, wondering if that meant he'd lose his bet. "Four of us should be enough."

"Agree. Only had two guards, plus Duane's crew. Even if they activate his medicine, Carlos carry him out."

Manny poured himself another glass of wine from the small bar. "How did you learn all this?"

"Because." Veronica took a few minutes to brush her teeth, floss, and wash her face. She came out and said, "I'm pretty and Rossi is malleable. He invited me to watch the fight from his private box, and afterwards return to his hotel room, though he's not staying at the Teatro."

"Are you—"

"Of course I'm not, don't be an ass." Veronica sat on the bed and slid her legs under the covers. "I recorded the conversation using the microphone and camera in my clutch purse. I caught him laughing about the Camorra clans. They're angry with him because he moved the tournament two or three years ago to Vomero, away from Secondigliano in northern Naples. He's doing it to intentionally infuriate the people every year. He wants strife because it's good for business, and the lesser soldiers can't break through his defenses."

Carlos said, "They gonna try anyway."

Veronica yawned and turned off the Tiffany lamp next to her bed. "I've had a long day, boys, and the Egyptian cotton sateen is calling my name. Talk in the other room please?"

37

Marcus and Carlos had stalked Mackenzie returning from the first fight two nights ago, so they knew the route—a hidden staircase and hallway skirting the hotel's major thoroughfares. The four infiltrators took up positions at a four-way intersection near the top of the staircase.

The plan was simple.

Kill the two guards, plus Duane. And anyone else.

Return down the stairs with Mackenzie and exit through the emergency door at the base.

Hide in the neighboring casino until Manny returned with their Fiat.

Flee to the airport, where Marcus's associate waited.

Fly home and execute Darren Robbins.

Easy.

When the staircase opened at 9pm, six guards walked through, each brandishing an assault rifle and radio, followed by Duane and Mackenzie, then a tall thin German dressed in tactical gear, Mrs. Chambers and a pretty blonde girl, and then four more guards. Mackenzie's wrists were shackled and he wore a bizarre black band on his left wrist.

Other than that, he wore only fighting shorts and he bounced lightly on the balls of his feet.

Marcus gave a little head shake and the four infiltrators turned away from the procession, hiding their faces around corners. Veronica wanted to scream—she was close enough to speak to Mackenzie. But there was no way to eliminate the entire contingent of guards before help was radioed. They hadn't expected this many.

Duane was talking to Mackenzie in a low voice. "I don't trust the fucking Japs. You know?"

Soon they'd marched around the bend of the passage, out of sight.

Veronica said, "Shit. Now what?"

"Gun them down from behind," said Manny. "And die young?"

"Not yet," said Marcus. "In this hallway, even catching by surprise, we'd be toast. Need to find better odds."

"So we're going to let Mackenzie fight the giant Yakuza champion?" asked Veronica, an edge of panic in her syllables.

"He'll win tonight," said Manny. "Mack a badass hombre."

"But the Yakuza have assassins in the crowd!"

Marcus said, "You two, get yo ass to the fight. The Japanese section. You see someone pull a gun, ace'em. Carlos and I stick around in case August comes back with a tiny guard detail."

Manny and Veronica ran.

$\sim$

MANNY KEPT his eyes on the Japanese spectators as he and Veronica prowled up and down the arena staircase, scanning for shooters. But there were hundreds of Japanese in the section, maybe thousands and the crowd was raging. It'd take a miracle for him to spot the assassins before they got a shot off.

Veronica tried to help him scan, but she kept sneaking glances at the cage. Mackenzie was winning, it appeared. He wouldn't let the sumo wrestler get up.

Near the end of the first round, they heard gunfire. Two shots from the section above. The crowd screamed as one.

Manny charged, gun drawn.

"There!" cried Veronica, pointing. She whirled back to the cage, searching for Mackenzie. He hadn't been hit, dancing away from the downed giant.

The two shooters stood in the front row of the upper-most section, long-barreled pistols held surreptitiously at chest level. Manny's first round went through the closest assassin's eye socket, and his next through his throat. The second assassin jumped in surprise and turned his gun on Manny, far too late. Manny fired his Beretta twice into the man's chest, and then he was close enough to press the barrel directly into the guy's forehead and squeeze the trigger. Loud and bright blasts in the darkness.

The speakers boomed as Ferrari, the master of cere-monies, called for order.

Most of the Yakuza crowd were screaming and recoiling away from the violence, but not all. Two accomplices behind the assassins went for pistols in their shoulder rigs.

Manny couldn't get both. He fired from the hip and leapt blindly down the staircase. More gunfire, missing him. He tumbled and slid to the next landing, hidden by the heaving throng. Security charged upwards in the direction of the gunfire bursts. The guards ran past him without a second glance.

Tenderly massaging his ribs, he rendezvoused with Veronica below. Several minutes later they watched Mackenzie electrocute himself and the Executioner.

"What. The. Hell," said Veronica. "Is he doing."

Medical staff for both champions hurried into the cage.

"Tryna save the Yakuza's life. Mack's heart bigger than his brain."

Finally Veronica found her voice. "The man I fell in love with," she said. "Is an absolute mystery to me."

"Look on the bright side, mamí. I just made a hundred grand."

"Good. I need it."

"Por qué?"

"I'm bidding on the champions," said Veronica. "Both of them."

38

"Those men over there. Crimson jackets, by the door."

Veronica and Manny stood at the round bar, their drinks untouched. The betting hub was buzzing with energy from the night's drama. Gamblers were screaming at officials, declaring because the Japanese champion still lived they shouldn't lose their money. The American hadn't won. But, explained the cashiers, safely ensconced behind steel bars, Signore Ferrari had declared the Yankee the victor. All bets were final.

Manny said, "I see them. So?"

"They're looking for me. Rossi wants me to attend his after-party."

"Ah. You going?"

"I am not," she said, punching numbers into her phone. "I'm bidding fifty grand on both champions, a record amount. I have to win one, don't you think?"

"I think maybe you need to find sex in healthier places."

She and Manny waited impatiently as the clock ticked down. The numbers hit zero and phones all over the room buzzed, followed by women groaning and laughing.

Veronica inspected her screen.

"I didn't win Mackenzie," she said in a whisper. "Someone bid over fifty thousand dollars for him. Unbelievable. I will kill that bitch."

"Who?"

"I wish I knew. On the other hand..."

She held up her phone for Manny to see.

>> THANK YOU FOR BIDDING. CONGRATULATIONS, YOUR BID WAS HIGHEST FOR O PRINCIPE, CAMORRA CHAMPION.

>> YOUR FUNDS HAVE BEEN SUCCESSFULLY PROCESSED.

>> PROCEED TO THE CONCIERGE DESK ON THE SECOND FLOOR TO MEET YOUR ESCORT. A REMINDER, YOU ARE ALLOTED SIXTY MINUTES ONLY.

"Veronica, *no intiendo*," said Manny. "Why're you doing this?"

"I'll explain when I get back." She placed her hand on Manny's shoulder. "Wish me luck."

"Buena suerte, mija."

Veronica ducked her head and strode from the room before she could be spotted by Rossi's henchmen.

Manny raised his glass. Caught the eye of a group of dejected Yakuza across the bar. Winked. Saluted them with the glass, and drained the scotch.

39

Her escort was a hulking man, head and shoulders taller than her, as strongly built as Mackenzie but fat, bald, with a prominent chin. Gold necklace and watch. He looked at her once, nodded, and then kept his eyes to himself.

"O Principe will not be chained," he said in an Italian accent as they walked. "You assume risk associated with the activity. Your safety is not guaranteed, and you may be injured if we subdue him. The metal bracelet he wears is for your protection and we won't remove it."

"I cannot imagine the Prince hurting any woman walking into his chambers for the purpose of sexual recreation," said Veronica.

The man made a grunt noise. "Rules are rules."

The guard led her past a door on the second floor marked with an American flag and her heart skipped a beat. Was some bitch inside? The Teatro di Montagna took Mackenzie's escape attempt seriously, it appeared—two armed guards stood outside his door, but none of the others.

Around three more corners, they found the Prince's suite.

The antechamber's walls were white, the carpet wine colored. Four attendants looked up at her arrival and she detected their approval.

She held her head high—I bid fifty thousand dollars for your champion. But it is he who is the lucky one.

Her escort opened the door to the inner bedroom and stuck his head in. Nodded to himself and stepped aside.

"You have sixty minutes," he pronounced.

Veronica entered the bedroom and said, "Close the door, please."

"For your safety—"

"I waive my right to your protection for the next hour. Thank you." She took the handle and closed it herself.

"Veronica, cazzo santo, sei qui!" cried the Prince, and he flew to her. He kissed her mouth, her forehead, her mouth again, and said, "Sei qui, non posso crederci, sei venuto!"

Veronica, it's you! I can't believe you're here!

She smiled as he wrapped his arms around her and lifted. "Ciao, Principe. È bello vederti."

It is nice to see you, Prince.

He spoke into her neck, rotating them in a circle. "Non mi hai detto che stavi arrivando."

You didn't tell me you were coming.

She replied in Italian, "It was a last minute emergency. I didn't know you'd be here. You are fighting very well."

He set her down and kissed the top of her head.

"Veronica, it breathes life in me to see you again. I cannot begin to tell you."

"Did the Camorra force you into Gabbia Cremisi?"

"No," he said. He took her by the hand and led her to the bed. "I voluntarily entered."

"But why? This is a horrible thing."

"So is all of life."

She stepped away from him to inspect his body. He'd showered and wore only shorts. He was a tall, hard man with muscles and ridges, and an open, mischievous face. Thick black hair and eyebrows, two days of scruff.

She said, "I don't see any wounds."

"I do not lose, Veronica. Except to you."

She laid her purse on the bed and moved to the window. Did Mackenzie have the same view?

Was he with the woman right now? The woman who bid over fifty thousand?

"Why are you here?" he asked.

"It's complicated."

"Say you will marry me," said the Prince. "I will win this tournament and we'll run away."

She turned back to him. Leaned against the window, rested the heels of her hands on the glass. He came to her. Started kissing her neck.

"My answer has not changed, Prince," she said.

"I will leave this life. For you? I swear I will."

"You entered a tournament expressly to kill other men," she said. "You are incapable of leaving the life. We cannot be together. You know this."

"But I am in love with you."

"I was a prostitute hired to please you." She placed her hands on his bare shoulders and pushed him away. "You fell in love with that woman. Not me."

"With you."

"You don't know the real me."

"I know we are meant to be together."

She refused to look him in his eyes, such a deep rich brown, so full of hope and pain.

"Prince," she said.

"We'll get on a plane."

"I've given you my answer twice. We cannot be."

"I'll be rich on Sunday. We'll fly to—"

"I am married, Prince," she said.

He flinched back, as if she'd struck him. But then he stood entirely still. Not even breathing for a long time. Not entirely unlike the statue of David.

Finally, "To who?"

"A man I love. From America."

"A client? Like I once was?" he asked.

"No."

"He cannot make you as happy as I can. As I did."

"What we had was special, Prince," she said.

"Yes."

"But it was brief. And an illusion."

"Not for me."

"It was for money." She took his face in her hands as tears leaked out of his eyes. "You're a king among men. But you are destined for another woman."

"Then why did you come? To torment me."

"I came to beg you."

He took her hand and kissed it. Closed his eyes. "I am a man you never have to beg, Veronica. All that I have and am is yours."

"Then please..."

"Yes?"

"Help me free the American."

He laughed. "The Yankee? You are joking."

"I am not."

"Why?"

"Because he is my husband."

His shoulders fell. He released her hand and stepped

backwards. Slumped onto the bed and slid off. Sat on the floor.

"No."

"He was brought here because of me," said Veronica, and she began to cry too. "It is me who should be killed, not him."

"I do not understand."

"I left Darren Robbins. I told you I would, someday. And I did. With Mackenzie's help. And now he is suffering, because Darren hired a hitman."

"This Mackenzie. We've spoken. He does not deserve you."

"But he does. He's the most remarkable man I've ever met. You would like him, in different circumstances." She knelt beside him and picked up his limp hand, hard and tough, and kissed it. "I'm so in love with him that some days I cannot function."

"I despise him."

"I know I am asking much of you."

"You are asking everything."

"I'm going to try," she said. "But without your help, I will probably be killed."

"I cannot help you. Rossi brought me to his room. Guaranteed me fortunes untold if I beat the American, and I promised. If I betray him? He'll kill everyone I've ever loved."

"Then you're still a slave."

"Always."

"You deserve better," said Veronica.

"That is the first lie you have told me tonight."

"Mackenzie deserves better too. Please."

"It cannot be done. We are surrounded by professional assassins. Watched by thousands of eyes. Much of our planet's corruption is concentrated in this city, and the men here are not to be trifled with. Shooting your way out would be impossible."

"During the fight, you can lose to him. He won't kill you. He's not that kind of man," she said.

"You insult me."

"No! I beg you."

"I do not lose."

"Prince—"

"And he is not worthy of you." He was pinching absently at the carpet on which he sat, near a heavy plate bolted into the floor. In Mackenzie's room, her husband would be chained to it. With the woman.

"He would spare you, if I asked him. That's the kind of man I want to be with."

"I am destroyed, Veronica," he said. "You ask too much."

"I know."

"If I lose, I throw away fortunes."

She shrugged, which always looked good on her. "Bet on the American."

"What do you mean?"

"Bet on the American and then lose. You'll be alive and rich. Mackenzie won't let you be killed. He spared the sumo wrestler."

"Mackenzie, I loathe this man. He makes a mockery of us. And now you say... Augh, never have I wanted to kill someone this much."

She squeezed his hand.

He said, "I cannot believe you are here. It fills me with life and despair. You are here, but not for me."

"I would spare you the pain if I could."

He said, "I will test him."

"What do you mean?"

"I will kill him in round one. If I cannot, I will kill him in round two. This will prove he is not worthy of you."

"What if you cannot?"

"I can. But should the miraculous happen, if he survives until round three..."

"Yes?" said Veronica.

"Then...because I love you, I will let him live. On a condition."

"Thank you, Prince."

"He will still die. The security will catch him. And there is a rumor of an assassin," he said.

"I heard the rumor. What is your condition?"

"If I kill Mackenzie during the first two rounds, you must marry me."

"Marry the man who killed my husband?"

"Marry the man who exposed him as unworthy," said the Prince. "I would kill a thousand men for us."

"I wouldn't love you."

"With enough time, I will win you over."

"Very well," said Veronica. "He will not lose to you. But if he does, you and I will marry. If not, you help me."

"The bargain is made. The best chance he'll have is to escape during the fight."

"That cannot be true. He's in a cage."

"Think about it, my love. Security will be busy with problems. The crowd will be rowdy and overflowing. You must create a diversion in round three. I will open the cage, and he can disappear into the bodies. All armed personnel will be in that arena. Once he is out? No one will catch him."

"How will you open the cage?"

"I know a way."

"What kind of diversion?"

He said, "A big one. A power outage. Find a way. But only in the third round. At the beginning."

"Prince, thank you."

"Do not thank me yet, my love. He will die. Because you are a woman worth killing for."

B right and early the next day, they sat around a wrought iron table in a nearby palazzo drinking caffè. Marcus was replaying a video on his phone, footage captured by Veronica's purse. On screen, Rossi was bragging about his invincibility and the helpless plight of the opposing Camorra clans.

Veronica asked, "You think it's enough?"

"Should be."

"I show them this," said Carlos. "They storm city and kill the *jefe*."

"But they can't get in. Rossi has all roads blocked until after the tournament."

"We find a way, Señora Summers."

"I got an idea about that," said Manny, mixing collagen into his coffee. "Carlos, you work up an army to attack the gate, I'll open it from the inside."

"How?"

"Pure Hispanic machismo. Just tell me when and where."

Veronica said, "Let's assume we can break down the

gates so the disgruntled local soldiers can get in. I think the Prince is correct—a power outage would work wonders."

"Got that covered too." He dug into his pocket and retrieved a phone. "This morning, while you fat lazy mafia crime lords slept, I went exploring." He punched up a few photographs and slid the phone across. "The power lines are underground. But this place, behind the hotel, near the loading dock..."

Marcus said, "What am I looking at?"

"Electrical boxes. Transformers. Power supply. All that."

"Ain't guarded?"

"Very guarded. Behind a sturdy fence. But still, Imma blow it up."

"That so," said Marcus.

"That so. Should knock out power, until generators kick in."

"You believe you can?"

"You offend me, mamita. I blow up what I wanna. You know how?"

Veronica said, "Pure Hispanic whatsits."

"Machismo."

Marcus held up five fingers. "First, raise the army. Second, bring'em in tomorrow night, cause a ruckus. Third, knock out power during the third round. Fourth, find Mack after he escapes during third round. Fifth, get the hell out of here. I'll have the car ready, and private jet waiting."

"Drumming up a mob is no easy thing," said Veronica.

"I won a small fortune off Mackenzie's victory last night," said Marcus. He rubbed his thumb across the tips of his first two fingers, a universal signal for money. "Gonna reinvest it into the cocaine shop down the street. Mob needs convincing? We'll coke'em up."

"That's a lot of cocaine."

"I bet a lot of money."

"What about the assassin?" asked Veronica. "Everyone knows the Kings hired one."

"Jump off that bridge later. I've asked a lot of my contacts. No one knows who it is. We get home and ace Robbins? Contract goes away."

A small white van braked to a stop on the cobblestone street and a gray-hired man in a vest leapt out.

"Look who I find sucking nectar in my palazzo!" cried the tailor. "It's you, the gods and goddess of my dreams. Aphrodite and her harem."

Veronica tried to rise and greet the tailor, but he pushed her back into the chair and knelt before her. "I cannot stay. I only stopped to worship. Because of you, fair-haired maiden nymph, my store is almost empty. The blushing billionaires came with open wallets and they purchased everything. They want to look like the blonde girl in the evening gown, the blonde girl with perfect breasts at the pool, the blonde girl in heels with legs that never end, and you send them all my way. Because of you, I am wealthy."

Veronica laughed. "Reaping what you sow, haberdasher. You gave us a fortune in fashion."

"I cannot stay. If I could, I would throw myself at all of you, such a gorgeous nubile table." He took her hand and kissed it twice. "But alas, I'm off to dress the champions."

She sat up straighter. "Both?"

"Both. I am the very best."

"You'll talk with the American?"

He said, "Of course. The man is so beautiful that I might linger."

"I need a favor, good tailor."

"Anything. I would slay a dragon for you. I would sacrifice my child, if I had one."

"Pass him a secret message, from me."

The man gasped and clutched her hand tighter. "Yes! Intrigue! Drama! Conspiracies and secrets, yes, absolutely."

"No names," muttered Marcus. "Just in case."

"I must fly!" cried the tailor, glancing at his watch. "Already I am late."

"Tell the American I'm here," said Veronica, and her voice betrayed her, choking with emotion. "And that I love him. And that I will release him. Tomorrow."

41

That night, Carlos flipped the lights on, the harsh unwelcome glare.

Veronica woke with the awareness that it wasn't time. She checked her phone and groaned. "It's two-thirty in the morning. What's wrong?"

"The Camorra clans," said Carlos, breathing heavy, tight red t-shirt threatening to rip at the seams. "They come now. There will be fighting."

The other bedroom light snapped on and Marcus appeared, rubbing his eyes. "Supposed to be eighteen hours from now."

"I show them the video. They are a mob ready to fight. Thousands," said Carlos. "They come to kill Rossi and they come to watch the final match."

"Watch Mackenzie?"

"Half love Señor Mackenzie. Half love the Prince."

"Look like I didn't need to buy suitcases full of cocaine," said Marcus.

"They are coming now." Carlos went to the mini fridge

and snatched a bottle of water. Twisted the top and guzzled half. "We cannot stop them."

Manny rolled out of bed and bounced on the balls of his feet a few times, awake and fresh immediately. "Where?"

"Coming up Tangenziale di Napoli."

Manny whistled. "The main gate."

"I snuck up the side. Rossi's police are at the barricade. The Camorra clans want to attack at three, Señor Martinez, and then move up Via Frencesco Cilea."

"Well then." Manny grinned and reached for a pair of pants. "We don't have a minute to lose. Carlos and I, we will crack open the door to Vomero."

Marcus nodded. "Summers and I stay here. The mob attacks? We might bust down August's door. Stay in phone contact with me."

Yanking on pants and shoving feet into sneakers, Manny laughed, flushed and gorgeous with energy and enthusiasm. "The game is afoot, amigos! This is the happiest I've ever been."

Vomero, the small town on the hill in the middle of Naples, essentially had one point of ingress—the four-lane ramp looping up the side of the mountain off highway A56. On either side of the incoming ramp the land fell away precipitously. The ramp intersected Via Frencesco Cilea on the brow of the hill. If you wanted to get a car into Vomero or if you wanted to move a lot of people into Vomero in a hurry, you had to go through that intersection, making it a natural chokepoint for the *polizia* and Rossi's forces to barricade.

Hundreds of glistening black uniforms waited with shields and gas canisters and firearms.

Up the long ramp came a small cavalcade of trucks and SUVs, occupying all four lanes. Marching boldly behind, in the middle of the highway, thousands of soldiers from the angry clans. The police used powerful spotlights from above to keep the soldiers in sight and to blind them.

Manny and Carlos emerged onto the roof of the closest residential building—a modern seven-story, pale blue structure set with glass balconies and windows. Two police nests had been hastily erected here, set around two of the powerful spotlights. Carlos quietly surprised the southern nest with his heavy shotgun, holding the barrel at their eye level and stumbling through his Italian; the police got the gist and they didn't move. Manny wrapped used elasticuffs to tie the hands of the officers, men relieved to be taken out of the fight.

The two insurgents moved through the darkness to the northern police nest and repeated the drill. Only one man resisted and Manny shot him in the forehead with his silenced HK.

Carlos turned off the radios and double checked the bindings while Manny crouched beside one of the spotlights. He unslung the rocket launcher from his shoulders and removed one of four RPGs from his backpack.

"This is so beautiful I could cry," he said, fondling the steel tube with affection. He had a recent Italian variant of the Russian RPG-7 launcher with a single-stage HEAT warhead, good for making a mess.

The eyes of the nearest subdued police officers widened at the weapon.

Carlos typed into his phone, communicating with his contacts in the Camorra mob.

Manny carefully slid the projectile into the launcher until the display beeped and turned green. He stood, weapon perched on his shoulder, and peered down at the dramatic diorama below.

Carlos said, "You ever fired one of those, Señor marshal?"

"First time for everything, Señor outlaw. Tell your amigos, I'm ready."

Carlos typed into his phone and hit send.

A minute later, the Camorra trucks and SUVs ascending the ramp accelerated to five miles per hour. The ranks of soldiers behind kept up. A quarter mile from the bristling barricade, coming around the final turn, the vehicles kicked it up to ten.

Manny aimed, one eye screwed shut.

He asked, "So lovely up here, you noticed?"

"I notice. Good temperature. Smells like cooking sausage. You doing that right?"

"Hope so." Manny's finger snaked around the trigger. "Bendita madre, guía mi furia."

The unguided rocket roared and leapt away, so quick and hot it was like magic. The next instant, the cluster of cruisers and cement roadblocks on the outbound lanes burst. Blacktop and tires were flung into the air, followed closely by the sound of a detonation.

"Touchdown!" laughed Manny, already loading another RPG into the tube. "I'm so happy."

The Camorra militias released a war cry and sped up, emboldened by the allied show of force.

The police and guards suddenly found themselves confused and surrounded. Discipline and resolve melted.

Manny aimed again...and fired.

Nothing happened.

Carlos reached up and shoved the projectile further into the launcher, and the display beeped green.

"Gracias."

"De nada."

Squeezed the trigger...and fired.

A hot blast and the second salvo punctured the barricade. The police turned and ran from the invisible foe raining death. Onward came the Camorra, their enemies dissolving.

"Mischief, take thou what course thou wilt," said Manny.

"Que? What?"

"I'm quoting Mack. But making a mess of it. Text Marcus, tell him the army is on the way. And let's me and you, *vamos*."

43

Veronica waited by the door, wearing the closest thing she had to battle gear - flats, loose palazzo pants, and a wraparound black linen shirt. She looked ready to attend a private runway showing of next Spring's fashion trends, except for the .380 pistol she slipped into her clutch purse.

Marcus stood at the mirror, examining the way his jacket covered the HK pistol in his shoulder holster. He hated those things, meant for the damn police, not him.

The first angry Camorra soldiers were already in the hotel—they'd witnessed the arrival from their window. Time was ripe to free Mackenzie.

Someone knocked at the door. Veronica froze. So did Marcus. They weren't expecting visitors.

The lock was activated with a master key and the door swung open. In stepped two security personnel that Veronica recognized—Rossi's men.

The first man saw her and released a long breath. He said, "Sei una donna difficile da trovare."

You are a hard woman to find.

"Ti ci è voluto abbastanza tempo. Cominciavo a pensare che Rossi avesse perso interesse," she replied.

Took you long enough. I was beginning to think Rossi had lost interest in me.

The guard, a tall and brooding Italian with thick eyebrows, didn't smile. In Italian, he replied, "Follow me, please. I will escort you to Signore Rossi's private box."

"His private box?"

"For the fight," the man said.

"But...the fight is not for eighteen hours. And we heard the hotel was being stormed by local thugs."

"It is. Those loyal to Di Contini, they are here to protest Signori Rossi."

"Rossi, your boss."

"Yes," said the man, and he looked unhappy about it. "Signori Rossi has decided the fight will happen immediately."

"Now?"

"Now."

"It is the middle of the night."

"Let me speak openly, ma'am," said the man. "It has not been pleasant since you left Signore Rossi's side. He blames us for being unable to find you. If you do not follow me willingly, you will be taken. Our lives are at stake."

"Oh."

"Are you alone?" he asked, frowning at the two beds.

"Yes. Except for..." Veronica snapped her fingers. Marcus, listening out of view, stepped forward. "Except for my body guard, Marcus. If I join Rossi in his private suite, he will accompany us."

"Signori Rossi did not mention a body guard."

"I am ready to follow. But if I go, Marcus goes."

The two sentries exchanged a glance. The second man shrugged.

"Very well. Follow me," said the lead guard. "The fight begins soon."

The two sentries bracketed Veronica in the passage and walked for the elevator. Sounds of shouting came from down distant hallways. Marcus took out his phone. While they walked, he sent a text to Manny.

>> **Ronnie and I, taken to Rossi's box. Fight starting soon. Get ready to cut power. Wait for signal.**

44

Timothy August and Sheriff Stackhouse sat at a dim booth at Blue 5 restaurant in Roanoke, Virginia, eating dinner and listening to the live band—soft jazz tonight. Long past his bedtime, Kix stared vacantly at the sax player. Uneaten pieces of mac and cheese were held but forgotten inside Kix's tiny fists, and his eyelids drooped.

Timothy August set down his martini and said for the third time that evening, "You think the kids are okay?"

Stackhouse smiled and squeezed his hand. "I'm sure of it, babe. That's a dangerous crew we sent over there. We'll get a text soon with a picture of them sipping drinks on an Italian beach. Try not to worry. Mack is fine."

Timothy nodded to himself. "I'm sure you're right."

45

Manny and Carlos bounced in the bed of a truck fishtailing through town near Castel Sant'Elmo. Such a ruckus was being raised by the invaders that Manny couldn't help joining in.

"Free the woman!" he cried.

Carlos fired his pistol in the air.

Manny continued, "Especially the fine señoritas!"

The phone in his pocket buzzed. With one hand on the truck's cab, he steadied himself. With the other, he retrieved the phone. Opened. Read the message from Marcus. Get ready to cut the power, it said.

"Time for more fun, amigo!" He pounded the roof of the cab and shouted in the window, "To Teatro di Montagna!"

46

Veronica's escorts were forced to take multiple detours to reach the top of the arena. The incoming Camorra soldiers clotting the passages weren't dressed in sharp uniforms like the hotel's security force, and they weren't powerful Gurkhas like Rossi's private detail. They were a motley crew in ratty jeans and soccer jerseys. Boots and ball caps. They carried old rifles, revolvers, and bottles of whiskey. Many were mere boys. But they were overwhelming in number, they were passionate about the Gabbia Cremisi, and they hated Rossi.

The higher they climbed, the faster Veronica's heart raced. All was coming to a head.

The two sentries led them into a final unadorned hallway and to a door marked with, "Suite Numero Uno. Solo Personale Autorizzato." He pushed it open, stepped inside, and closed it. A moment later, it opened and the man beckoned them in with a jerk of his head.

They entered into the lounge of an opulent private suite high above the stadium floor. The lounge was furnished with divans and settees and short tables; a portion of the lounge's floor was thick glass, looking down on the cage. Beyond the lounge, only reached by walking over the glass floor, was an open-aired seating for watching the match below. The farthest part of the suite, to the right of the entrance, was a bar and serving area—attendants were bringing out platters of food and the bartender was pouring a dark cocktail into a highball glass.

Rossi was at the bar by himself, half-sitting on a stool. A corpulent and darkly pink man, every inch an Italian, dressed in white linens and moccasins. His short gray hair was pushed back and held with product. His eyes were partially pinched closed between his cheeks and heavy brow, and his neck spilled over the collar, hiding much of a gold chain.

Mackenzie, Veronica thought, would crack a joke about him being one of the Sopranos.

Next to Rossi stood a soldier Marcus recognized as a Gurkha—no mere hotel security guard, but Rossi's private mercenary. He held a Beretta ARX crosswise across his abdomen and a scowl on his granite face. His head was shaved.

Making a subtle motion with his thick arms and short fingers, Rossi beckoned them over. In Italian he told Veronica, "You disappeared."

A slow phlegmy voice.

Veronica replied, "That night, over the bar, the meeting with your rich friends was boring. I am a girl who likes action."

"Did you find some?"

"No. I was hoping you would come after me," she said. She eased onto the bar stool next to him, somehow invading his personal space while looking like she belonged there.

She crossed her legs and took a proprietary sip of his drink, all calculated moves signaling she belonged to him.

Without looking at Marcus, he said, "Who's this."

"My bodyguard. I'd like him to remain."

Rossi shrugged. "You think I can't protect you here? Look at my sentries. They displease me? I feed them to tigers."

Marcus, acting his part, took up station next to the door with two other hotel security guards. This wasn't going according to plan, he thought. Trapped in the suite with Rossi, a fucking Gurkha, and two hotel sentries. Not ideal.

Through the glass floor he monitored the arena. The stadium was filling with both the wealthy and the violent. The master of ceremonies, Ferrari, identifiable because of his shock of white hair, was running everywhere. Soon his voice issued from a thousand speakers and the orchestra began to play, the strange combination of electric guitar and cello and violin.

Rossi made a wince and a shrugging motion. "It's a shame, this thing happening in the middle of the night. We're all tired. Won't be as good a show. Not even hungry."

"Are you worried about the division in the Camorra clans?" asked Veronica.

"There's always division. Part of life, part of the system, division. Good for business. The buildings in Vomero get damaged, we rebuild. You know who gets a piece of reconstruction?" He pointed at himself with his thumb. "More guns bought. Who profits? Me. War is an engine making me wealthy."

"Are you in danger?"

"Some." He shrugged again and drank his Negroni, a dark and swirly cocktail. "My helicopter, it's on the roof, ready. After the fight, we'll slaughter some of these kids.

Enough to scare the leaders. Send them back home to their mamas. I'll be gone. We'll be gone. That's how it is."

Veronica made no discernible changes to her face, yet somehow she looked smoky and inviting. "That's how it is."

Rossi's right hand snatched at her blouse. The wrap-around design came halfway loose, revealing her red bra underneath. Veronica didn't flinch.

"Red," he said. A heavy grunt caught in his throat. "I like red."

"I thought you might."

"I get bored later? I tell you to take it off? You do as you're told," he said.

"Yes Rossi."

Standing by the door, one of the hotel's security guards next to Marcus released a faint snort. Shook his head slightly and stared at the floor. Sensing disgust, Marcus whispered to him, "What happens she don't wanna undress?"

The guard whispered back, "My English? Bad. Rossi asshole. Rossi kills her."

"Damn."

"Kills you too. Feed the tigers."

Soon the arena was far over capacity, the energy like a wave ready to crash. Chants caromed off the walls and flags began burning. Ferrari worked them into a frenzy and introduced the champions. The Prince came first, his entourage shoving back the rabble. Rossi and Veronica went to the glass window to watch, while the sentries stayed put.

In Italian, Rossi said, "The Prince. One of my finest soldiers."

"He is loyal to you?"

"He loses? I kill his whole family. Smart people, they stay loyal."

"The American is strong, though."

"You root for the American?" he asked in a soft voice.

"I am from Switzerland. I root for a good time."

"The only reason you're alive, after running away from me, is that we're going to have a good time. You please me? I'll make you rich."

Veronica took his hand. "You are in good hands. We'll have the best time of your life."

"Yeah."

"I'll make you the happiest man alive. So happy you'll beg me to stop."

For the first time, Rossi smiled. "Begging you to stop."

"Yes."

"Girls from Switzerland look like you, I might send for some more."

Ferrari's voice changed pitch and he introduced Mackenzie. The crowd ramped up the volume. Camorra soldiers began firing guns into the air, punching out the lights. More flags were set on fire and waved.

"Look at them, shooting up my hotel." Rossi spoke to one of the hotel security guards behind him. "Gun. Give me your gun."

The man obediently opened his crimson jacket with his left hand and retrieved a black pistol with his right. He placed it in Rossi's meaty palm. Rossi waddled into the open-aired seating and his face tightened with concentration and he aimed from the hip. He squeezed. Paused and emitted an indignant snort.

"Next time you take the safety off," he said and did it himself. He held the pistol belly-height and jerked the trigger five times, shooting down into the crowd in what he considered the direction of the rabble breaking his lights. Veronica flinched each time.

Marcus and the other guard at the door each shook their head slightly, marveling at the violent and entitled stupidity.

"Who do you fire at?" asked Veronica.

"The fuckers shooting up my hotel." Rossi handed back the pistol and told him, "You, go find them. Any still alive, kill them. Quickly. No peasants get to shoot at my ceiling until I say it's time."

"What if you missed?" asked Veronica.

"I don't miss. Trust me."

The man left, speaking into a radio. One guard down, thought Marcus. Now only the second hotel security guy and the Gurkha remained.

Still not great odds. But they'd gotten better.

Rossi indicated the bar. "Get a drink."

But Veronica only had eyes for Mackenzie, making his way through the throng. He looked healthy and energized, a king. He was taller than most, his shoulders heavier, his neck thicker. The people loved him, the security team feared him, that was obvious.

Mackenzie's cuffs were taken off and for a brief moment he paused. As if she could read his mind, she knew—he was debating breaking free. It was chaos down there and his handlers weren't paying enough attention.

"Run Mackenzie," she whispered. Yet she knew something else—he wouldn't. He wasn't a man who backed down from a challenge. He wasn't a man who ran away from trouble, but towards it. In the midst of his incarceration he would've found a way to remain autonomous and independent, and running now would admit he'd been helpless. She didn't know him well but well enough to understand he'd rather die standing up to cruelty than die running from it.

He leaped into the ring and her stomach twisted in a knot.

There came a knock and the security guard cracked the suite's door, nodded, and threw it wide.

A man and a women entered.

The man looked like a younger and less fat American version of Rossi, and the woman was stunning, thought Veronica.

Duane and Emile Chambers. Marcus recognized them, Veronica didn't, not immediately.

The man stopped in the doorway and exclaimed in a raspy voice, "Marcus! The hell are you doing here? Got'damn."

Marcus shook the man's hand, somewhat caught between his role of bodyguard and his true identity, which Duane knew. He grinned and said, "Here with Veronica. Don't think you know her. We heard about the American, so we figured we needed a vacation."

Duane was more animated than Marcus'd ever seen him, hopped up on cocaine. "The American. Mackenzie, you mean. Listen, Marcus, I should have talked with you about that. About him, you understand. It's my call, but..."

Rossi, watching the interaction and understanding half the English, made a grunting noise. Veronica squeezed his hand and redirected him in Italian, "The fight is about to start, my dear."

"Those two," said Rossi. "Know each other?"

"They've worked together before, I think. My bodyguard is well known. I don't know the second man."

"Duane Chambers, a King from the States. He brought the American, and he's about to owe me three million euros," Rossi informed her.

Marcus was telling Duane, "Forget it, Chambers. All good. We came to watch August. Win or die, we having a good time."

"I'll be honest, Marcus," said Duane, taking him by the hand again and squeezing with genuine enthusiasm. "It's damn good to see another American. These fucking wops? Everywhere. You picked a helluva night to join, though. This got'damn place is in the middle of an uprising."

Emile Chambers came to stand next to Veronica, her chin held high. She was an inch shorter and she made Veronica feel underdressed. Veronica hadn't known she'd be hobnobbing with criminal royalty. Emile eyed her blouse, still open where Rossi had twitched it, and said, "You're the topless woman from the pool."

Her accent was French.

"That, and more," said Veronica.

"You're a whore."

"I'm a good time."

"I don't hate many people, but I hate you, my love. Effortless beauty and those legs. A rare combination."

"It only required ten million lunges."

"I didn't know Marcus Morgan took up with whores."

"Just the best ones."

"Rossi invited you here?" asked Emile.

"Of course. The man has taste."

"You're quite lovely. Enjoy it while you can, darling. You've got a few more years, no? Before you're too old and you're forgotten," said Emile with a tight smile.

"Nonsense. In another decade I'll simply buy a new face, like yours," replied Veronica and the two women laughed, a tight and forced sound.

Rossi went to the bar. He returned with twelve large bricks of euros, wrapped with cellophane.

"Duane Chambers," said Rossi, and he set the stacks onto a cushioned chair. Another trip to the bar and he came back with a white velvet pouch, cinched with string. He upended it onto the stacks of cash and six red-tipped diamonds spilled out. "Il mio lato del patto."

Duane paled. He nodded to himself and gulped. "Good, yeah. A bargain is a bargain."

Rossi smiled without humor, his eyes almost disappearing, and raised his hands, palms up—*and?*

Duane went into the hallway and took a suitcase and a pouch from a man with tattoos up his neck. He returned and closed the door. Set the hard-shell briefcase onto the adjacent seat. Popped the two locks, opened it.

Barely, Veronica managed to not gasp. She'd never seen so many hundreds. Green for days.

Sweating, Duane carefully upended his own pouch. Six aurum. If he lost the bet, it'd set him back five years.

"Three million and six," he said.

"Buona," said Rossi. "Good."

"Good." Duane wiped his forehead. "Yeah, good."

The speakers blasted, beginning the fight. Duane grabbed Marcus by the jacket sleeve and dragged him into the outdoor seating area. They stood against the railing.

"Think August can win this thing?" Duane asked but didn't wait for an answer. "Can't believe I let that fat bastard talk me into this."

Rossi went to the bar and came back with another Negroni and watched the fight with pale eyes.

The Gurkha stood at the entrance to the open-aired seating—even he watched the combatants.

Veronica had a hard time breathing. To her, the fight looked like high-speed gymnastics. The Prince was nimbler, quicker, but he looked like a teenager next to a full grown man. A rapier versus a broadsword. If Mackenzie connected once with all his strength, it'd be over.

The third round, Mackenzie. Survive until the third round.

"They are beautiful," said Emile. "Beautiful violent men."

"You enjoy the violence," Veronica replied and it wasn't a question.

"Look at the American. Look at the shoulders, the chest, the blood on his back."

"I see."

"The other fighters, they are criminals. Cruel but undisciplined. They are hitmen and used to easy victories. But the American, he is like a god, no? He fights not to hurt, but to win. He has people he loves, to get home to, and it makes him...what is the word in English, impervious? Such a man. Like a thoroughbred horse. I cannot break his spirit," said Emile.

"You've tried?"

Despite her best efforts, Veronica's fingers began to tremble.

"Of course." Emile's smile was proud and mean. "The man has been in my possession for a week, chained. A bridled stallion in my pasture."

Veronica cleared her throat. "Chained? I like mine to run free."

Rossi, admiring Veronica and her deep breaths, asked, "Voi due e il vostro stupido inglese. Che cos'è?"

You two and your stupid English. What is it?

Veronica answered, "Lei sta ammirando gli uomini."

She is ogling the men.

The fat man grunted.

His Gurkha chuckled.

Veronica asked him in Italian, "Do you always watch the fights alone?"

"Who is worth watching with? Who deserves the best seats? Only me."

The buzzer sounded and the two men separated, each moving a little slower and gasping for air. Maniacs attacked the fence and Ferrari sounded delirious. Mackenzie's body shone with sweat and his corona of dark hair was mussed.

"And now," said Emile slowly. Her skin was flushed. "For electricity."

"You're twisted, Mrs. Chambers."

Emile turned to face her, away from Duane. "Without danger, life is nothing, no? If my husband knew what I have done to the American, he would kill me."

"What..." Veronica stopped and took the drink out of Rossi's hands and finished it. The man looked pleased and signaled for another. "What have you done to the American?"

"His arms were stretched wide, in chains," said Emile in a hushed tone, oblivious to Veronica's wide eyes and trembling lip. "Unable to move. Unable to resist."

"And?"

"And I molested him," whispered Emile.

"You raped him?"

"Not to my entire satisfaction. Yet. But I have it arranged, after this fight. A room specially prepared. With enough money you can buy anything, you know. Or maybe you don't. He will be taken there and chained. If he wins, of course. Do you not envy me? That muscular monster under my control. I'm weak, thinking about it. And he will enjoy it too, I'm sure, in the end."

"You plan on subduing Mackenzie and having sex," Ronnie heard herself say.

"Quiet, my love," said Emile with a wicked smile. "Our secret."

"Of course."

"You think he'll enjoy? I hope so. My lovers always do. But who cares about the whore, yes?" she asked with a smirk.

Veronica nodded to herself, as if making a decision. Went to the bar and asked for a white wine. Picked up her clutch purse and walked back.

Marcus was texting. He looked up from the phone, eyed her, eyed the Gurkha, eyed the purse, and shook his head slightly at her.

Not yet.

A member of the security team, just a boy in peach fuzz, sat unmoving against the cinderblock wall under the threat of Carlos's heavy shotgun.

"You don't move," said Carlos.

The boy shook his head.

Manny carefully guided his penultimate rocket into the launching tube until the display beeped and turned green.

"Ay dios mio," he said. "Such a sexy sound."

In the surrounding neighborhoods, gunfire crackled, but no one bothered them in the dark behind the hotel.

His phone buzzed. A text from Marcus.

>> August doing well

>> Almost time. Get ready to light this shit up.

Manny grinned.

The Prince was injured. Even Veronica, a newcomer to blood sports, could see it. Mackenzie had him pinned to the mat with his knees, and the man writhed. Rossi hurled his cocktail glass from the balcony into the crowd below and shouted, "Prendi il cazzo!"

"Finish him!" Duane sounded like a man dying of tuberculosis. He pounded on the balcony's parapet. "Kill that wop!"

Yan-kee, Yan-kee, chanted the crowd.

The Prince got a sucker punch into Mackenzie's throat and he fell near the fence. His metal bracelet burst and he staggered, electrocuted and disoriented, but the Prince couldn't take advantage. His shoulder was out of socket.

Rossi's face was deep red with displeasure.

"Look at the American," said Duane, hoarse. "That's what you can do with freedom and democracy and steroids and grass-fed beef. Makes me wish I had a son. God, I can't take this. This shit is rough on me."

"Maybe don't bet the farm, next time," said Marcus, arms crossed, eyes on the fight. His right hand, tucked under his left arm, was pressed against the reassuring bulk of his pistol.

"Fucking Rossi goaded me. Man's a pig."

The round ended and the fighters went for more water. Again the fanatics attacked the fence and the security team responded. The cellos and electric guitar played louder.

The third round, thought Veronica. Finally, after an eternity, it's time. She and Marcus exchanged a glance. He nodded and punched a message into his phone.

"You are rooting for the American," said Emile.

"If I had to choose," replied Veronica. "I would pick him, yes."

"Don't get your hopes too high, love. He's a dead man. As assassin awaits. After I'm through with him, of course."

"Who is the assassin?"

"We don't know. It's too bad," said Emile as a small table rose from the cage floor for the fighters. Metal weapons, barbaric tools. Mackenzie's mouth was bleeding. "Because I may wish to keep the American as my sexual toy."

Duane had been listening. He cocked his head and stared at his wife. "The fuck you just say? Sexual toy? The American? What do you mean, sexual toy?"

Emile Chambers's breath caught, the cruel smile frozen on her lips. She didn't respond.

Rossi's hand slid between the folds of Veronica's blouse and he said in Italian, "Me and you, we're leaving. Without your African bodyguard."

"As soon as the fight ends?"

The buzzer rattled from the speakers like an alarm.

Round three began.

The crowd raged.

Veronica dropped her wine glass. No one noticed, so fixated they became on the two men in the cage. The fighters weren't moving. Rossi shouted at the Prince. So did the Gurkha.

Veronica's hand slipped into her clutch purse and wrapped around the pistol grip.

And that was when the power in the Teatro di Montagna went out.

PART III

Carlos and Manny watched the transformers blaze and spark, the launcher still on Manny's shoulder but empty, their faces dancing with firelight.

"That worked," said Carlos.

"So pretty, right? Something magical about Naples at night."

"Señor August, we need to find him."

"Let's go, amigo."

The powerful lights and speakers inside the stadium snapped off. The sudden dark hit me like a physical thing. There was a hush, ten thousand throats closing in surprise and wonderment. Even I, an intrepid investigator with seemingly preternatural insight into the future, was caught off guard.

Meg cried, "Mackenzie!"

The Prince waggled his nasty hammer at me. I barely saw it.

He said, "I honor my promise. You survived and even worse you beat me."

"Neat trick, with the lights."

"You have committed allies," he said.

"Do I."

"We have only seconds. Your plan?"

"To escape," I said. "And go down in a blaze of glory and derring-do with verve and élan."

He grinned. Looked like it took a lot out of him, poor guy. "You know I cannot understand your American words."

"Get one of those calendars, a new word every day, you know the kind? People will like you more."

"The power is out, but even if the cage is still on? The gate never is," he said. He turned suddenly and, using his good arm, he swung the hammer and smashed the locking mechanism. Once, twice, and it broke off.

"That's precisely what I was going to do," I said.

He dropped the hammer and picked up the heavy short sword. Cut himself deeply across the chest, wincing.

I winced too and sucked at my teeth.

Mackenzie August, vicious monster, weak stomach.

"Go," he said as blood spilled down his abdomen. "And be worthy of her."

"Her who?"

Members of the mob, driven to their mammalian instincts, were ascending the cages, trying to climb over top. And then? They hadn't thought that far ahead, I bet.

The Prince laid down on the mat and released a fake groan, like an Italian soccer player would do. The stain of red spread beneath him.

The power snapped back on, backup generators kicking in, the lights dim.

All was chaos.

But I was already gone.

51

The power snapped back on, backup generators kicking in, the lights dim.

All was chaos.

The Prince lay on the mat, bleeding heavily and barely moving.

Of Mackenzie there was no sign.

"Hah!" cried Duane. "The Prince is dead. Or close to it. I win your got'damn bet, Rossi."

Rossi's face looked nearly purple. "Il tuo combattente è fuggito!"

Moving smoothly, Veronica withdrew her little .380 pistol and pressed the barrel into the soft underbelly of Emile's jaw.

"My husband's not a horse. I need therapy, I know, bitch, but I don't handle competition well," said Veronica. She closed her eyes and flexed her entire hand, squeezing every finger muscle. She fired twice, wet muffled blasts. Emile went over backwards into Duane's arms.

Marcus removed the HK from his shoulder holster, forced to admit the easy reach was handy. Duane was close enough that he couldn't straighten his arm. He set the barrel at the base of Duane's skull and fired once. For good measure, twice more into the spine.

He and Veronica both turned their guns on the Gurkha but the hotel's security guard gunned him down first. He shot the Gurkha at the base of his spine, beneath the ballistic vest, and then three more blasts in the head.

"What the hell," said Marcus. His ears rang.

The security guard said something in Italian, which Veronica translated, "Says he's wanted to do that a long time."

The man nodded and kept his gun trained on Rossi.

Tattoo Neck opened the private suite's door, pistol drawn, come to investigate the gunfire. Saw Duane and Emile already dead. Looked at Marcus.

"You work for me now. Keep watch outside," said Marcus, wearing authority naturally.

Tattoo Neck paused, thought for a second, nodded, took another look at Duane's corpse, and closed the door.

"Tell you what," said Marcus. "Just us lowlife scumbags here. What do we do 'bout Rossi?"

Veronica stepped away from the Italian crime lord, fixing her wraparound blouse and keeping her gun trained on the remarkably calm bartender and servers. They wouldn't do anything stupid, which was good because Veronica would never shoot at them. She was already on the verge of being sick.

The remaining Italian guard said, "What? My English..."

"Rossi," said Marcus and shrugged.

Veronica translated, "Cosa dovremmo fare con lui?"

What should we do with Rossi?

Rossi's face had gone from purple to gray. He was

pressed against the railing, trying to keep his moccasins from soaking up blood. "Spara a loro, fottuto idiota!"

Shoot them, you fucking idiot!

The guard grinned and said, "Rossi? Le persone dovrebbero decidere. Gettalo tra la folla."

The people should decide about Rossi. Throw him to the crowd.

Rossi turned from the guard to Veronica and spat at her. "You whore! Bitch! Kill you! Kill family!"

Marcus stepped around Duane and Emile and threw a hard left, breaking Rossi's nose.

"I hate violence," said Marcus, shaking his fingers.

Rossi staggered backwards, holding his face. The guard came across the room and hit Rossi again. Pushed him backwards against the golden balcony railing. Grabbed the fat man by his knees and lifted. The parapet acted like a fulcrum and Rossi tipped back and upside down. He tumbled onto the stadium seating twenty feet below, a collision unhealthy for all parties.

Marcus leaned over enough to watch. "Ain't gonna go well for the guy, folks realize who he is and that his bones broke."

"Good," said the guard. "Killed my brother."

Indicating the chair with his gun, Marcus said, "Take the euros. Should be three million. We in a hurry and can't carry that much anyway."

"I don't...my English."

Veronica translated, "Prendi l'euro. È tuo ora."

"Veramente?"

"Sì, prendi i soldi.

Take the money.

The guard fell to his knees. Took a golden cross out of

his shirt and kissed it. Thanked them in Italian. Tried not to cry.

Marcus picked up the twelve aurum and deposited the diamonds into his pocket. Snapped the briefcase closed, assuming ownership of the American currency.

"Time to go, babe."

"Mackenzie," said Veronica, watching the heaving throng below. "Where's Mackenzie?"

52

F irst things first.

Beat the hell out of Ernst, the stupid German bounty hunter. Vital? Possibly not. Important? Deeply.

For the moment I was hidden by the raging riot but the locals were recognizing me in a hurry. My loud shorts were a dead giveaway.

A lot of things didn't make sense.

How had the Prince known the power would go out? Yesterday he'd told me to survive until the third round. He'd known then. But why not the first round?

Could he be working with Meg, the physician? The tailor had told me the blonde girl was on my side. Yet she didn't strike me as possessing enough moxie to arrange a coup such as this. There must be a third party involved, but who?

The fuming security chief (guy with flashing Bluetooth earpieces) and I saw one another at the same time, a few feet apart in the mayhem. He had a two-handed grip on his black Benelli pistol, and he brought it around in a sweeping motion. I got my left hand around the barrel, ducked under and pointed it skyward. I brought my right fist up between his arms, an uppercut into his chin. His jaw and teeth clunked, a sound unlike any other, and his head snapped back.

"Shouldn't you be congratulating me?" I said. "I won."

There'd be no congratulations. I was a prisoner to him, a frequent pain in his ass, and he the warden.

I hit him again—he dodged his head to the side but I still caught his cheekbone. He was stuck; if he let go of the gun, he was dead; if he didn't let go of the gun, I'd keep pounding him.

He tried head-butting me but I popped him in the nose first.

"Not so fun when your prisoner isn't shackled, is it."

We rotated around one another, him jerking at the pistol, firing at the ceiling. Overhead, pieces of the stained glass broke. Bam bam bam, I hit him three more teeth-rattling uppercuts.

He released the pistol with his left hand. Awkwardly kicked at me, and went for a second pistol on his thigh. It was a good move. I jerked the black Benelli pistol out of his right hand. He stepped back and drew the gun off the thigh holster. A small Glock.

One of his goons materialized. Young guy, but big. Shaved head. Wearing the crimson jacket. His pistol was out so I spun away, moving to his left. He closed his eyes and pulled the trigger twice. Missed me, but didn't miss the crowd behind.

Guns are dangerous, awful things. More screaming.

Bluetooth had his Glock up, fighting through the crowd towards me.

The goon with a shaved head was going to shoot again,

hurt more people. I lunged, pushed the newfound Benelli in my hand firmly against his shoulder and shot him.

He was no pro. He dropped the gun, screwed up his eyes and screamed at the ceiling. Face turned purple. It wasn't so much the pain, but the disorientation and stomach drop that comes with being shot. He'd live.

Some inner alarm rang. Too much time with my back to Bluetooth. I dropped and twisted. Landed on the floor, gun held with both hands, straight out between my knees.

Bluetooth fired and missed over my head.

I shot back. His ear puckered, the lower half bursting into a red pulp. The flashing earpiece broke and popped free.

Sweet poetry.

He still held his gun.

I shot him in the thigh and he dropped, like both legs quit working. Gun clattered away.

I stood. His goon had fled into the maelstrom of people. I crouched next to Bluetooth and put the barrel at his temple.

"Shoulda let me go. Truce? Or death. You get a choice," I said.

He spit blood at me. I whipped him in the mouth with his own Benelli.

I smiled happily.

"Truce?"

"Truce," he said.

"Oh boy!" I jerked two full pistol magazines off his belt. No pockets in which to put the magazines, how embarrassing, so I slid them under my super tight shorts.

The locals were fighting against the hotel security forces and the Camorra soldiers loyal to Rossi. It'd started as shoving and shouting, but more gunfire was breaking out. I was one drop in the sea of heaving humanity.

Still came the chants, Yan-kee Yan-kee! The men around me pounded me on the back.

This was a mess. A farrago of which I wanted no part.

Where was Ernst?

Overhead, the speakers turned back on. Power being restored. Ferrari declared me the winner. The Prince was being attended to by his medical team. The orchestra, somehow, someway, still played and made everything worse with its frenetic driving beat. I shoved my way through the crowd far enough to fire twice with Bluetooth's pistol—I shot the cello and I fired over the head of the musicians.

The music abated. Finally.

On to more important problems.

Where was the fabled assassin sent for me?

And how the hell did I get out of here?

53

Marcus Morgan, Tattoo Neck, and Veronica paused in the hallway at a stairwell leading to the roof. Howling down the corridor was the sound of a helicopter warming its engines. Maybe more than one helicopter.

An Italian chant none recognized was reverberating through the floors and walls. It was loud and haunting and portended only bad things for the structure and beautification of the Teatro di Montagna.

Men in crimson jackets ran everywhere. Other hotel staff hid in doorways.

Tattoo Neck, still a little spooked by the death of his boss, stepped into the stairwell and looked up.

"Yo Marcus, you sure we can take Rossi's chopper?"

For the moment, he was ignored.

"Where is Mackenzie?" said Veronica.

Marcus had a phone to his ear. "Manny ain't answering."

"I'm going to look for him," she said, still gripping the .380.

"No. We'll go secure a ride first. Manny will..." Marcus quit talking because Veronica had already left.

54

The Yan-kee cries had stopped and I was no longer being patted on the back. At least for the moment. The swelling fight between Rossi's men and the hotel security team and the other Camorrista occupied all of their scant attention now. Strife had blossomed into full civil war and the Teatro di Montagna into Gettysburg. Their hero, one Mackenzie August, couldn't be worshiped while they fought.

Fame is a fickle friend.

I ran up one of the stadium's wide exits like an Olympic sprinter. A sprinter who couldn't run fast, one who'd made the Olympics through a technicality, one who had few functional joints.

I heard a crack and the painted concrete wall to my left issued a puff of fragments. Someone had shot at me from behind. I tucked my left shoulder under and dodged to my right. A sudden move, intended to throw off the shooter's aim.

Obviously.

Ernst charged after me. The German bounty hunter was

tall and thin and he ran like a giraffe. He was a sniper, not a fighter. Graceless and gangly, and he didn't shoot well on the run.

However the electrical burns on my wrist hurt. My lips were bleeding and swelling. My groin still ached. My throat burned. I was exhausted from lack of sleep. Excuses, but real ones.

I returned fire at Ernst and I missed. He fired back and missed. A couple of pros, we were.

I kept moving to my left, sidestepping, pistol steadied with both hands, my left arm pinned against my ribs, my right arm nearly straight, slightly cocked at the elbow, keeping the pistol at eye level.

Another round from Ernst. I felt it score along the right side of my abdomen. The bullet hadn't penetrated, or if it had not deeply.

Behind him, a blonde woman. Meg. "Mackenzie!" she screamed.

"Told you to run, Ernst," I said.

I squeezed the trigger. The gun kicked, a bright roar. His ballistic vest buckled. He was moving at a run and the bullet's impact with his chest caused him to miss a step. His gun arm trailed upwards and his next shot went five feet over my head.

I quit sidestepping. Steadied. Fired again and the vest crinkled at his stomach.

My shots hadn't penetrated but the impacts hurt. He lost control. Moving too fast, like a man on stilts unable to stop. He fell to his knees near me, put his left hand out to halt his collapse, tried to aim with his right.

I stepped forward and hit him in the face. An awkward left hook/uppercut swing, because he was below my belt. Caught him in his right eye.

He fired wild, desperate, missing.

From twelve inches away I yanked the trigger—one blast and the slide locked back. Empty. I ejected the spent clip, pulled a full magazine from my tight shorts, slammed it home, chambered a round, and fired twice more.

Three total blasts. I hadn't missed. Ernst was dead.

"Mackenzie!" shouted Meg again. She came up the ramp, medical backpack bouncing.

"Where's Duane?"

"In the suite, I guess," she said. "Ernst shot you."

"I'll live."

"You're a mess, Mackenzie." She peered at Ernst and put a hand to her mouth. "I might throw up."

"I bet you were a hoot during your emergency rotation in school."

"Sit down. You need medical care."

"Not yet. First we finish this."

"You're losing more blood than you think." For the moment we were in our own self-contained universe. The fighting felt distant and we didn't have to shout.

"I'm going for Duane. A promise to keep."

"Okay, but first," she said, and she set her backpack down. Got on her knees. "Let me administer a bandage to your stomach and an epinephrine shot."

"Perhaps you failed to notice how triumphantly masculine I am," I said, but she wasn't wrong. I felt lightheaded and my shorts were getting slick with blood.

"You need to lie down. Hold this," she said, placing a bandage in my hand.

"Meg," I said. She flicked the top off a syringe and jammed the needle into my abdomen. A sudden motion, and her hand was shaking. "Epinephrine?"

She didn't answer, pressing the plunger.

Uh oh.

I smacked her hand away. She gasped and the needle broke.

"Meg."

She didn't look up. Stayed kneeling, tense, her shoulders hunched, leaning forwardly, staring at the ground.

"What'd you do?" I asked.

No response.

I felt the familiar numbing sensation spread through my body. Muscles going dead. I half sat, half fell onto the floor.

"I'm sorry."

"Do you know," I said, slumping against the wall. I tried operating my body but it was sluggish, like from a remote with dying batteries. "How tired I am of your concoctions."

My words slurred.

She wouldn't look at me. Pulled out another needle and vial of liquid. "I really am sorry."

"Darren Robbins?"

"Yes."

"You're the assassin."

Yourethsassin.

"No," she said. "I'm not an assassin. I'm a physician in a mountain of debt and no way to get a job, due to misunderstandings. After today, however, those problems are gone. Darren contacted me and his offer was very generous."

"I'm disappointed in you."

"Don't you dare." She lowered the syringe and glared. Maybe more of a pout. "You, with your perfect life. Tall, strong, muscular, perfect health."

"You noticed."

"Loving family and friends. You've never struggled," she said. "You've never gone without. It's hard being a woman. It's hard living in a man's world and doing what I must to reach the top and then being shamed because of it. You'd do the same, in my shoes. You underestimated me, because I'm a woman. You defeated the men but didn't think twice about me."

"No. I overestimated you. Expected better."

"Yeah, well, you're in a long line of men I've disappointed," she said, and she drew medicine into the syringe.

"Do me one favor."

She stopped. Kept her eyes steady on the vial. "What."

"Pass my son a message."

"I can do that."

"Tell him my doctor sucked and to sue for malpractice," I said.

"You think you're funny."

"I really do."

"You don't deserve it," said Meg. "But this will be painless."

"If you try to inject me, I'm going to bite you."

M'gonbitew.

"You can't move, hotshot."

"My mouth can. A little."

"Time to sleep, Mackenzie. I really am sorry about…"

Her eyes widened.

Someone kicked her in the face. It wasn't a great kick but Meg shrieked and tumbled backwards. A woman stepped between Meg and me. A trim woman, strong, great architecture. She raised a gun and fired it.

Meg screamed again. Held her breath. Patted herself. Peered up in disbelief.

"I missed," said the woman with a gun. "I can't believe I missed. Hold still."

"No!" shouted Meg. "Please, I'm a physician."

"Not for much longer."

Meg scrambled backwards. She closed her eyes and screamed again. The woman with the gun fired a second time.

Missed.

"Are you kidding me," she said. "This is harder than it looks."

"Stop, please, oh god, I'm so sorry, please don't."

"Let her go," I said. "Let her be crushed by financial obligations."

Fancelobagations.

The woman with the gun kept it trained on Meg. Waited. Said, "I'm tired of hearing gun shots. You're in luck. Run away, bitch. And don't ever touch my husband again."

Meg stood. Looked as though she wanted to say something. Instead she turned and fled.

The woman with the gun remained. Oh, what a woman. Long legs, great ankles showing. Tawny hair piled in an updo. Her eyes were the color of the Mediterranean, waves of blue, sparkles of green. She was part southern belle, part Los Angeles starlet. The muscles of her jaw were strong, the skin tight and flawless.

A woman I was in love with.

She lowered next to me.

"Hello Mackenzie."

"Hello Ronnie."

Big fat perfect tears formed in her eyes. "You're so beautiful my heart could break."

"For our honeymoon, I brought you to Naples."

"I hate it here."

"Me too."

"The men smell," she said.

"That is not my primary complaint."

"You're shot."

"I'll live. Plus I was just pumped full of anesthesia."

She pulled the broken needle out of my side. "I should have executed that little blonde harlot."

"I politely disagree. I prefer mercy over retributive justice."

"Do you still like me just because you do?"

"Yes, but the list of reasons I do is growing. How did you find me?"

"I'm kinda rich and cute. I get what I want. What I want most of all? A sexually active relationship with my husband. Can you walk?"

"I cannot. What kinda kinky sex would that be, anyway, walking?"

Behind her I saw Gennaro, my second favorite little boy, running up. "Here! I found him!"

Ronnie looked up. "Manny," she said and her face widened into a magnificent smile. "There you are, I need help."

"You brought Manny?" I said.

Gennaro stepped aside, beaming.

"Hola, Mack," said a familiar voice. Manny came into view and squatted next to me. "I dig your new tattoo."

"Shut up."

"Congratulations on winning the Gabbia Cremisi, mijo."

"Thank you. Cross that off my bucket list. It's great you two are here. Almost makes us even," I said.

"Carlos and I, we're carrying you out," he said.

"Make sure you tip Gennaro. Is that a rocket launcher on your back? What buffoon thought it wise to give you a rocket launcher?"

"They pass these out like party favors here. Mack, this place, Naples, it's no place for honest amigos like us. But I love it," he said.

A man named Carlos, a Mexican of whom I was fond, knelt at my waist and pressed a bandage against the bullet wound. "We must go. More soldiers and police are coming, and the hotel is on fire."

"First," I said. "You got another missile for that thing? I promised Ferrari I'd knock this whole place down."

"Only one rocket. Not enough."

Eying the stained glass window high above, I said, "I know. But I have an equally grandiose and effective idea."

55

Carlos and Manny locked arms behind my back and under my thighs and I contributed very little. They carried me to the roof, where the sky to the east was purpling. Three helipads were in use, and several more choppers hovered nearby, waiting their turn.

Marcus Morgan approached us and shouted, "Rossi's helicopter is already gone. Need another idea."

"You were going to take Rossi's?"

"Good to see you, August. Long story."

Manny said, "Could take my stupid tiny Italian Fiat."

"No," said Carlos. "Only one way into Vomero. It's closed by police."

"So we hijack one of these choppers. Need to go soon. Place gon' burn up before long."

"Hey, it American!" shouted a woman. Or rather, three women. Chinese, by the looks of them, and quite attractive. "It American, we bid on you!"

"Bid? Or bet?" I said, eyeing them. Because that's about all I could do.

"Both! Haha!"

The women laughed and took turns kissing Manny and Veronica on the face. Manny and Veronica kissed them back.

One week with me gone and everyone goes nuts.

"Our helicopter was taken," said Veronica.

"You come us!" shouted one of the beautiful women and she waved us to follow, towards a turquoise helicopter. *Turquoise.*

"Yes!" shouted her friend. "We love you! So pretty! We have sex American! In plane!"

Veronica laughed and shouted over the rotor wash. "He's my husband."

"Husband? You bid on Italian! You have sex Prince!"

"No," said Veronica and cleared her throat. "That didn't—"

"We saw you name!"

Marcus muttered to me, "Another long story."

We boarded a helicopter, one of those luxury business models. We fit but not comfortably. I was buckled into a seat by the window, and one of the Chinese women sat on my lap.

"You get blood on dress!" she cackled. "We crazy bitches!"

"We have American! In plane!"

Veronica sat across from me, smiling. A deeply happy smile, enjoying my confusion. Without enough room, she was partially resting on Carlos.

Marcus moved to the cockpit and our helicopter threw itself into the violet sky.

"Mackenzie, you can go to sleep," said Veronica. "You're safe."

The Chinese woman's nose pressed into my cheek. She

wrapped an arm around my neck and said, "You go sleep! We won't touch. Much!"

The helicopter banked over the city. Flames were visible through the hotel windows, and police lights flashed in the surrounding neighborhoods. As the helicopter climbed, we saw the Teatro di Montagna in all its monstrosity. The great stained glass dome on top was shattered, demolished almost completely by Manny's final rocket. As though the hotel had lost an eye.

56

I woke up to white noise. The faint hiss of air conditioning and cabin pressure. The steady drone of turbines. Soft voices.

A private jet. I'd been on this one before.

My head was in the lap of a sun goddess. Her chair was reclined backwards and she slept against a pillow, magnificent in repose.

I sat up inch by inch, testing and flexing each abdominal muscle. Swiveled to get my bare feet to the floor. And stood.

Yeeeeouch. There was no part of me that felt healthy.

Manny and Carlos slept in chairs on the other side of the aisle. Through the window the sky was a watery blue.

I went to the aft restroom. My face looked swollen. Lip puffy. Throat bruised. My shoulders throbbed. A bandage had been attached to my abdomen and the flesh underneath felt hot.

I found a suitcase with clean clothes. Silk shirts—must be Duane's. I stripped out of the fighting shorts, stiff with blood, and pulled on a pair of his boxers. The shorts were too big and I couldn't find a belt, so I pulled on one of his t-shirts and hoped no one minded the man in his underwear.

Marcus Morgan was up front talking on a cell phone and typing into a laptop. He had the front section to himself. Across from him, lying open on a leather chair, was a hard-shell briefcase overflowing with money.

He saw me, said, "Call you back," and hung up.

I shook his hand. His fingers were long and firm, and he wore a silver Tag watch.

"Look like hell," he said.

"Wrong."

He grinned.

I said, "Thanks for coming, Marcus."

"Summers wouldn't hear otherwise."

"She's the best."

"If you'd seen all the stunts she pulled to get to you?" he said. "You'd find a better word."

"I am an independent and self-contained man. But some girls are worth letting in, I think. Because otherwise I'd be dead. You killed Duane?"

"I did."

"I told him I would do the job."

He shrugged. "You and me always been a little symbiotic."

"I guess it still counts, even if you did it."

"Does. Maybe you didn't, but the pack did. The pack of which you a member."

I waffled my hand. "A pack? Didn't I just say I'm an independent, self-contained, and complete human being."

"You an independent human being got himself in some deep shit and needed help. And now? Bout to become a legend."

"I wasn't before?"

Marcus pointed at his laptop screen. "Camorra still chanting about the Yankee who won the tournament, spared the Prince, killed Rossi, and burnt the place down."

"Not bad, right?"

"Not bad at all. Especially cause I made a fortune betting on you."

"That's the money in the briefcase?"

"Naw. That's Chambers's money. I'll check on his next of kin. Or maybe keep it."

I said, "This is Duane's plane."

"Kings' plane. Mine for the moment."

"That so."

"I reported the demise of Chambers. Temporarily, I have his seat on the board."

"The King's board of directors? Moving up in the world," I said. "The sick, twisted, mercenary, polluted world of the mafia."

"Till they vote. But I like my chances. And like this sick world or not, you in deep now."

"Malarky."

"You kidding me? You won the Gabbia Cremisi. You killed Rossi. Deep as deep can get."

I said, "Your friends on the board aren't gonna be happy with me after I deal with Darren Robbins."

"Darren called me. Knows we're coming home. He said you two square. You survived two contracts, so all's even."

I made a tsk'ing noise.

"Yeah," he said. "I know. It ain't even."

"Tell him I'm coming. And hell's coming with me."

"That a quote?"

"You betcha."

I got up and walked to the rear of the plane. Laid down and rested my head in the lap of Veronica Summers. She issued a soft murmur.

Like music to my ears.

The End

A note from the author

You guys are great! (I assume) Thanks for reading.

I wrote three Mack August books between the months of January to July, 2018. (It was the best. I love being inside Mackenzie's head. My wife says sometimes when she texts me it's like Mackenzie texts her back)

(It may interest you to know that my wife and I are at the end of a long adoption process, as of mid 2018, and soon we'll be flying to India to bring a little girl home, out of an orphanage. Her name's Rima.)

This was Mack's most intense story yet, on the wild and surreal side. I hope you enjoyed reading it as much as I enjoyed writing it. But I'm glad he's headed home. Leave your thoughts on Amazon or GoodReads—it helps me stay in business.

Final thing—I wrote a short story about the honeymoon of Ronnie and Mackenzie in the Bahamas. It takes place after *Only the Details* and involves a minor mystery, and it didn't fit in the book. So if you'd like to read it, **click here and I'll email it to you for free. The short story is called A Ghost in Paradise.**

To simplify, here is my recommended reading order:

1) August Origins (Book One)
2) Desecration of All Saints (Book One and a Half)
3) The Second Secret (Book Two)
4) Flawed Players (Book Three)

5) Last Teacher (Prequel - I'll email you the book for free)
6) Aces Full (Book Four)
7) Only the Details (Book Five)
8) Ghost in Paradise (Short Story. I'll email you.)
9) Good Girl (Book Six)
10) The Supremacy License (Manny/Sinatra, Book One)
11) Wild Card (Manny/Sinatra, Book Two)

In my opinion (which is important, because I'm the author), you should get the free short story and then move on to *Good Girl.*

Preview of *Ghost in Paradise* — A mystery during Mackenzie's honeymoon.

Chapter One

Marcus Morgan, a burgeoning big man on campus within the District Kings organization, directed the private jet on which he flew to land in Roanoke, Virginia. The Gulfstream was a shared investment by four wealthy businessmen and criminals, including Duane Chambers. Duane, however, had been shot in the skull and spine and left for dead with his wife Emile on a burning balcony inside a hotel in Naples, Italy. Marcus, having administered the gruesome execution, assumed an easy ownership of the Gulfstream. He communicated via email with the other three owners, who congratulated him on the ascension up the corporate ladder and assured him the private jet wasn't needed in the next eight days.

His prized cargo—Mackenzie August, the infamous and reigning underworld fighting champion. Millions, perhaps billions, had changed hands on his startling upset at the Gabbia Cremisi tournament. Marcus himself profited immensely, to the tune of nearly four million.

And now? Now Mackenzie needed medical attention and a proper honeymoon, as directed by his wife.

Mackenzie's best friend Manny Martinez realized the extent of Mack's injuries when there came no protest about a trip to the doctor after they touched down.

Manny's car had been left at the airport and he drove Mackenzie and Ronnie to a private house in the city, following Marcus's big Lexus. A physician and a nurse met them at the door—concierge medical attention; they were being paid for their service and their silence. The house was zoned as a residence but used exclusively by wealthy visitors for private and sometimes ignominious emergencies.

The physician spent fifteen minutes with Mackenzie in a patient room and pronounced, "Good news, you're going to live."

Mackenzie said, "Never in doubt."

"However..."

Click here and I'll email the entire short story to you for free.